THE PARADE

APOCALYPSE SURVIVORS

MATT J PIKE

****

****

Edited by: Lisa Chant

Cover design: Matt J Pike

Published by Zombie RiZing Books

Paperback Edition: June 11, 2023
ISBN: 979-8-89074-464-7

Cover design: Matt Pike

Big thanks to Lisa Chant for her editing skills - you're awesome!
Also, Imogen Taintey, Jan Pike, Katie Lowe, Lauren Dawes, Kylie Leane, and my children Sophie, Sam and Abby Pike.

...as well as anyone who reviews this on Amazon or Goodreads.

****

Also in this series:
Apocalypse: Diary of a Survivor 1
Apocalypse: Diary of a Survivor 2
Apocalypse: Diary of a Survivor 3
Apocalypse: Diary of a Survivor 4

****

Other books by Matt J Pike

Starship Dorsano Trilogy:
Kings of the World
War & Quel

Hart & Sol

Zombie RiZing:
The Beginning ZR1-3
Death's Door ZR4-6
Dragon's Wrath ZR7-9
Death's Door ZR10-12

****

For news on promotions, competitions, appearances and
future releases, sign up to Matt's mailing list at www.mattpike.co

ADELAIDE
FORMER CITY LAYOUT
PRE-12/4 COMET

AUSTRALIA
(Current shape unknown)

ADELAIDE

EDINBURGH
AIR FORCE
BASE

NORTHERN
SUBURBS

COMET FRAGMENT
TRAJECTORY

WESTERN
SUBURBS

NORTH ADELAIDE

ST VINCENT
GULF

AIRPORT

NORWOOD

ADELAIDE CBD

ADELAIDE
HILLS

SOUTHERN
SUBURBS

TSUNAMI
EST HEIGHT:
100-150m

BLAST WAVE
EST SPEED:
4500kpm

NORWOOD
FORMER CITY OF ADELAIDE
INNER EASTERN SUBURB
POST 12/4 COMET

TSUNAMI:
HEAVY DAMAGE

TSUNAMI:
PEAK

TRINITY
GARDENS

STEPNEY

MAGILL RD

MAYLANDS

FULLARTON RD

GUN STORE

BEULAH
PARK

STORAGE
FACILITY

NORWOOD
OVAL

PORTRUSH RD

KENT
TOWN

THE PARADE

OSMOND TCE

KENSINGTON

SYDENHAM RD

NORWOOD

KENSINGTON RD

ROSE PARK

TOORAK GARDENS

◀ CITY
(0.8-2km)

◀ WESTERN
WASTELANDS
(2.5-9km)

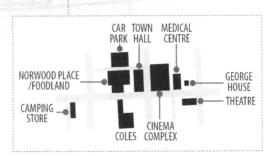

CAR TOWN MEDICAL
PARK HALL CENTRE

NORWOOD PLACE
/FOODLAND

GEORGE
HOUSE

THEATRE

CAMPING
STORE

COLES CINEMA
COMPLEX

###
PREFACE

I remember always wanting to write a book. It was definitely a calling for me in the old world. But it never happened. Hell, I never even started one. I guess there was never the time or drive or inspiration or whatever that thing is you need. Truth be told, I probably didn't even really know what time or drive or inspiration really meant back then. Not at the level where your life depended on it. Not like now.

Everything has changed.

Some called it rock night, some impact night. I've also heard epoch rock, the great impactor, an end of days event and probably a dozen more terms, each with its own variants, depending on who you talked to. Where I come from we called it by the date it occurred – 12/4. I guess that's 4/12 in other parts of the world but, given how close we were to action central when it all went down, we'll stick with 12/4.

Not only did 12/4 change everything, the pace of that change was so rapid and monumental it's really hard to know who I was back then. Less broken, that's for sure.

I wish, every day, that I could go back there – pre-12/4 – but I know that's impossible. I also know the version of me who has survived it all, well, that is the new me, and no amount of wishing back the past would want me to wish her away. I like her, despite everything it took to find her.

I also wish every day that different choices had been made between then and now. I wish those of us lucky enough to survive a comet the size of a mountain slamming into our world at an insane speed took that miracle mortal dice roll to help shape who we were for good as we rebuilt out of the ashes. That didn't happen. Not in the way you'd like to believe it would. Instead, out of those ashes of the end of the world we somehow found the worst in ourselves. I may never come to terms with that.

Perhaps, like the scars left on the very world we live on, the scars left on our species will take decades to heal – centuries even.

That is a big part of what this book is about – healing. Now that the dust is starting to settle on what remains of our society, like the ash is settling from the sky, it is time. Time to start on the next journey, one that may take longer than my remaining days to reach a conclusion. But we have to start, so here's a start.

I've also been inspired in part by a young man I've come to know in recent months. A true survivor. A rebuilder. A crucial part of why New Adelaide is shaped the way it is. There are debts there that can never be repaid.

He – Jack – kept a diary of his days from the moment the world found out the end was coming, through the destruction, through the darkness, until he started to find hope once more. I have read every word. It is powerful and inspiring, a testament to human spirit and hope.

It is a reflection of life as it is in the new world.

This is what I want from the words to follow here. I want to tell the stories of those I know and knew. How we were drawn together by the end of days. How we who remained somehow survived the darkness in all its forms to eventually make it to a place of hope, and the sacrifices so many others made so we could.

I have spent many weeks talking with those who survived, to make this the most authentic record of the reshaping of our city as possible.

May this act as a chronicle of the events that changed the world as we knew it and the lengths people went to to ensure humans lived on. May it also act as a memoir to those who gave their lives so the ideology of hope and community survived. May they also act as a warning that, if we are ever pushed to the brink again, we will be smarter, kinder, better.

It is good to hope.

My name is Zoe Carter, this is my story, and the story of all the members of the Norwood Hub during and after the impact of Comet 2014DM3 in April 2014.

May I – we – be forgiven for what we have done.

###

###

CHAPTER 1:

WHISPERS

Looking back over the lead-up to impact night, there were a lot of things that were hard to process in real time. There was just so much going on. A comet was headed to Earth – impact inevitable and the results would be catastrophic to our way of life.

That alone was enough to wrap your head around. Shock – that was a big part of it. It was not an easy truth to acknowledge, let alone accept.

The universe had found a way through humanity's paper thin defences in the direction it should have been keeping a bigger eye on all along. I could go on about astronomy, near Earth objects (NEOs), dark comets, monitoring systems, government funding, politics and a hundred other things that might have changed our fate, but it doesn't matter now.

The bottom line is an astronomical level of bad luck was about to smash us in the face, and one of the first reactions people felt, along with shock, was a sense of being completely let down by the system.

Not only that, it also took the best part of two days to become public knowledge. And when you have only got a handful of days left, that is an entirely big deal. That time – those stolen two days – represented a chance to get to where you wanted to be in this world, and for those who wanted to be there with you to do likewise.

It was a sense of betrayal from everyone in charge. J Citizen doesn't matter. You're on your own. Ironically, this theme would soon become a way of life.

That was the backdrop to processing the high likelihood your days were numbered. For billions, that number would be less than a week, for billions more, a few months. That was the first truth you couldn't avoid in those disorienting, numbing days that felt almost like an out-of-body experience.

I was one of the last to find out. The young man Jack I mentioned, well, he was at the other end of the spectrum. While not a significant player in the early parts of this story, he influenced it in more ways than he may know, stretching right back to the very beginning, or is that the end?

*

It could've been any morning in the inner eastern suburbs of Adelaide, except it wasn't. Down the centre of the suburb of Norwood ran a strip called the Parade, slowly stretching its arms out and yawning itself into life for another week day. In amongst the cafes and fashion stores two supermarkets began their daily operations. In one of them a young man with a loaded trolley played harbinger to the dark truth that this day was the start of something different.

The woman on the checkout did her best to rein in the look of bewilderment she knew had crossed her face as the teen approached. He responded with a smirk. It was his third run through the cashiers, each with a trolley loaded with cans and long-life goods.

She ran his purchase under the scanner in silence. He looked like he'd had a big night. Maybe he was on something; it would explain a lot. He returned the final bagful of cans to his trolley and fished out a credit card for payment – a different one than before.

Curiosity got the better of her. "What, is the end of the world coming or something?"

"Yeah actually, there's a comet coming, we've only got three days to live."

She let out a nervous laugh as she finalised the transaction. "Well, you won't be needing all that food then."

"Stress makes me hungry," he said, as he completed the payment.

They looked at each other for a couple of awkward seconds, while the transaction disappeared into the ether to seek approval from the bank gods. Eventually, it chirped the sound of success and the mysterious teen with the odd purchases went on his way, but not before giving her a subtle cowboy-like salute.

Two tills over, fellow cashier Em had witnessed the whole interaction and was trying not to laugh. Crazy purchase – this had all the makings of a moment worth capturing. She tried to remember every detail for accuracy of retelling in her break. She smiled for choosing the shift over her economics lecture. Sometimes, it's the little things.

*

Sixty eight hours to go.

###

###

CHAPTER 2:

RUMOURS

Billy was still tucking his uniform in when he spotted Liv at the cigarette counter. Things were still pretty quiet, even for that time of the morning. He felt a slight wave of relief and took a moment to fix his hair, pushing his curly brown locks behind his ear. He took a breath to refocus and hone his charming smile before he loped towards his in-all-likelihood-annoyed flatmate.

Liv looked him up and down, seemingly disappointed with what she'd seen. "You're late."

"Is it fair to say eastern suburbs girls are at least 11.38% hotter than the average?"

Liv gave his attempt at deflection a look of disdain. The fact she almost matched him in height added a little extra sharpness.

He gulped. "Last night got away from me, to be fair."

She stared at him, deadpan. "Have you got any idea how loud you were?" she said.

He opened his mouth to say something funny, but the look on Liv's face stopped him in his tracks. "It was probably a little late... in the end."

"3am is a little late?"

"You know what Hayden's like when he's had a few."

Billy hadn't finished the sentence before her expression told him blaming other people wasn't going to cut it. "I'm thinking of cutting down on the sessions. Well, the Tuesday ones."

The deadpan stare continued.

"Mondays as well."

"Did you clean up the lounge before you came in?" asked Liv.

Billy's expression answered in the negative. "Have I mentioned how nice you look today?"

Liv sighed and turned her attention back to her workspace. "Oh, Steven is looking for you." Her voice was noticeably lighter.

"Shit." Billy scanned the aisles for their manager. Then looked to see Liv smiling at him. "Bitch!"

He faced another unimpressed look. "Sorry. For all the things."

She nodded her acceptance and they found their truce for the morning.

"Oh, before I go, did you see Em's post in the chat?" said Billy.

Liv shook her head.

"We've been smashed in the freak of the week comp. Like, smashed. Get this, some kid walked into Coles earlier and bought three trolley loads of cans and shit. All long life stuff – full-on prepper vibes. Anyway, one of the oldies served him, asked him what he was up to and he said, wait for it... it was the end of the world!"

A smile crept across Liv's face as she absorbed the details.

"Like, he wasn't even joking – he thought it was the end of the fucking world."

"Spent nearly a grand. On fucking cans! Is that not the craziest shit you've ever heard?" said Billy.

"Forget freak of the week, Coles have got the year covered. We may as well wave the white flag now."

"Totally screwed," agreed Billy. But even as he said it, his voice trailed off, distracted.

Liv followed his gaze to see what had caught his attention. She set her expectations to low, given Billy's easily distracted nature. Approaching the nearest checkout, a woman in her 30s wheeled a trolley loaded with canned goods, topped with as many packs of toilet paper as physics would allow.

"You have got to be kidding me," said Billy.

"You don't think?" said Liv.

"There's only one way to find out."

He lifted his collar in an attempt to make his Foodland uniform look more spy-like, gave Liv a wink, then headed over to investigate. At least that was his plan until...

"Ah, Billy, good of you to join us."

It was Steven the manager.

*

Despite the best efforts of those in charge, rumours started and word spread. Talk was soon gaining momentum on the 'net which soon became a conversation too credible to ignore. One message became a flagship for those early hours. Twitter, new account, 0 followers.

@NASAinsider14

Comet 2014DM3 is real. 5km wide. This is catastrophically bad people and you're not being told. We have 65 hours until impact. Friday – 4pm GMT. Tell those close how you feel and make peace with your life. #2014DM3 #cometrumour #endofdays #truth #NASA

It was the right message in the right moment. The unstoppable information was now out in an unstoppable way and nothing would be the same again.

*

My head pounded. My mouth was dry and my tongue felt like it had been encased in a woollen sock protector for the last five hours, or however long I'd managed to not be awake for. I wanted to gag. Thoughts came flooding back as I killed the alarm. Vomit levels of drunk on a work night – well done me.

I saw the photo of me and Craig I had been using as therapy the night before. We stood in each other's arms, the backdrop of Monaco a slice of perfection from a couple of years ago. I'd added a few extra details the previous night, including a Hitler moustache, unflattering eyebrows and the word cheater across his forehead. I smiled at the additions I didn't remember adding and flipped him the bird before throwing the frame across the room.

I thought about pouring a coffee and calling in sick. Instead I took the less reality-confronting option and went back to sleep.

The phone rang. I ignored it.

Yep, that's where I was at the start of the end.

*

"C'mon, pick up, pick up, pick up."

"Zoe's AWOL, leave a message."

Claire sighed. "Zo-zo. Me again. Give me a call, huh? Look, it's... just call, OK?"

She looked at Alex and gave a defeated shrug, then took a sip of her coffee. Alex turned her attention to her pram to make sure her son was still asleep. They gave each other an uncomfortable smile. Both well dressed, the pair looked as at home as anyone on the strip that morning.

April was delivering a kind autumn morning. Jackets were hung over the back of chairs as they watched the traffic idle up the Parade. Ideal as the weather was, the weight of the empty seat dominated the mood. Pre-work coffee on Wednesday was a ritual I hadn't missed in the longest time.

Alex's eyes followed a young waiter as he headed back inside after clearing a nearby table. "I honestly think that ass is defying gravity. Do you think it's defying gravity?"

Claire cleared her throat. "I... I haven't really thought ab–"

"Do you think he'd donate some of his collagen?"

Claire was a veteran of Alex's comments, designed to rattle the unsuspecting. She adjusted her glasses and absently flicked her auburn hair. "Ass collagen? I'm not really su–"

"I'd make it worth his while."

Claire gave a nervous laugh, Alex stared longingly at the counter area, her finger circling the rim of her coffee cup.

"How's Kendrick?" said Claire.

"We're not talking about him today."

The conversation paused for sips of coffee and a round of people watching.

"As for Craig, who does that?" said Claire, eventually.

"An asshole," said Alex. "No, asshole... that's not quite right. A taint!"

Claire smiled awkwardly, aware Alex's volume was at her usual I-don't-care-who -hears-this level.

"No, taint doesn't really nail it either. I haven't moved it far enough to the front. He's a total, total, c–" Alex left the word on her lips. Her attention turned to her baby, now awake and smiling at her – an interaction as sweet as pie.

"So, what do we do about Zoe?" said Claire.

The waiter made another lap of the outside tables. Alex turned her gaze to his collagen farm as he passed by.

"Earth to Alex."

"What? Sorry, I got distracted by River."

"I think the waiter's name is Reed, actually," said Claire.

"Is it?" Alex shrugged with indifference. "I don't care which part of the water catchment area he's named after, his collagen is mine."

Claire nodded, confused. One day Kendrick was the most amazing husband on earth, the next Alex was obsessed with the waiter. Time had taught Claire it was not worth her energy to analyse it any deeper. "And Zoe?"

"Look, she'll get through this. And better this happened now than after they were married."

Claire nodded. "You're right, big picture, it's not the end of the world."

At that moment a kombi van puttered past, the horn beeping. From the open passenger window a woman emerged. She was topless with the words 'the end' written in red paint across her breasts and stomach. "The end of the world is here!" she yelled. "Woo-hoo!"

Claire, Alex and everyone else at the cafe stared. Some laughed.

"Well, fuck me," said Alex.

They chuckled as the van beeped its way up the street.

###

###

CHAPTER 3:
REALITY

"Yes, boss?" said Billy, in a tone that left Steven not knowing if he was being genuine or having a lend.

"That's three shifts in a row you've failed to get here on time. What am I to do about that?"

"Well, if you're asking for my advice, I'd suggest a promotion."

Steven stared at him. Billy smiled.

"Unconventional, I know, but it would definitely keep me engaged."

Steven was now locked into his pose and stare. It appeared nothing would change it, leaving Billy confused as to whether he'd gone too far or not far enough.

"What can I do for you, boss?"

Steven sighed. "Someone's just put a serious dent in our canned goods stock. All of it needs topping up from out back. Should keep you busy for a while."

Billy sighed. "Yes, boss."

*

While we were all just life-ing with varying levels of success, the unknown reality was that we were all just ticking down time until 2014DM3 became a truth in each of our realities.

Even as we remained unaware, that process was happening at a pace that could now not be slowed. Science and rumour were overpowering suppression and control. Out of it shined the dark truth of what awaited us – and that dam of truth was about to burst in spectacular fashion.

The President of the United States scheduled a press conference that would change the world.

Back on the Parade, it would trigger another chain of events that would connect many realities in ways we could never have imagined.

*

Patrick emerged from the ensuite, grabbed the pants folded out on the bed and started getting dressed. He whistled his satisfaction in the moment and patted his ample belly before doing up his shirt buttons. There was a flush of the toilet and Olivia followed moments later. He slapped her naked ass as she walked past. She squealed and laughed. The two got dressed on opposite sides of the bed, careful not to leave too much of a footprint on the space.

"This old guy's still got it," he said. "That was seriously hot."

"Seriously," Olivia agreed. "On both counts."

"To be fair, you're only as old as the person you feel."

"So, I just took 17 years off your life?"

Patrick smiled.

"In that case, you're welcome."

Olvia's heart was still racing from the moment and for all the risks they were taking. "So, when am I going to see you again?"

"I'll be back in the office mid-afternoon."

"I meant to see you."

"Not sure. Family things this weekend. Obviously I've got the Fiji trip with Hayley and the kids and their families next week..."

The words drifted into the air as they continued getting dressed. Olivia toyed with how to respond, Patrick prayed she wouldn't. He had his shoes on and tied before a response had come. "It won't always be this way, you know."

They exchanged a smile that was equal parts doubt and assurance, and way too much to process while they closed up the property post open for inspection. "That's the third time the Brewers have been through. I reckon them, the young couple and the oldie with the cane are all big potentials."

Patrick hmmed with a tone of interest, but he was lost on his phone. He laughed, then stopped just as quickly. "Wait, what?"

Olivia looked at him, confused.

"Facebook post from James Parnell – Restrover boy – in the wine game, played golf with him for years. Anyway... clued in... I thought... but listen to this. 'Read this link, reliable source says it's legit. Pass it on to friends and family and pray. A lot."

They stared at each other. "What's the link?" said Olivia.

Patrick read out loud. "Comet 2014DM3. Expected impact on April 12 – shit. Has the potential to cause worldwide destruction. Inconceivable loss of life... and the way of life we know. Use your last days wisely."

"What site was that posted on?"

"Some sciencey blog thing."

"Not news?"

"Googling now."

*

Billy placed the final four cans onto the shelf, aligned all the labels, then sighed. Like he told his friends way too often, it really was the world's most pointless and unrewarding task. He'd lost count of the amount of times he'd barely left the aisle when his work was undone by the customers. Still, at least his work would pass muster with Steven when he checked up, which he would definitely do.

"Excuse me," said an old lady, in a tone that didn't match the pleasantness of her words.

She didn't even wait for Billy's response before she was pushing her way into his space. He smiled thinly at her as he backed away and gave her access to the baked beans. As he turned to his trolley filled with empty cartons he heard the thud of tin on tiles, followed by another 'Excuse me".

He turned back and picked the can up off the floor, offering it to the old lady. She had already selected an undented tin and was shuffling on her way.

"Rude much," he whispered, before shoving the deformed can as far back on the shelf as he could without ruining his display.

"Excuse me?" said the old lady again.

Billy froze in surprise at her laser-like hearing. "I didn't say anything."

She stared at him for an uncomfortable amount of time before muttering something under her breath and moving on.

When he finally felt she was a safe distance away, Billy sighed, then turned his attention back to the trolley and making his escape from the aisle.

"No Mum, all the cans."

Billy stopped in his tracks and turned. There, a man in his early fifties with a trolley laden with food cartons and long-life drink containers shooed the old lady away from her trolley. He ushered his partner – or daughter, Billy couldn't be sure – in to help and the two started loading cans into the old lady's trolley.

He watched on in stunned silence. As he saw his fine stacking work being dismantled, his mind ticked over to the next move. He approached the man, clearing his throat as he arrived. It was a failed gesture. "Excuse me."

"What?"

The man's terseness threw him. He was sweating. Profusely.

"What are you doing?"

"Shopping. You got a problem?" He made eye contact with Billy briefly, before returning his focus to the cans.

"They don't pay me enough to have a problem, man. Just wondering if what you're doing has something to do with the end of the world?"

The man stopped to eye Billy. "What do you know?"

*

It was the most watched piece of television of all time, both live and in the hours afterward. The numbers dwarfed what the global population would soon become. The US President made the rumours of the comet official. But, really, by the time that happened, it kind of felt like everyone pretty much knew anyway.

We were given details like the predicted impact spot – the Indian Ocean – as well as being told the comet might break up on entry, meaning it could potentially impact a much wider area.

The president announced an internationally coordinated missile response, hoping to divert the comet's trajectory and probably a dozen other things that are forgettably meaningless now.

I guess they wanted to give the impression everything was getting handled. The thing is, though, no one really had the sense it was. So, if it was designed to give us comfort, it didn't work. If it was designed to keep the population subdued, well, as the nights ahead would prove, that didn't work either. It all seems a bit ludicrous now.

Once the President had done his thing, we heard from our Prime Minister a couple of hours later, then the State Premier a few hours after that. All similar messages with a slightly more local flavour each time.

Then the media did their thing, replaying press conferences and getting expert analysis. It didn't amount to much more than a ra ra pom pom pushing cheerleading act. Humanity was going to save the day, apparently.

Spoiler alert – this book.

*

Mind you, this was all still yet to be news to me – I was still off the grid, while the rest of the planet went to defcon 5… or is it 1? Whatever, the worst defcon.

The scramble was definitely on. How that scramble manifested was different for each person, based on a million individual factors. But, hearing from others' recollections, it boiled back to some simple needs/actions – be with family, protect family, prepare for survival, make peace with God, serve community.

Sure that doesn't cover everyone, because the anarchy that played out over those final days – even just those things reported on – was horrific. It was the same story all around the world. In the face of the unthinkably large, where others were taking stock spiritually, others acted out.

Of course, watching the media tell our collective truth you'd be excused for thinking we were community and family focused as we spiritually prepared for our fate. But that was only a half truth.

It's not our best trait as a species. We can literally look right at a complete something and see only the bits we want. Our blindness to the truth right in front of our eyes is utterly spectacular to behold. The mirror we look at ourselves through is so sophisticated in its design it only reflects the half of the image we want to see, letting us nod back approvingly.

It seems to be a centuries-long human tradition that is probably very unhealthy on a lot of levels. Given where the world is at now, it's time to start telling more accurate stories of our reflection and our history.

Sure, noble, kind, beautiful and touching things happened towards the end, but so did a whole lot of horrible, deceitful, cowardly, remorseless shit. There were those who lost all sense of care and responsibility – their last few hours seemingly driven by two words – fuck it. Or maybe fuck you. Not in the good way, either, in the dangerous one. Really dangerous.

Then there were those who were driven by revenge, their last days dedicated to getting even with whoever for whatever.

That was a part of the social backdrop in our final days. Every person was living with tunnel-vision-purpose, perhaps like never before. There were so many overlapping and conflicting goals – some noble, some horrible. It was all playing out in a world where information was flooding you, whether true or not, and it was impossible to absorb it all.

While you're living out what you think could be your last few days, well, that's a lot. It came with a feeling of detached numbness. It was a feeling soon to swamp me and a feeling I've since found out was shared by many, many others.

###

###

CHAPTER 4:

DESCENT

I pressed my headphones into place, hit play on my phone then opened the door for the first time in four days. I hadn't listened to Metallica's *Black* album for years. It was on the outskirts of my heavy listening range and that's what made it seem so right for this fuck-Craig-I'm-going-outside-again moment.

A tune from my attempted rebellious teen years. The phase perhaps never really suited me that much. But, then again, neither did towing the line. All I had left from that period was a few photographs I'd rather not see again, a small tribal tattoo with similar visual appeal that could be concealed under my jeans and a few albums that collected dust at the back of my collection.

I apologised to Rage Against the Machine for having them play bridesmaid as the opening riff of *Enter Sandman* rang through my head.

I made my way to the street and started into a light jog. The run would help. Clearing my head would help. Anything to distract from Craig would help.

It was a nice day for me to reemerge, I thought.

I let my feet find a rhythm with the music and tried to shake out the cobwebs. I decided I'd head down to the parklands on the city fringe and track through a few of the footpaths that criss-crossed the grass before heading back up the Parade to home. If I managed to run for the full album's length, I'd be happy. Especially if it came without any of the thoughts that had been completely occupying my mind for the last few days.

Why did they call it the *Black* album, by the way? There was no mention of the title in the artwork nor on the spine. iTunes tells me it's called *Metallica*. But no one ever called it Metallica. A self-titled album that wasn't the debut album – that must be rare.

I wasn't sure how common it was, but I was happy with the early start to my thoughts and my run.

The morning peak hour traffic was noticeably thinner than usual as I waited for the pedestrian lights to invite me across DeQuetteville Tce and into the parklands. I could already see the sirens in the parklands ahead. Instead of cutting through and around the pond, I followed the terrace up to Rundle Rd before making a left into the city. My legs were heavy – it'd been far too long between runs. *Sad but True* was the track that escorted me around whatever was happening in the parklands. I could make out two police cars as I headed past the commotion on the Rundle Rd side. Despite the decreased traffic, it was backed up all the way to East Tce – very unusual for that time of the morning.

Before the song finished I was on the fringe of the CBD at East Tce, I saw the reason why. There was another set of police lights further down Rundle St. As I drew closer I could see the street had been blocked. Patrol cars and police tape were stopping anyone from getting through. There was a cop on the East Tce intersection, directing cars away from Rundle. What the fuck was going on?

Whatever it was, I knew my best move was to get well away. Something big had gone down, that was for sure. It was eerie. Not-Adelaide eerie. Not just the police; there was something about the traffic being down, something about all of it. Big things just don't happen here. I desperately needed coffee and some latest news. I turned my back on the east end and followed my path back towards the Parade. As I reached DeQuetteville Tce again, there was another round of sirens, this time headed towards the CBD from Kent Town, on the wrong side of the road. Police again, but this time motorbikes. They were leading a convoy of other vehicles. I decided to stop at the corner and do some stretches to get a better look.

The patrol car slowed as it reached the intersection. Once the cross traffic stopped it accelerated again. Behind it, I counted nine army trucks of various sizes rolling in. Two of the car-sized ones had soldiers manning massive guns behind the driver's seat. Another two looked like tanks – again with guns – but they had wheels instead of tracks.

Seriously, what the fuck was going on?

The military parade had rolled past at speed, bookended by two more police bikes. I watched as it joined with the confusion at the East Tce intersection before it disappeared into the traffic and other sirens along Rundle St. I gave the scene in the parklands another look before returning to my jog to the final bars of *The God That Failed*. As I was preparing to cross the lights back out of the city, the sound of the next track was drowned out by something different altogether – an army helicopter. Then a second, followed by a third.

What the fuck was going on?

It could wait no longer. I picked up the phone and dialled Claire.

*

Billy juggled his backpack around as he tried to do up the buttons on his uniform, while trying to keep pace with Liv. The degree of difficulty was made harder by the phone in his hand and the sunglasses temporarily secured in his mouth. The hangover didn't help either. He mumbled a futile and inaudible "wait up", but nothing was slowing Liv down.

The streets of Norwood were different that morning. It wasn't the look, but the soundscape. Sure, they could hear distant sirens, more than they could place, but it was beyond that. There was something completely different in the audible landscape of the path they'd walked several hundred times. It created an unsettling eeriness out of the mundane. Nothing was right.

Finally, Billy had his uniform ready to go. He wiped the drool from his shades before putting them on, collecting himself and moving into stride next to Liv. "It's going to be mental, isn't it?"

"Probably."

Conversation drifted off as they both set themselves for whatever they would face at the other end of their short walk. Billy was buried in his phone, flicking through Twitter. When he found something interesting, he'd lift his shades back to read it. "2014DM3 is expected to impact in the Indian Ocean, although the shape of the object is leading some experts to believe it will break up in orbit, making the final impact point harder to determine."

Liv didn't reply.

"What the fuck are we doing?"

Liv didn't reply.

"We have, like, two days left – that's it! Why the hell are we going to waste it working our asses off?"

They reached the corner of the Parade, two blocks from the entrance to the shopping centre, yet only about 20m from the back of the queue lined up to get in. On the other side of the road, another queue stretched out, presumably for the Coles, directly opposite the Foodland. Dotted along the outside of the queue, members of the army stood in watch. About halfway down the river of humanity a scuffle broke out, no doubt around positions in the queue. It soon turned into an all-out brawl between a number of people. Amidst the chaos a girl in a yellow princess dress screamed before her mum swooped in to protect her from a stray body or punch. The nearby army members rushed in.

Billy took his shades off to take in the scene. "Oh, fuck."

Liv didn't miss a step in her march, leaving him in her wake again.
"Liv," Billy yelled out, as the gap between them stretched out. "Really?"
"Really."

After another look over the crowd, the army and a rapidly departing Liv, Billy collected himself. He swore to himself then chased after her.

*

"What do you mean, you're going into work?" said Hayley.

"I've got business to take care of."

"You've got business to take care of here."

Patrick sighed. "Look, honey, there's a lot going on. This thing is huge."

"Exactly! Your family needs you."

"It's bigger than that."

"What? Real estate?"

"I just need a few hours. Tie up some loose ends. Got a couple of irons in the fire that could help us out."

"Are you hearing yourself right now?"

Patrick looked at her, speechless.

"Look at the TV. I don't think your commision is the answer to that!"

"You don't understand."

"I think I do. We need to pack our shit, now. We need to get to the shack, now."

"No! We need to stay put and come up with a plan. We need to get all the information before we make a decision."

*

Slumped on the couch seemed to be the best place to be at that moment. Routine would've meant a drink of water followed by a shower, then work or shops and brunch, depending on the day. But there was no routine for me today. There was just slumped on the couch with sweaty skin forming a sometimes sticky, sometimes slippery relationship with the leather underneath. I just found the least uncomfortable way to deal with it while watching the rolling TV coverage.

I was fully consumed in my detached numbness now and frantically playing catch up with the rest of the world.

The countdown was on to the launch of the European Space Agency's rocket, and there had been plenty of replays of the Chinese one going up in a frightful explosion after peaking at a height of approximately 30m above the takeoff pad. There were updates on the latest from world leaders and the latest from NASA. Locally, it was about the violence the night before, the calls for calm, and the efforts to maintain civil order, as seemed to be the term in use by police, politicians and media. Then there was the mayhem at supermarkets and shops – the problems with supply and the purchasing restrictions. Between all that and the ticker at the bottom of the screen rolling out more facts from further afield, it was all too much to get my head around.

It was too much to handle alone.

Thankfully Claire was on her way.

Until then, I'd just sit and watch in real time as my world that had figuratively been destroyed prepared to get literally destroyed. At some point I laughed. It was an acknowledgement to my ex and to the heavens who had somehow joined forces to mess my shit up. Well played, I thought – just far too good. All I could do was laugh.

*

Billy and Liv were ushered by army members through the small gap created down the middle of the waiting throng. There was someone addressing the crowd the pair didn't recognise. The same message was being repeated over and over through a megaphone. "Please remain calm. Please remain patient. Customers are limited to $150 of purchases."

Once at the front, a couple of security guards nodded the uniformed pair through.

Inside, there were more security and army personnel. The army members were brandishing rifles. It was no different to those outside, but being at such close range, with eyes directly on them, made Billy and Liv feel the full weight of the weapons.

"Holy shit," whispered Billy, removing his shades.

"Yuh-hu," replied Liv, in similar hushed tones.

"I've never seen a gun before."

"Me neither."

It was difficult to know whether to look at, or away from, the weapons. Fortunately, there were new signs covering almost every free surface in the entry area of the arcade. They dotted every free piece of real estate on the short walk to the Foodland entrance. It was the same three messages as the woman on the speaker was uttering outside – remain calm, remain patient, purchases limited to $150.

"This has most definitely escalated."

Liv gave Billy a nod as they neared the store. "How are they going to stop people buying over $150? I don't want to be doing that."

"I think the guys with the guns will be there to help you." Billy nodded at the final soldier.

They were soon past the security guards and into the store, where Steven had the staff gathered. He was a far cry from the version of the manager they were used to seeing. He looked like he hadn't slept all night, his eyes were wired and he was sweating. "...once again, we don't know how today is going to play out, but we're going to have to be on our toes, and if anything is going wrong, I need to know about it straight away. Got that? Straight away."

He paused to wait for a verbalisation of agreement.

"Very well. And if you can't get me, Kris or Kelly are your go-tos. Ah, welcome Liv and good of you to join us, Billy."

Billy shot Liv an expression of injustice before fixing his attention on the manager.

"We'll have two of the security team stationed near the main counter all day. We'll have soldiers close by as well. If we can deal with it, we'll deal with it fast. If not, we have support."

Steven paused to make eye contact with as many of his staff as he could. "This is going to be some sort of day. I'm told more stock is going to be rolling in all day – Evan, your team out back needs to be working overtime."

Evan nodded.

"Team..."

Billy hated it when he said team.

"...the next couple of days are going to be remembered for a long time. This team, my team, here at Norwood, are going to do what needs to be done to get as much product out the door as possible. People are going to be scared, angry, tense... just, be prepared for anything. Remember though, what we're about to do here will make a difference."

After a quick consultation with his watch, he shared more eye contact around his team. "Seven minutes. Time to rock."

"Hang on a sec! Boss, what about the food guarantee? If we work all day, don't we get a free shop?"

Steven shot Billy an unimpressed look. "The company will be following the protocols for shifts longer than eight hours."

"Have you seen the crowd outside? There'll be nothing left!"

"You'll get your supplies. We're told new supplies will be coming in all day."

There was an awkward silence.

"There better be some cheese sticks left."

###

###

CHAPTER 5:

PLANS

The door opened to reveal Claire, armed with some flowers, a bottle of gin and a bag full of snacks, tonic and lemon. She didn't say anything, just offered me a warm smile.

Although I'd thought I'd be ready for the moment, I was lost for words as well. More than that, the moment triggered a wave of emotion I'd thought I'd dealt with through several bottles of wine across previous evenings. Tears flowed.

"Thankfully I bought all this the other day, else I'd still be in the queue," said Claire. She grabbed my hand and led me to the kitchen, where she dropped her gifts and we embraced. This triggered another level of tears. We stayed in the moment for some time.

"Fourteen phone calls and 43 messages," said Claire.

I laughed through the tears.

"And not a thing from you."

"I just needed a moment," I said, as I sniffed some of the tears away.

"Newsflash – we might not have that many moments left."

We separated and smiled at each other before Claire turned attention to her care package. "We're going to need a drink."

I hit the kitchen to grab some bowls for the snacks. "My body says fuck no, but my brain wants a double."

"Double it is."

Once she'd taken the cling wrap from her nibbles tray and poured the chips into a bowl, I checked to see what I had in the fridge to add to the bounty. It was a grim and sickly looking wasteland within, the door shutting quickly.

"Alex should be here any minute. She's got Jacob with her."

"Cool," I said. "How's everything with Kendrick?"

"She hasn't really said much. I think he's in Singapore. The team had a friendly in Japan that was cancelled. Most of the team headed back to London.

He pulled the pin and was trying to scramble for a flight back home. Not sure how he's going to pull that off."

"Shit... she OK?"

"You know Alex."

"Yeah, probably going through turmoil, doesn't show it."

We both took a moment to ponder our friend in silence.

"So, are we talking Craig now, or do you want to wait for the final guest?" said Claire, eventually.

"I'd rather not at all."

"It's going to happen, you know it."

"Well, I only want to say it once."

"We'll wait then. That just leaves surviving the complete destruction of the planet as the other order of business," said Claire as she took a large swig of her gin, also a double.

I laughed. "Sure. What's your plan?"

"Don't laugh, I've been doing research."

I had a quick swig before I added another round of laughter.

"I'm serious. We can do plenty that'll make a difference if, you know, we survive tomorrow night."

The comment was enough to have me nodding with approval. "I'm listening."

Claire pulled an iPad from her handbag. "Right, first things first, we need to—"

The doorbell rang.

I opened it to reveal Alex – pram in one hand, bottle of gin in the other.

"Let's get pissed, bitches."

While we laughed, she leaned into the pram and apologised to her baby for the language. "What are we talking about? Comets or fuckface?"

*

"Twelve hours!" said Billy as he grabbed his shopping bags and followed Liv from the store. "Who works twelve hours?"

"Harden up, man," she said, nodding to the army guy, bored with the stagnant queue he'd watched all day.

"If we survive this shit, I want a medal."

Liv sighed, reaching her limits. "How much attention did your mum actually give you as a kid?"

Billy stared her up and down. "Plenty, I'll have you know. Saw the trend coming and was well ahead of her time. Smart woman, Mum."

Liv's response was delivered in the language of groan. A sense of claustrophobia hit her as they worked their way past the queue and to the door.

A nod was exchanged with the bouncers at the main doors before they headed outside. They continued to follow the queue up to the Parade until they turned right for the walk home.

That's when they saw the queue in all its glory – every bit as long as when they'd passed it half a day ago.

"Holy shit," said Liv as she took in the enormity of the numbers and the matching line for the Coles opposite. "They're going to be here all night," she added, quietly.

"No shit," said Billy at similar volume as he gazed into the distant crowd. "Hey, remember that brawl this morning?"

"Yeah."

"There was some girl in a princess dress caught up in it. Anyway, I literally saw her and her family at work an hour ago."

Liv shook her head and walked in silent contemplation.

"Nearly the entire day doing that! This lot will be here 'til morning."

"Your shift was quicker than lining up."

"Shit! So it was."

"There you go, you got a food medal."

*

"Gentlemen," said Patrick as he addressed the gathering. "...and lady. Firstly, I want to thank you all for your attention at very short notice in a very crazy, unprecedented time."

He looked around the table. Connections he'd known for years, many as far back as when his dad was establishing the business. Fourteen leaders of society and business, knowledgeable and powerful. They had a lot of sway in the Norwood area of the city.

"Time is precious right now so I won't keep you too long. Look, we don't know what's about to go down, nor how it will impact us here. But what I do know is how each and every one of you and your families have made this area what it is."

He looked around the familiar faces – Ratherfords, Petersons, Heagraves, Riccis – families that were the backbone of the area in both business and development. There wasn't much that happened along the Parade without the involvement of one or more of them.

"I just wanted to make sure whatever happens, we do as we always do. We work together to ensure our families and this area stays strong."

"How are we going to do that?" said Percy Peterson.

THE PARADE: APOCALYPSE SURVIVORS

"You would've seen the invite to the chat thread I sent though this morning. I set it up as a space to keep each other informed. If you get information that will affect us, share it. The more informed we are, the more likely we are to get through this. Share anything you find out. Between us we have connections to council, business, government and media. If we can pool the knowledge we gather, we raise our chances of getting through all this with a minimal impact."

"Or we could all die," said Angelo Ricci, with a smile.

Patrick nodded at him. "Or that. Look no one knows how any of this is going to play out. I'm looking to do everything I can not to end up dead. And that's exactly why we're here.

"Right, let's look at some scenarios."

*

"And this one!" Alex flashed her phone to the others to show off the pic she uncovered. "She's there as well, that's ten months ago."

Claire and I studied the picture.

"What an asshole," said Claire, before noting my reaction and squeezing my hand.

"So, at least seven months, but possibly ten, maybe more," said Alex, as she took her phone back for further investigation.

I took a large swig of my second gin. "Alright, you know what? Fuck it. Fuck him. I… can we talk about something else?"

I chased the rest of my drink down as the others came in to console me. It was at that point the tears flowed again. I just wanted any other conversation than this.

Alex pocketed her phone. "Shit, sorry Z, was just trying to help."

"I know. It's what I've been doing for the last four days. Stalking him, trying to find a why."

I laughed, full of self-loathing. "How sad is that?"

"It's not sad," said Claire. "You've got to do what you've got to do."

"Well, it didn't get me far. Waste of time."

"Craig or the four days?"

"Both."

Alex ended the generous remains of her own drink, collected the glasses and moved to the kitchen to pour another round. "Man, four days. If this shit goes tits up, that's, like, two-thirds of the rest of your life. I think."

She looked at her toddler sleeping in the pusher, his slumber negating the need for an apology.

I sighed. "Thanks for that insightful perspective."

Alex winked and gave a cheeky grin. It was too annoying not to like. She turned her focus back to the drinks. "Double?"

"Obviously," I said. "One for each day left."

"Man, two days. How the fuck do you process that?" said Claire.

"With a double," said Alex, as she slid one to both of us across the table and went back for hers. "In good news, Kendrick reckons he's got a flight back to Aus."

"Brilliant! How?" I said.

"Pulled in some favours with the sponsors, spent a lot of money. Anyway, looks like he'll make it before they kill flights. He's headed to Melbourne, but that's a whole lot better than on a different continent."

"To homecomings!" I said, as our glasses were raised in celebration.

I sipped deep. "If he can manage to get home, we should do something, you know, in preparation for what's about to happen."

That statement was followed by nods of agreement.

Then silence.

"Don't all rush forward with ideas."

More silence.

"At this rate it'll take us two days to actually think of an idea."

"Pressure, much?" said Alex. "You know I don't work well under pressure. Last time I was under this much I called for an epidural."

"Technically, it's not even two days."

"Seriously, Claire, you're not helping."

"Just trying to get some facts right. Isn't that what you're supposed to do?"

"Fine," said Alex. "Less than two–"

"Just over 32 hours."

"Thirty…. Shit, really? That's all? OK, so we've got tonight and tomorrow."

"To come up with a strategy?" said Claire.

"Yes."

"To prep for a potentially life-eliminating event?" I said.

"Yes!"

That ushered in a quick end to the conversation, followed by a long pause.

"We're fucked, aren't we?" said Alex.

###

###

CHAPTER 6:
COUNTDOWN

"That's the last of it," said Billy as he admired the pantry. "I reckon we've got ourselves at least two weeks of food if it all goes pear-shaped. When you add that to what we already had that's…"

He paused to do some mental arithmetic. Liv paused for the inevitable punchline.

"Two weeks and one day, all up."

"That's reassuring," said Liv, with a large lavishing of sarcasm.

Billy gave the pantry one last loving stare before closing the door. "Obviously, it's not going to matter much if we're incinerated in a 40km crater."

"Any time you want to shut the fuck up, that'd be great."

"What? It's true!"

Liv paused on the words. In the background, the TV went from one fact to the next. She tried to close her mind to it all, but every angle from every subject matter returned her mind to the same thoughts.

"Look, don't you think we should talk about this?" said Billy.

"About what?"

"All the things! Seriously, we can't just focus on selling groceries until the world blows up."

"We're not just doing that! We're partying."

"Yes, and that's great. Totally down with that plan. But, you know, we've got to talk about stuff."

"Stuff?"

"Yeah, like all the stuff." He pointed skywards. "Like that." Then the TV. "And that. All the things."

"I would much rather talk about anything else right now."

"We don't have many hours left."

"Exactly! I'd just like to spend some of them not thinking about stuff and things."

"Me too. But... I don't know... don't you think we should come up with a plan?"

"What plan?"

"Like... just... something."

Liv rolled her eyes, grabbed a cigarette and headed out to the balcony. Billy followed, grabbing a pinch of tobacco then playing with it in some rolly paper. "I don't have a plan. I want to talk to you about making one. Are you watching what's going on?"

"Of course I bloody am."

"I mean, what's really going on?"

Liv lit up and inhaled deeply. She looked through Billy as she slowly gave her response. "We are all probably going to die."

"Exactly! Well, maybe, perhaps. Maybe not. And then what?"

"Beyond pray?"

"Look, just humour me for a few minutes." He lit his rolly. "In case you're not up with what's going on, all these missiles they're sending out are almost entirely likely to fail. Well, maybe if you're watching the TV you'd think there's a chance, but have you been reading some of the threads on reddit and twitter?"

Liv had her eyes fixed on the small part of the city skyline she could see from the balcony. She blew a plume of smoke out in its general direction.

"It's... well, pretty grim. Mainstream media is just sugar coating shit."

"How is telling us a massive comet is coming to destroy us sugar coating it?"

"Just... you need to think details. They're trying to say things that keep the people calm."

"Isn't that a good thing?"

Billy spat in an attempt to dislodge a piece of tobacco from his lips. "I'd rather know the truth, thanks."

"So, what you're seeing on twitter is the truth, then, is it?"

"Exactly. It's the shit they don't want you to know."

"When have you become such an expert in... space stuff? And politics? And the media?"

"Since I started paying attention. Look, it's not me, I'm just trying to source the best information I can, so I can make the best decisions I can." Billy pointed to the TV inside, not that Liv was looking at him still. "What they're telling us... it's more for show to keep us as calm as possible right up to the last minute.

The government is totally messing with our shit so we don't go mental. But it's totally going to go mental. Look at the queues today."

He paused, waiting for a response. He was left disappointed.

"And that's just the tip of the iceberg. Shit's going to get, like, way worse and we need to make the best moves going forward."

"You think you're going to read a tweet that's going to save your life?"

"No… I'm just saying, the more we know the better we can plan."

"Plan what exactly?"

"To live… it's kind of an important thing to me."

"Look, Billy, I know you mean well and all, but I'm struggling."

"Me too, I'm just trying to help."

"I just need… I don't know… a bit of mental space," said Liv.

"I get that. I do. But, what are we going to do?"

"My plan is to stay busy. I'm going to work to do my bit, and when I'm not there I'm going to do my best not to think about it."

"OK, sure, but, like, have you thought about what you're doing when shit goes down tomorrow night?" said Billy.

Liv opened her mouth to speak but no words came out.

"You going to go to your parents or anything?"

"Fuck that."

"Fair enough. Well, good for me. I'm not entirely Adelaide connected. Fancy spending the last night on Earth with me?" said Billy. "I heard there might be some parties happening."

*

Alex reeled as the gin hit her throat. The pour was too rich, even for her seasoned tastes and tolerance levels. "So, the government is telling us jack shit, the shops are crazy, so we can forget about stocking up on food, we have no idea where the best place to ride out the night is and we have no idea what's going to happen nor how to prepare for the aftermath. Oh, except if we do survive, we have no idea whether we think it'll be better to be in the city or not."

She looked to the others for visual approval of her summation. "Oh, one more thing, we haven't come up with one single idea that's in the least bit useful in any of the above circumstances. Is that a good read of the room?"

"Pretty much nails it," I said.

"So… any ideas?" said Claire.

"Well, our point of difference seems to be not actually planning at all," said Alex, as she took another swig. "Even if we started meaningfully preparing

33

now, we still wouldn't catch up to where everyone else is. So I say we lean into our ineptitude a little more. Tomorrow night, come to the apartment. We're not going to get a better view of the city. Let's just get smashed, talk shit and watch the end of the world."

Claire and I looked at each other. I shrugged my shoulders then nodded my approval. I mean, why not?

Claire followed suit. "We're in."

"Brilliant," said Alex. "We can all sink on the same ship."

"Maybe it won't go down like that," I said.

"And if we wake up the day after, we're all smart enough to figure something out then, right?" said Alex.

"Sure," I said.

"Totally," said Claire.

We cheersed the plan that involved not actually planning and the responsibilities we hand-balled to our future selves, should we live long enough to be them.

*

Patrick wiped the sweat from his brow and looked at his reflection. He couldn't believe how much weight he'd gained in the last few months. He tried to breathe in and twist his body in a way that minimised the appearance of the extra kilos.

Behind him, he saw the reflection of a naked Olivia walking into her ensuite. She looked at his pose and laughed. "Mm-mmm grandad bod."

Immediately after uttering the words she froze, stunned they had fallen from her mouth and hoping they would be received in a way they were intended.

Patrick studied her for a moment, before returning his attention to his torso. "Needs some work, doesn't it?"

Olivia breathed a little easier. She'd seen Patrick in enough situations to know he could go on the attack when he perceived one aimed at him. There was a rage somewhere in there that simmered just under the surface. She cursed herself in silence for daring it to come out, while offering him a smile, then an embrace.

"So, when am I going to see you again, handsome?"

"Hayely's been trying to get us to head down the coast for tomorrow night."

"Oh."

"Heading to Normanville is a very bad move."

"Well, they're trying to evacuate Perth, I saw. Tsunami they reckon."

"I was talking about staying close to where we're strongest, staying closer to you. Makes the most sense."

34

It was the first time Olivia had heard him mention her name in relation to anything related to events after the impact. With all the unknowns, it was a positive to hear spending time with her was part of his thinking. She kissed him for what she hoped wasn't the last time.

###

###

CHAPTER 7:
LAST DAY

Time didn't seem to obey its normal rules. That day – the last day – seemed to go on forever in one regard and flash by in another. I'm not sure I'm explaining it properly.

Everything from the previous couple of days had escalated – the mayhem and lawlessness at night, the queues for food and supplies, and the need for quality information on what was about to unfold and the acceptance there was a complete lack of it.

Intertwined in all of that was a sense of being let down by the powers that be – in every direction really. There was a palpable resentment and anger you could feel with almost everyone, everywhere. You only had to see new coverage of the shopping centres to know how messed up things were. People were fighting over even the most basic stock.

Toilet paper. I'll never fully understand how this had become one of the most valuable resources in the universe in those few days – but it was. Seeing people fighting over toilet paper (among other things) still stays with me as a symbol of, well, everything above.

It just gets more bizarre to think about over time. I mean, in the months to come, food would be the new economy. A constant thought – consuming it, sourcing it, ensuring a supply – these things were soon to become reality. But toilet paper? Not once, not ever, have I had a supply issue with toilet paper.

People were feeling like pawns without control of their destiny, I suppose. Awaiting a fate no one asked for with limited ability to change their version of that fate in any meaningful way. It was disenfranchising. It was more than that, though. It was lonely.

I mean, I was alone in completely different ways, but even those who weren't through those days tell me they experienced the same thing. So you did what you could to feel like you had a purpose and it connected to something bigger about you, your beliefs, your way of life or those you loved. The thing is though, no matter how much praying, prepping or partying you did, you couldn't fill your head with enough things to escape the brutal truth – the end was coming fast. This stupid freak of fate had become a fuckening of everything your reality was based on. And no matter how much you connected outwards you had to process that alone. No one could escape those thoughts. All thoughts led to Rome.

It was a unique kind of loneliness.

So, that's how the people of Earth spent those last moments in time before the world changed. It was more connected and real than probably any other moment in history at one level and the loneliest at another.

Maybe those who were destined to survive were being conditioned to what they would face on the other side of it all.

*

For the people of Adelaide, the impact would fall in the very early hours of Saturday morning 12/4, so early it may as well have been Friday night.

It was going to be an end of the working week like no other.

###

###

CHAPTER 8:
LAST NIGHT

"You're late," said Alex, as she picked up the phone.

"So sorry," I said. "I'm still with Claire and her folks. We've literally had three goodbyes already. We're getting there, slowly."

"Am I on speaker?"

I looked at Claire, her brother and her parents, huddled together, tears all around. "You are."

"Good. I know you're slowly getting there but the comet is not. The TV is super depressing and between that and the lack of adult company I'm nearly a bottle of red deep already. Hurry the fuck up."

I mouthed sorry to Claire's mum. She smiled, then nodded her approval of their immediate departure.

"Hello?"

"Alex! Sorry, we're on our way."

"Now?"

"Now."

*

"You coming or what?" yelled Liv at a volume capable of being heard through Billy's door and over his music.

There was no response. As she turned her back to leave, the door opened and Billy stepped through. He was wearing a black T-shirt with the letters SHTF across the front.

"Ready!" he announced, before he looked down at his top. "Like it? I wanted to be, like, super on point tonight."

She rolled her eyes before investigating his latest creation.

"Don't look too closely at the edges," he said.

"Is that one of those shit punk bands you listen to?"

"What? No! SHTF!"

She stared at him, blankly.

"Shit hits the fan. You know, this. This... everything. End of days! SHTF!"

"Are you high?"

"Obviously."

Liv groaned and headed to the door.

"What? It's party prep 101."

Liv locked the door after they'd passed through. They headed down the stairs to street level. All the while she was as careful as possible not to encourage further conversation from Billy, which failed dismally.

"Anyway. This shirt – talking point. Just saying."

Silence.

"Man, end-of-days party. It's going to get seriously loose, right?"

Silence.

"Like, the sort of loose where even I go, 'shit that was loose'. That level of loose."

Silence.

"You know Em's gonna be there tonight."

"I was literally the one who told you that."

"She's..." started Billy, before making noises of satisfaction.

Liv made a vomit noise in response.

"What? She is. Little blonde pocket rocket of yum."

"If I could live the rest of my life and not hear you say those words again, that would be about the perfect amount of time for me."

"Whatever. Just saying, a few drinks, the right music, the fear of dying horribly in an apocalypse, a quirky on-trend T-shirt – it could be the perfect storm."

"I'm pretty sure the perfect storm means when a whole bunch of horrible things happen at once."

"And?"

"Well, I guess if you're happy for that frame of reference for your sex life..."

"Good point. I guess it's a fair step up from the current frame of reference."

Liv absolutely knew the exact amount of encouragement to offer at this point of the conversation was zero. She also knew it wouldn't stop Billy responding.

"I'll give you a clue, it's a Star Wars character."

Silence.

"Well, close enough to one."

Silence.

"Hand solo."

"Ewww. Did it ever occur to you that being constantly stoned, your homemade fearmongering T-shirts and the general vibe of desperation is what causes the situation in the first place?"

"Say what you want about me, but don't bring the T-shirt into it. He's an innocent in all of this, aren't you buddy?"

"Besides, what makes you even think Em is into guys?" said Liv.

"Because she dated Sal... and Zane."

"I mean just guys, maybe her spectrum is wider than you think."

"Whoa, whoa, whoa, are you doing what I think you're doing?" said Billy. "Not cool! I saw her first! Bro code."

"I think you're very confused with the jurisdiction of this bro code," said Liv. "And the fact that you want to align with anything that has the word bro in it should eliminate you as a chance with Em from a quality control perspective."

"Excuse me, quality is my one wood."

"Eww," said Liv.

"It's a golf term, means I'm good at it."

"Oh."

"Anyway," said Billy. "If you are right about her spectrum and you're telling me you'd be interested, you'd still be competing against me."

Liv went to respond, but a snort-level laugh quickly replaced it.

"That was supposed to be a threat," said Billy as they stepped onto the footpath and into the last night.

*

"There's been no mention of it anywhere," said Hayley.

Patrick took a sip of his scotch. "All I'm saying is if a tsunami is going to be a complete disaster for Perth, we can't in any way say the coast is going to be completely fine here."

"I told you I've looked into this. The tsunami is supposed to be coming down from the Indian Ocean. There's no way Normanville would be affected."

"They also said the comet is unstable and may break up in the atmosphere. What happens if something lands closer?"

"We can't guarantee anything. What if the comet ploughs right into Norwood?"

Patrick met her frustration with a look of bewilderment. "Look, I'm not risking it down by the coast. End of story."

"Asshole," said Hayley, before venting a noise of displeasure and exiting the room.

Patrick waited a few seconds before pulling out his phone. He typed, 'Good news, I'm staying local', then sent it to Olivia.

He looked up to see Hayley looking at him, full of judgement.

He slipped his phone away in the most nonchalant way he could muster. "It's the right call. We'll get through this. We have so much support around here. Whatever happens, it's our best shot."

Hayley didn't respond with words. She held her judgmental look a few seconds longer before leaving the room once again.

*

"I don't want to go," said Sara Mochizuki.

She watched the hills approaching in the dusk light. The streets were as quiet as she could remember as her dad drove. She turned her attention back to her phone and the stream of messages coming in.

"It's just one night," said Yamato, trying to hide his impatience in soothing tones.

"The last night is not just one night."

"It is a night for family."

She groaned her displeasure.

"I want to be with my friends."

"You have friends up here."

She groaned again. "It's not the same."

Sara was soon back in her messages, before returning to the conversation with a frustrated sigh. "You just don't get it."

Yamato ignored the comment, keeping his focus on the road as the city grid of straight roads gave way to the windy incline that would lead them to their destination for the evening. The silence was a good chance for his daughter to let her anger settle.

"And you look ridiculous."

Or not.

He pulled the car to the side of the road and eyed her. "Enough!" he snapped.

"Please accept what is happening. We are five minutes away from the Jamesons' place and I want to walk in with my daughter and spend these last few hours with people I know and love."

It was not often he took a tone with Sara and her body language told him she understood the gravity of his words.

"Any number of things could happen tonight – from very bad to very lucky. I love you. Very much. Ever since your mum died… she… she would want this."

41

He dabbed the moisture from his eyes.

"If the worst happens I want you there. Maybe we get lucky and everything is fine, whatever that is, but for every outcome in between a disaster and a miracle we need to have each other's backs. Possibilities and people you can trust is all we truly have right now."

Sara nodded as the enormity of the night finally grabbed her. Yamato noticed her shift in mood and reached out his hand to hold hers. She looked at it briefly before taking it.

"There is nothing more important than family. There is nothing more important than you."

It was Sara's turn to wipe away a tear. Once satisfied with her work the two made eye contact again, both soon in embarrassed laughter at the emotions of the moment – Sara dressed for a casual night out, Yamato wearing a white suit, accentuated by red detailing. The highlight of which was a rising star on the centre of his shirt.

"And I do not look ridiculous, thank you. There's only one missile left that can save the world, so I'm wearing the old national colours to back our rocket in."

Sara gave him an incredulous look.

"OK, maybe it's a little ridiculous."

*

"About time!" said Alex, as she opened the door to Claire and I.

It was hard to not be somewhat envious of Alex's apartment. It was on the upper levels of a highrise on Greenhill Rd with ridiculously good views of the city and beyond. It was modern and spacious, every inch of it enhanced by Alex's eye for design and art.

She led us to the kitchen, where a second bottle of red was already well under way. She set it aside, lined up three glasses and proceeded to make gin and tonics all around. "Jacob's down but it won't last, he'll need another bottle soon. Don't worry about noise or anything. Doubles for you two? I'm not ending this world as the most pissed bitch."

We smiled as we unpacked our bags of snacks and drinks, then settled into the bar stools.

Soon, the round was issued out, with all the glasses raised.

"Here's to…" said Alex. "Actually, I've got nothing."

"That's not like you," I said. "What about, good friends?"

"Good start," said Alex.

"And, erm…"

"Surviving?" added Claire.

"That'll do," said Alex. "To good friends and surviving!"

We clinked glasses and consumed.

"Any updates on Kendrick?" I said.

"He made it to Melbourne. Was one of the last flights to get out. Just a matter of getting home now. He's trying to sort out a car. Hopefully he's already on his way, but he reckons it's mental, like, everywhere. He's on a standby list. Worst case he hits the road in the morning if he didn't manage to get something arranged tonight."

"When did you speak to him last?"

"Just after I spoke to you. Haven't been able to reach him since. The phone network is pretty fucked right now."

We offered reassuring smiles, but felt for the angst she must've been going through. At least he was back in Australia.

"Anyway, enough of that," said Alex. "Let's get smashed before the comet does it for us."

*

"The fuck are you looking at?"

Billy was thrown by the question from the random skinny guy with the blonde-tipped mullet and wispy moustache. They were gathered around a firepit in the backyard of the place rented by a friend of Liv's friend. Things had been getting loose from early on and the firepit was their refuge from the craziness in the back lounge room that spilled onto the back verandah.

The tunes were cranked to a level only achieved when everyone was sure the cops had a million more important things to deal with than disturbing the peace. Whether it was dancing or singing or arguing or making out, everything was being dialled up to eleven. The result was an uneasy feeling that things could go south very fast.

Mullet boy represented all of that in a sentence, asking the most dangerous question and staring at Billy, waiting for him to fuck up his response.

On a positive note, Billy and Liv had been in conversation with Em and her friend Ashley, both giving similar weight to the evening. Down side, Em and Ashley were holding hands.

Billy shared a looked with each of the girls in turn before returning his attention to mullet boy. Every cell in his body knew it was an extremely bad idea to inflame the situation, but no matter how aligned they were on the topic, there was a part of his brain that had the deciding vote. That also happened to be the same part of his brain that could not resist making smartass comments. Especially when pushed. This was doubly true when put in a socially awkward situation, where his brain would challenge itself to say the most inappropriate thing he could think of.

It was a compulsion Liv knew well, which would explain her shaking her head and mouthing 'no' when he looked at her seconds earlier and pantomiming a preemptive facepalm.

He gulped, then looked back at mullet boy. "I'm not entirely sure. Best guess is some variety of bipedal primate, but anything beyond that would be pure speculation."

Behind him he heard Liv groan. In front of him mullet boy took several seconds and facial expressions to distil the sentence. He watched as it was eventually filed in the category of fighting words, prompting a charge towards him.

Billy jumped out of his chair, ready for the attack. It was at this point he cursed his brain for being so predictable, especially knowing fighting was far from a strong suit.

"There he is!" said an older teen over his shoulder.

"Get him!" said another.

Billy didn't know whether to turn to the new potential threat or keep his focus on mullet boy. Fortunately, as mullet boy rounded the last part of the firepit that separated them, the two new players tackled him to the grass.

The crunching sound of impact was soon followed by rolling bodies and flying fists.

Billy watched on for a few moments to be sure the threat to him was extinguished, then turned to the girls. "Shall we go?"

"Good call," said Em as she grabbed her jacket from the back of her chair.

Liv stared at him as she made her way to her feet. "You literally can't help yourself, can you?"

"What?"

"Some variety of bipedal primate? Really?"

Billy gave a cheesy grin, designed for maximum Liv annoyance, before the four of them headed for the house and their exit. Billy, bringing up the rear, even managed to swipe a couple of bottles of alcohol from the bucket in the laundry as they went.

They were soon on the tree-lined street out front of the house. The music was still loud enough to have to raise their voices to hear each other.

"Every time I start to think you may be smarter than I give you credit for, you pull something like this," said Liv.

"Me? I could've said anything. He was looking for a fight regardless."

"What about I don't want to fight?"

Billy shrugged. "Maybe that, I guess."

Liv groaned.

"Anyone getting any signal?" said Em, playing with her phone.

"The network is pretty grim," said Ashley.

"So, what are we doing?" said Billy. "We've still got a couple of hours of life on Earth."

Em and Ashley looked at each other and shrugged in silent conversation.

"Come back to ours," said Billy.

"Either that or I get a cab," said Ashley.

"The cab network will be slower than the phone network right now, you'll be here all night. C'mon, we're only a ten-minute walk from here."

Another silent communication shrug.

Billy revealed the bottles he'd swiped from the party house. They clinked together as he presented them to the group. "We've got drinks – plenty of options – and I've got a few juicy buds left too, if that's your thing."

It was enough to resolve the unspoken conversation.

"Done," said Em.

"Boom!" said Billy, as he gave Liv a sly wink.

She rolled her eyes as they made their way home.

###

###

CHAPTER 9:

COLLISION

Whoever we were, wherever we were, and whatever we were doing come the moment of impact, we were all doing the same thing. One eye on the sky, the other on the TV while praying – in whatever prayer mattered to each person.

Time had run out.

There was no escaping what would happen next and that thought alone was enough to rip a hole in the pit of your stomach that could not be filled with any amount of company or words or alcohol or happy pills.

We watched the shot on the TV that will be seared into every survivor's memory for as long as they live – the satellite camera vision of the comet punching into the atmosphere and glowing so bright the entire screen went burnt-out white.

Then nothing.

We were all still alive!

The news reports struggled to relay any useful information, while we celebrated.

In Adelaide, our celebrations would be very short-lived.

*

Elsewhere outside the city, there were so many things that would stay with Yamato from that night. While many of them were yet to play out, the first truly eerie sensation was the sound of silence. Sure, the TVs still blared information, but the room full of people watching on at the Jamesons did not make a sound. There must have been forty people there. And silence. He wrapped his arm around his daughter and pulled her in tight. She reciprocated.

Any pretence of the social normality they'd been experiencing for most of the night had evaporated. Even the TV coverage was eerily light on words as the minutes turned to seconds. There was nothing left to do now but wait and let the cards of fate fall where they may.

Helpless.

The last words he remembered from the coverage between the wait and life-changing forever was, "To every soul watching on, in this extraordinary time for humanity, may fate be kind and may we see each other on the other side."

All eyes were fixed on screens, both inside and out on the balcony. As the dust settled on the moment of impact on the coverage, a buzz of noise started rising out of the silence. Anticipation built. No one wanted to speak for fear it would somehow change their collective fate. After a slow motion ten seconds, someone eventually said, "That's got to be good, right?"

Someone else yelled "Yes" from the core of his being, which opened the path for a collective round of screaming in wild celebration. They were not dead.

Yamato squeezed his daughter again with everything he had. She turned and buried into him with a hug.

That's when the night outside lit up like day. Those not already on the balcony rushed to see the action.

Yamato and Sara also raced to see what was happening, cramming up in the packed space next to a teen boy, Jack, who was taking photos of the sky and the large chunk of rock floating through it.

Yamato gasped. "It's massive."

Jack nodded while Sara gripped her dad tighter.

That massive object was a small fragment of the comet.

*

"Oh shit!" said Billy as the sky pulsed as blue as a summer's day.

He was crammed onto the tiny apartment balcony with Em, Liv and Ashley. The seconds passed in slow motion. All eyes were drawn to the small wedge of sky visible from their townhouse. Through hand holds, the four of them stayed connected as they watched the moment unfold.

The slither of blue sky turned yellow, red then white, before a rock, almost golden as it burned through the atmosphere, sailed in and out of view. It was blinding, but mystical. Impossible not to watch.

The light show ended as quickly as it began. It was soon replaced by the noise, distant and godly. The sky had been ripped apart, literally ripped. It groaned into the night, deep, guttural and reverberant. The noise echoed around the broken sky, then up and down the streets, around everything. Through everything.

The apartment building shook.

The balcony complained. A small deposit of mortar dropped from above onto the railing.

"Get inside!" yelled Liv.

*

The sound of a baby crying was barely audible over the TV in Alex's apartment. Even that was being ignored as the three of us stared out at the views of the city and beyond. The shaking had stopped at least. While the darkness had swallowed the lightshow from seconds earlier, the night looked different now. Shooting stars streaked in from the south west. Dozens of them, mere seconds apart.

"What in the actual fuck was that?" said Alex. "Was that the comet?"

"Think so," I said. "Or some of it at least... I guess?"

"Some of it? That was some?"

"I... I don't know."

"What the fuck is it doing over Adelaide?"

Neither Claire or I responded. We didn't know.

Out of the window a streak of orange light connected the sky to the ground. An object smashed into the plains west of the city. While the impact was hidden from our view by the CBD, the explosion in the aftermath was not. A ball of fire ripped out into the atmosphere, silhouetting the buildings in the city for a few seconds before receding from sight.

We had just seen a tiny piece of the comet smash into some spot in the northern suburbs. Something that would've killed a lot of people. I remember the silence that followed as everyone processed what they'd seen, what it meant and how real everything had now become.

"Oh fuck!" said Alex, eventually.

*

"Oh fuck!"

Yamato wasn't sure who said it, but he was sure it spoke for the group watching the mayhem from the balcony. There was something in the tone of the statement that perfectly reflected how he felt as the explosion tore through the western suburbs. It was matched in quick time by fragments of the rock ploughing into parts of the Adelaide plains north and south – long and lethal glowing orange tracer missiles from the heavens. They were sitting ducks now. No control over their fate. Exposed. Doomed. That was the tone of those two words.

He held Sara closer and prayed in silence to a god he didn't believe in that they'd be spared.

Time played tricks. It bent around the fear and reality of the moment. It distorted the seconds. There were no seconds, just a helpless void where time should be. It was too much to quantify and impossible to measure as the jetsam of 2014DM3 rained down. Any moment was potentially their last, likely before any awareness it was even happening could form.

The moment just was. Until it was no more.

The impossible-to-measure seconds passed. The chaos abated, as unannounced as it had come.

No one dared speak. No one dared seal their fate with words of pessimism or positivity. No one dared jinx the moment. So, the hopeless tone of the "Oh fuck" hung in the air, across distorted time, until it did not.

Yamato felt his daughter's squeeze on his hands tighten again. It was strong. It burned. It was pleasant. It reminded him he was alive. In that moment, he couldn't have asked for anything more.

He reached a hand out to the young man in front of them, briefly flicking through the images he'd taken on his phone. He knew him through connections and knew his parents were out of town. The touch on Jack's shoulder was a way to check in to see if he was OK. Jack turned, gave a thin smile and nodded a silent yes.

*

For all the things that were destined to happen on the Adelaide plains in the aftermath of the events of that night, I have to remind myself of the paths that crossed on a balcony in the foothills at that moment in time. Maybe life was tipping its lid, maybe it was an Adelaide thing because everyone seems to be connected to everyone somehow, or perhaps it was destiny. Whatever the case, time and events would give the moment Yamato checked in with Jack weight no one could have appreciated in the moment.

It gives me shivers whenever I think about it.

*

It had been over a minute since the townhouse last shook. The first rattle had been from the passing of the rock, the others, no one knew. Ash cuddled Em on one couch, Billy and Liv held hands on the other. They looked at each other in silence.

"It's over, right?" said Liv.

"I think so," said Billy. "Fuck! I really should not have had that last cone."

He stood up. Paced back and forwards a couple of times before heading to the balcony sliding door and wandering outside. All was dark and clear and calm. A handful of stars stared back at him through the slither of city-blinded sky. Apart from the distant sounds of sirens and the sounds of the neighbours, it could have been the middle of the night on any given night. "Whooo-hoooo!" he screamed into the dark stillness before heading back inside.

*

"What the hell?" said Alex as she looked over the wounded city, rocking her baby in her arms. Behind her the TV coverage was confirming the impact point as the Bay of Bengal. "Seriously, what the actual hell?"

"They said it might break up on entry. I guess that was the smaller bit," said Claire.

"The smaller bit? Jesus."

I had my attention on the TV and told everyone to shush.

"There are reports coming in of a smaller fragment landing in the Melbourne area. In the vicinity of Frankston," came the report from the TV.

We looked at Alex, not knowing what to say.

She stood in stunned silence for a moment. Looked at us in turn, then at Jacob. She shook her head. "No."

"No, no, no, no. no, no."

She repositioned Jacob so she could draw the phone from her pocket, repeating the same word over and over. She dialled Kendrick.

I walked over and offered to take Jacob off her hands. "He was getting a car, right? He could be hours away from Melbourne by now."

Alex shook her head as the phone rang. It went to message bank. "Kendrick. No, no, no."

"It's the phone lines," said Claire. "Everything's down. It doesn't mean anything."

*

But it did.

The Melbourne impact changed everything. The destruction was real. There was a whole lot of new realities we had to come to terms with in mere moments, but Melbourne's demise made everything that was happening very real for every Australian survivor.

You can't live in Australia for any period of time and not know someone from Melbourne.

The city did not lay in ruins. It simply was no more – vaporised, no doubt, along with its four million residents. Probably only a crater remained – a new coastline – a reshaping of our country. Gone.

The reality is destruction was coming to all corners of the earth in its own way and time, but straight out of the gate we were hit in the face.

While some celebrated their moment of survival in Adelaide, the news of Melbourne was already hitting hard for others.

Watching your friend get struck by that in real time was a moment seared into my memory for all time. There are plenty of those moments these days, but that was the first. Then came my own grief at my memories of Kendrick and the aching hope he'd made it out. As all of that was punching me in the gut my mind kept recalling people I knew who lived there. Thoughts of a dozen people hit me straight away, but memories of others kept coming at me throughout the night. I stayed silent, as it wasn't a patch on what my friend was experiencing, but they all hit me.

It was a brutal initiation into the new normal.

*

"Yesss!" wailed Billy into the night.

He was back on the balcony again, searching for his stash in the mess that had been made of the table and its contents in the shaking. The others filtered out to join him again.

"Hells yes!" came the voice of a random neighbour in response to his cry.

"Whoo-hooo!" screamed Billy at the acknowledgement, a grin of pride shared with the others. "Boom!" he added, as he located his stash.

He soon found himself in a group hug. They danced around the small table in an awkward and elated four-part circle. Laughing into the night.

*

"Hi, Kendrick, me again. Can you please pick up? Please. Seriously. Just pick up." Alex shook as she left another message, Claire and Zoe holding her.

Her message continued. It got awkward and lost, then drifted into silence. Eventually she dropped the phone and wailed.

Claire and I squeezed her and Jacob tighter.

*

Yamato embraced his daughter and the two laughed at the craziness. At surviving. He saw Jack again nearby and called him over.

"So, you're good, yeah?"

"Yeah, think so."

"If you need anything, we're here."

Jack smiled at Yamato and Sara. "Thanks."

The room around them buzzed. Steve Jameson was doing his best to focus everyone on a plan of action. It was a tough crowd to organise as families gathered together, some sharing their relief at survival, others scrambling to their phones to make contact with loved ones in Melbourne. It was a mixed bag of reactions as people processed all the happenings in whatever way they presented. The television coverage continued around them. Lots of information, little news. Melbourne was lost. Beyond that, it was doubt and speculation and unknowns.

###

###

CHAPTER 10:
DESTRUCTION

Of course, the new world, showing itself as it was, wouldn't allow us much time to dwell on the enormity of Melbourne. It had plenty of tricks up its sleeve yet. And the next of those was already headed our way.

We didn't know it yet, but from the Melbourne impact point a blastwave had pulsed out in all directions, eating everything in its wake. It would lay waste to thousands of kilometres of countryside before it was done.

Not only that, but ejecta had torn from the hole that used to be Melbourne. Molten projectiles of rock and impact debris had shot into the air... into the atmosphere. So big was the strike on Earth, those missiles would rain down around the rest of the continent and the rest of the world.

Any thoughts of some miracle result of breezing through the comet strike unharmed as a planet and a species had already evaporated in what we'd seen. Shit was real. And we didn't yet even know what was headed our way from the Melbourne blast.

*

Alex lay in the foetal position on the couch with Jacob curled up on her chest.

Claire and I had let her be while we turned our attention to the view. Fires raged in several points across the city where smaller pieces of comet had impacted the suburbs.

We found ourselves holding hands as we surveyed the damage in silence.

Soon after, the entire building started to rattle and we gripped each other a little tighter. Something about the noises the building made didn't fill anyone with confidence as to its structural integrity. Not that anyone said anything out loud.

"Oh my god!" said Claire as the view over the hills caught her eye.

I leaned in closer to the window, tracking where she was looking. "What the hell is that?"

A blastwave rose up from beyond the hills and shot projectiles of all sorts over the Adelaide plains. The first thing my mind thought of was the Melbourne blast. Every sense told me this was the aftermath. Claire and I pondered the brutality in silence.

"What's going on?" said Alex.

She sensed something was not good and headed over.

"Oh shit."

*

It had been racing towards us in the minutes since the Melbourne blast. An all-encompassing concussion shockwave of wind and energy, tearing up – or down – everything in its path. Just over 650 kilometres separated Melbourne and Adelaide, and it only took what we now think was 12 minutes to reach us.

It would be impossible to imagine the ferocity of energy that initially shot out from the Melbourne impact. But even after travelling across a fair chunk of the country, losing power and momentum at every step, it still hit us like a hurricane.

The winds picked up on the Adelaide plains, sucking towards the hills that protected us to the east. But it was just the precursor of what was about to be unleashed. The Melbourne blastwave front soon hit the far side of the Adelaide hills. It exploded out and over the Adelaide plains in a wall of dust and debris the likes of which I'll never see again.

Soon, all matter of broken objects shot into the air above the city's east and rained down over the plains. No object was too big to be caught up in its forces. Trees, cars, stobie poles, people, animals all shot up hundreds of metres into the air before beginning their final dive towards the ground.

The city was pummelled in an assault that lasted several minutes. Houses were destroyed and fires raged as the cloud of destruction rose up and up until the hills were obscured from view.

Not long after the ejecta, hot molten rocks that had exploded out of the Melbourne impact site and into the atmosphere started raining down their destruction as well.

It was a show of force that will not only stay with the survivors who witnessed it forever, but also served as an apocalyptic level statement from the skies that said – you are no longer safe.

It really was a moment that made everything real. I mean, it was one of many, but this was the moment that let everyone know that whatever happened hundreds of kilometres away in Melbourne, and thousands of kilometres away in the Indian Ocean, could not be kept from our door. It was too astronomically big and the world too connected.

While seeing the fragment of comet pass over us was the harbinger of global destruction, this was the harbinger of death coming to our door.

*

Yamato and Sara watched the city below from the crowded balcony. Trees, cars and all manner of objects rammed into buildings near and far. The house rattled from one nearby impact or another. No one felt safe but no one wanted to leave their vantage point over the destruction.

The markings on the street below were now barely visible through all the debris that had rained down upon it.

Seconds later, a fiery ball of destruction hammered into the suburbs just to the south of the city centre, then another one out north. The ejecta started delivering its own brand of destruction.

"What the hell is that?" someone called out.

There was no response.

Another high-speed piece of molten rock slammed into a nearby suburb, triggering an enormous explosion that must've taken out several blocks.

Yamato leaned into Sara. "We need to get inside," he said.

"I want to go home," she replied.

Yamato nodded and headed inside to grab his keys, Sara at his side.

"Where's the water gone?" called someone from the balcony.

It was enough to stop him in his tracks.

*

The impact of the comet wasn't done with Adelaide yet. It had one more play to make on our city and it would be the most devastating of them all.

Tsunami.

Even though there was a general warning to get to higher ground to be safe from the tsunami threat across the country, all the modelling that had been presented in the lead-up to impact night showed Perth as the only city under any real threat, given it lay on the fringe of the Indian Ocean.

Of all the capital cities in the country, Adelaide should have been the safest, given it was positioned halfway up a gulf, well away from the oceans.

I'm not sure we'll ever fully understand what triggered the tsunami that rolled in that night but, regardless of the cause, the result was devastating.

A wall of water anywhere from 100m to 150m high (depending on who you believe) rolled straight over the beachfront suburbs and headed east. Nothing was spared. The entire west of the city had no hope.

It was surreal watching the first wave. It dwarfed everything in its wake. Every few seconds the wave front energy would appear to abate and you would assume it was starting to slow down, but it didn't.

Everything our city had been built up to be over the generations was coming apart before our eyes. And we had front row seats.

That's when Claire started repeating, "No, no, no!" over and over again.

At first I thought she was feeling what I was as we witnessed our city's destruction, but it soon became apparent her focus was on her parent's home in Prospect. If the city fell there would be no hope for Prospect.

Another layer of a sick feeling washed over me when I finally worked out the ramifications.

I just watched in silence as the tsunami rolled over 8km of suburbia and crashed into the city centre. I didn't even want to think about the kilometres of housing north and south of that point that had fallen to the waters. I just held Claire's hand as she repeated the same word over and over.

The tsunami didn't stop at the city either. The first wave pushed all the way to the Parade – as far along as Osborne Tce – another 2km east. Everything in its wake was a wasteland. Well, certainly in the western suburbs, where almost no buildings survived the bombardment. Most buildings still stood in the city and the affected areas out east, but few of their occupants would've survived.

It was an event that would shape the future of the city like no other.

I didn't know what to say about the moment. I didn't know what to say to either of my friends about their losses. I didn't know what to do. Or who to be. I didn't know anything.

*

"What the fuck is that?" said Billy.

He had already been staring at the changes around him in disbelief.

"Oh my God," said Liv. "It can't be."

"What else could it be?" said Billy. "What the fuck do we do?"

By now he, Liv, Em and Ashley were all standing on the balcony, while watching the wall of water approach. No one said tsunami, but they all knew. The word had been mentioned enough in the media during the previous three days to be front of mind.

"Could we make a run for it?" said Em.

"There's no way we're outrunning that," said Liv. "It'll be here before we've even gotten down the stairs."

"What about the roof?" said Billy, as he looked up and studied his climb options.

"No time for that either," said Liv.

They all turned back to the water rushing towards them, nearly on top of them. The front seemed so harmless as it hit the building's brickwork on the lower level. Soon it was pressing against the ground floor windows until they gave way under the weight of it all.

Around them, the sounds of destruction and screaming bounced around the smothering tones of torrents of water.

They started to hear the downstairs door rattle, followed by a scream of help.

"That's the old lady!" said Billy as he tried to lean over the edge for a better view of the lower level.

"Maryanne!" yelled Liv. "Maryanne!"

"What do we do?" said Em.

They looked around for a solution. The water continued to inundate the area, rising every second, and fast.

"We can't go down there, it'd be a death run," said Billy. "Have we got anything we can throw down to her to help?"

"She can't get the door open!" said Liv.

"Do we have a rope or something?" said Billy.

"Rope? No!"

Even during the course of their conversation the water had continued to claim the apartment brick by brick. Now it was at the top of the downstairs front window.

It kept rising. Soon, the ground floor was inundated and the water suddenly threatened their first-floor perch. They stood in silence as it rolled in, thoughts of what in all likelihood had happened to the old lady downstairs turning to their own fates.

Soon the water topped the balcony. Within seconds their feet were drenched and standing became difficult as the balcony rattled and the torrent did its best to take their feet from under them.

"What do we do?" yelled Em.

"I think it's levelling out," said Liv.

"You sure?" said Billy.

"I… think so."

Water flooded into the apartment as they gripped the balcony railing. It lapped up to their shins, but its progress had noticeably slowed.

"I think she's right," said Em.

"So, what do we do?"

"We either head inside or make a run for the roof. If we can can climb on the railing here we might be able to use the top of the balcony to get to the roof," said Billy

The balcony seemed to shift and the four stumbled slightly before regaining their feet.

"I cast my vote for inside," said Liv.

"Agreed," said Billy.

With that, the four inched their way from the balcony into the lounge room. The water was at shin height. It had pushed the couches, TV cabinet and coffee table up against the kitchen counter.

Liv waded her way to the counter, then climbed on top. The others followed. Once settled, they held hands in silence.

*

Yamato and Sara returned to the balcony at the Jamesons to see the tsunami roll across the city. Moonlight reflected the water as it swallowed suburbs, eating its way inland. Light went out in the water's wake – the only visual indication of the damage they could see from the foothills. It was an eerie reality to process. Everyone watched in silence, the occasional gasp of disbelief the only sound spoken.

When it hit the city, cries of anguish could be heard. They increased as the tsunami raged into the eastern suburbs.

Yamato's heart sank as he watched the advance. Their home in Rose Park was on the fringe of the city's parklands. The heritage home on tree-lined streets now looked totally exposed as the waters marched east.

He squeezed Sara tight as the waters pushed past the CBD. Faint hope soon turned to no hope.

"Where's Rose Park?" said Sara, as she leaned into her dad.

She knew the answer. They had spotted it plenty of times from the exact balcony they were on but, despite the night making placing locations over the Adelaide plains more difficult, it was clear their suburb had fallen.

Yamato started sobbing to himself. Twenty five years of memories – gone.

"Dad?"

The pair exchanged a look, confirming what Sara already knew. She cried and the two embraced.

*

Claire, Alex and I watched the waters rush in from the west. Within no time they claimed the city and soon the lower stories of the apartment building we were in were surrounded by water.

We watched each wave as it rolled in, surging over the top of the previous one as it started to withdraw to the west. Cars were tossed around and piled together along Greenhill Rd.

The building shook, rumbled and groaned.

In the distance, we saw city buildings collapse under the water's weight.

Silence was the expression of the disbelief that filled the lounge room.

"Not my place too," said Claire, eventually. "What am I going to do without a home?"

"Well, we're completely fucked then, aren't we?" said Alex.

"I now have nothing left," said Claire.

Before anyone could respond the power went dead.

*

"Here comes another one," said Billy.

They were gathered by the sliding door to the balcony that no one trusted to put body weight on any more. It soon became clear the new wave was bigger than the last.

"Get back!" said Liv.

"Shit!" said Billy.

Liv retreated to the kitchen with the others in tow.

She was soon on the kitchen bench again. "Grab hold of something!"

Billy grabbed the candle now lighting the lounge room before jumping up beside her. He offered his hand to Ashley, while Liv helped Em. Once everyone was perched on the counter, they turned to the door and waited for the inevitable.

The water didn't burst into the house frothing and foaming like the whitewater lip of a wave, it oozed in – a silent killer presenting as benign.

Em screamed as the silent shapeshifting killer oozed inside.

"Should we have shut that?" said Billy.

"No," said Liv. "We might need that as a way out. Better open than jagged glass."

Billy nodded at the logic and strengthened his grip on the benchtop. "Hold on!"

In a matter of seconds the water was climbing over it.

"We stay here as long as we can," said Liv. "If it looks like it's headed above ceiling level, we'll need to make it to the doors, get outside, then try to work our way up to the roof. Got it?"

She got a round of nods.

Billy looked down at everyone's footwear, finishing on Liv. "Are you going to be able to swim in your docs?"

She swore, then started working on the shoelaces to take them off. By the time she was finished, the water was another half a metre over the kitchen benchtop.

They exchanged glances and prayed for the deluge to end.

"When are we going to call it?" said Billy.

"If it gets to the top of the sliding door. That'll give us enough time to get out before it reaches the ceiling."

"Cool by me. I've been counting. It's climbing a ruler length every five seconds or so. That'll give us about 10 seconds until we need to hold our breath."

They watched as the waters continued to rise.

"I'm scared," said Em.

"Me too," said Liv. "You know what we have to do though?"

"Yeah."

"You good?"

Billy had his eyes on the sliding door. The dark water kept coming in, narrowing the gap to their marker to flee. "C'mon, c'mon."

It became clear no amount of words or positive thoughts were going to stop the force of nature and the focus turned to timing their escape.

"We don't have long," said Billy.

"OK, this is it," said Liv. "Wait for my word. Stay in a group. Stay hold of each other. Keep your heads up until you no longer can."

"The roof should only be a couple of feet above us when we get out," said Billy.

"Stay together," said Liv. "Two, one, go!"

###

###

CHAPTER 11:

TSUNAMI

Alex had her face pressed against the window, hunched over and weeping uncontrollably. I rubbed her shoulders and offered words of comfort I could tell she felt weren't anywhere near the gravity of the moment.

"What in the fuck do we do now?" said Claire.

Silence was the only answer to her question.

Whatever feeling of detached numbness I felt before this moment was now dwarfed. It wasn't real. It couldn't be real. Even as I was experiencing that moment in time I wasn't. And what Claire and Alex had lost – I couldn't even comprehend the enormity of it. This was my first taste of the new world and my initial reaction was that it was doing everything in its power to suck the spark out of the people still existing in it. That would be a read that would hold true for a long time.

Alex had collapsed under the weight of it. Claire seemed to have decided to keep herself busy to get through it. There was no right or wrong, just what was happening.

Claire started pacing back and forwards. "Have you got candles?"

Again there was no response.

She decided to scout for them herself and something to light them with. She refilled her drink as she reached the kitchen.

"Alex, talk to me," I said. "We're here for you, but we need to make some decisions, like, fast."

It was no use. Alex wasn't responding. I gave her a kiss on the forehead then joined Claire.

By then she had found some candles in the pantry.

I took another swig of my own drink before I set about rifling through the kitchen drawers in search of a lighter.

We came together and lit two of the candles.

"Ideas?" said Claire.

"Unless there's anything else to deal with, I say we wait out the rest of the night here."

Claire nodded. "And tomorrow?"

"I have no idea," I said.

"I don't think I have a home any more," said Claire, before the emotion consumed her too.

I gave her a hug. "I know. I'm pretty sure Alex can't stay here either."

"I guess that leaves my place, but who knows how far the waters went east," I said.

It all became too much for me at that point. Seeing what we'd seen was overwhelming. Thoughts of Kendrick were overwhelming. Seeing my friends now essentially homeless was overwhelming. Thoughts of Claire's family and my friends in Melbourne. And those things were just the top of the charts. There were countless other large scale thoughts circling that were too big to consume. At some point you just can't do it any more, but at the same time you can't think about anything else.

I put all of my energy into the embrace with Claire, wondering what the morning would bring.

*

Liv inched her way through the lounge room, one arm pressing against the wall and the other the ceiling. She could still move with her entire head above the waterline, but it was at the point where she had to angle it up to ensure her mouth was free to take in breaths. "Hang on! Nearly there."

Billy had one hand on her belt, the other pressing against the roof to help the group's momentum – a pattern that was mimicked down the line with Em, then Ashley.

Billy turned to give Em and Ashley a reassuring nod. That's when Liv screamed.

He turned back to see what was happening. Liv had moved her lead hand away from the ceiling and was using it to thrash about in the water. "What's happening?"

Liv continued her struggle without responding. With the candlelight now well and truly extinguished, it took a few seconds for Billy to discern what was happening. Eventually he saw an arm sticking out of the water. Not Liv's, not alive.

"Gross, gross, gross," said Liv as she pushed the body away.

Behind Billy, Em screamed.

It stopped as quickly as it started and she soon gurgled before coughing up water.

He soon realised he was going to struggle to take in another breath – he'd have to go under. He did so and used his wall hand to reach out for Em to drag her forward.

Up front, Liv had repositioned the body to her side and pushed it further away, giving her a burst of momentum forward. It was enough to hit the wall above the balcony door. She pressed her mouth up against the ceiling, yelled, "Go", then took in one last breath before diving under the surface for the sliding door.

In the chaos of the moment, she had no idea if the others heard her, but there was only one way out of this. She fumbled around for a couple of seconds before she got a sound grip on the top of the doorframe. Below the surface, the water moved in little eddies, swaying her about and doing its best to disorient her.

She let her hand on the frame be her guiding light and pulled the rest of her body towards it. The resistance through the water gave her confidence Billy still had a grip on her belt.

Her head ducked under the door frame and she pulled her body through to the other side, where she resurfaced and sucked in a large breath. Any eddies in the water in their lounge room had nothing on the undertow outside. She felt her body being dragged off to the side of the balcony before finding a grip on the frame to hold her location.

Suddenly, the flow of water seemed to pivot direction with a force that took it to a new level once again. It took all her strength to hold on.

Seconds later Billy surfaced, gasping for air. "Where… are… they?"

"Aren't they behind you?"

"Water… smashed… us," he said, before swearing, taking in another deep breath and diving under once more.

Liv fought to keep her grip as she counted the seconds for a head to reemerge. She hit 16 when Billy then Em surfaced in quick succession, both gasping for air.

Em was weak. Billy handed her over to Liv, knowing it was the only chance Em had of clinging onto the balcony.

"Got her!" said Liv as she gripped on, then started pulling Em in. "Go! Go!"

Billy sucked in deep breaths before diving under once more. Despite the change in the undercurrent direction, water levels were still rising. Liv doubted any air pocket remained in the lounge – Billy and Ashley were running on whatever remained in their lungs. Who knew how long Ashley had been holding her breath for now.

Liv gripped the balcony and Em hard and started counting once more. She was soon at 16 again – no sign of BIlly or Ashley. The seconds passed in slow motion – 24, 25, 26…

That's when she saw a head emerge.

"Billy!"

He gave her a look and she instantly knew there was no sign of Ashley. She looked at the water level and what little space remained above water on the balcony. She knew the seconds were precious. She could see BIlly preparing to go under once again.

"Billy! We've got to go!" she screamed.

As if on queue, the balcony shifted at the will of the water. It dropped a few centimetres with a crunch and a groan. Gone was the reliable structure they were clinging to. It now felt like a matter of time before it was claimed by the raging torrent.

Billy stared at the violent waters, hoping a head would resurface, before swearing once more and letting the waters drag him to Liv's location. He hit her and Em with a wet slap and grabbed them tight.

Em was weak, barely conscious. Billy and Liv shared a look – survival was up to them.

The water continued its barrage, trying to rip them away from their now flimsy perch. Past the balcony the waters fell into a larger torrent that flowed between the two apartment blocks. It was doing its best to suck them in.

"You alright?" Billy yelled to Liv.

"Yeah!"

"If we don't get to the roof we're going to get sucked into that."

"I know!" said Liv. "Can you see a way up?"

"On it."

He plotted a path in his mind before turning to Em. "You good to climb up?"

Too weak to speak, she nodded her affirmative.

Billy helped guide her through the water to the edge of the balcony structure, where she was able to reach out to the top of it and the roof gutter. Liv used her strength to keep her grip on the balcony post with one hand and Billy with the other.

After some manoeuvring, Billy found something to press his legs against, then pushed his weight into Em.

Em lifted herself so her stomach lay on top of the balcony structure before she lifted her knee onto the same beam.

The balcony groaned its displeasure

Billy roared as he channelled all his energy into supporting Em's lift.

With another effort, she was clear of the waterline and slumped down on the roof.

Billy and Liv looked at each other.

"You go," they both said at the same time.

"Hurry up," said Billy. "We don't have time to argue."

The water had risen further, making the climb to the balcony top an easier undertaking. Though drained, Liv had more strength for the move than the other two and was up on the balcony and ready for her step to safety in seconds.

The balcony cracked under the water pressure once more. Liv screamed as she slipped towards the water again. She managed to push her upper body forward in the fall, so it landed over the roof line. Her ribs screamed in pain.

Salt water splashed everywhere as she fought through the pain and kicked herself free with her legs.

"Billy!" she screamed as soon as she landed.

She turned to see no sign of him in the water.

"Billy!" she screamed again.

Seconds later, Billy resurfaced, gasping for air. Under the surface, his hand had gripped a nub of balcony timber still connected to the apartment. He had floated a couple of metres from where they were and Liv reached out her hand.

Billy reached his too – it was enough to close the gap.

Liv spotted that a section of roof tiles had been torn away. She turned around, gripped the joist underneath and backed her leg into the water until she felt a hand grip it.

Billy grabbed on tight then pulled. Liv screamed through the pain in her ribs and held on tight. Soon, Billy was at the roof's edge, before climbing over her to safety.

The two stepped back several tiles from the edge, dragging Em with them. The three collapsed back, trying to get oxygen to their lungs.

Too exhausted to talk, they kept their eyes on the waterline as it climbed the tiles.

They were about to step back further onto the roof when the progression of water slowed to a halt. No one spoke.

Eventually, the water level started to abate. Seconds after first noticing it, the gutters of the roof could be seen again. It continued to drop from the sides of the building.

"Fuck," said Billy in between heavy breaths.

"Fuck," agreed Liv.

They gave each other a hug. Soon, all three were in an embrace.

"So, what do we do now?" said Billy.

"I say we stay here and pray that was the biggest wave we'll see," said Liv.

"Works for me," said Billy.

"I'm cold," said Em.

She was shivering – they all were.

"Stay huddled," said Liv. "Looks like we're here until daylight."

*

While the second wave was the biggest, they kept coming in for some time. They washed over the city well into the night, some of the bigger ones also sweeping out into the eastern suburbs.

In a few hours our city had been reshaped. Most of it was swept away by tsunami, some of it destroyed by ejecta, comet fragments or collateral damage from shrapnel from the Melbourne blast. And everything east of the hills had been flattened by the blast wave.

No one will ever know the true death toll that night in our city.

Daylight would bring a new Adelaide. A fraction of its former size with a fraction of its former occupants.

For those of us who made it through that night, we had become survivors. We had survived a moment. Of course, we had no idea what that tag meant at the time, or the baggage that would come from it. That was all to come. Had we known what would become of our world, I know many would've been happy if the waves had taken them away.

###

###

CHAPTER 12:
NEW WORLD, DAY 1

"Four suitcases?" I said.

"I've narrowed it down as much as I can," said Alex.

I think I must've just stared at her in disbelief for several seconds before I remembered I could talk. "OK, well, let's assume your car is still actually in the carpark after what we saw down on the street last night, and that it even works. We've still got to get all of that down 14 flights of stairs. And if we have no car, we're left with whatever we can carry."

"This one is clothes for Jacob, this one's got nappies, food and formula and the other two is my stuff."

"Two bags?"

"Clothes, make-up… and memories."

I went to respond but didn't know how, given what she was going through.

"What about food and medicine? I think we need to take that, don't you?" said Claire.

Alex groaned at the thought of having to think about it all. "Oh, I've got no fucking idea, you tell me."

"OK, what about this," I said. "You guys pack the food and medicine. I'll head down to the carpark to see what the status of the car is. If you're done before I get back, maybe you can see if we can find any way to get some news. Do you have an old radio or something?"

"Pfft, doubt it," said Alex. "Maybe Kendrick had something."

Seconds later she lowered herself to the floor, leaned up against a suitcase and started crying again. Claire and I consoled her for a few minutes before we exchanged glances and nods, then I grabbed Alex's car keys and headed for the stairwell.

*

Patrick surveyed the damage at the front of his property. A van and two cars leaned into the bay windows at the front. The wall had given way under the pressure and bricks piled into their front lounge room. Two gaping cracks shot out from the impact point – one into the roof and the other to the corner of the villa and around the side.

He walked back to the front of the house, the grass piled with debris in parts, ripped away in others. He watched his feet as he walked, trying to step on the more stable looking piles of debris, knowing from experience his feet would sink through the sodden surface if he stepped on whatever ground level currently was.

Everything smelled like rotten seaweed or something. Until he reached the house, where the aroma of sodden carpets and dank filled his nostrils.

Once inside, he saw Hayley going through their clothes and loading anything still dry into suitcases. They hadn't spoken much. She was still in shock at the damage so far inland and the thoughts of their sliding doors survival moment.

He left her to work through that space while they busied themselves getting ready to leave their world behind. He had been right. They were alive. The silence spoke volumes.

*

Yamato kicked the tyre in frustration. Having spent half an hour putting the spare on another puncture, he'd only made a few hundred metres progress before it all happened again. He continued on for a bit until the grinding sound coming from underneath the car got too much to bear.

Sara looked at him. She couldn't remember the last time she'd seen him angry. "I'm fine to walk Dad."

"What about your asthma?"

"It'll be fine."

Yamato nodded. "I really don't want to leave the car here."

She looked around the street – it was quiet, traffic wise and the bitumen was covered in all sorts of debris. "I really don't think anyone is going to take it."

She smiled at him and after a few seconds he returned the look and nodded a concession she was right.

Then Sara started laughing.

"What?" said Yamato.

"Your suit."

Yamato looked at his eye-catching white suit with Japanese-themed flare. He looked ridiculous, doubly so in the current circumstances. He laughed, too, then shrugged his shoulders.

He grabbed all the valuables from the car, except the golf clubs in the boot, then clicked the lock button. He looked at Sara. "Ready?"

She nodded and they began their walk downhill into the destruction.

*

Claire opened the door to see my face, immediately knowing the outcome of my car reconnaissance.

"No chance," I said in case there was any doubt.

"What do you mean, no chance?" said Alex, on the couch holding Jacob.

"I couldn't even describe it as a carpark anymore. Most of the vehicles down there were piled up by the far wall. It was still half filled with water. It wasn't even water really, just a soupy mess."

"Great!" said Alex. "Just fucking fantastic."

"Then I popped my head out onto Greenhill Rd. It's a mess. Chunks of road are missing and what is there is covered in all sorts of shit. Even if we got a car, we wouldn't get far. It'd be a lot quicker to walk."

"Walk?" said Alex. "What about my stuff?"

"I think we're going to have to rethink your stuff."

"Seriously, I can't deal with this shit. Sorry Jacob, Mummy shouldn't swear. She's just disillusioned with the entire universe right now. It's being a total c—"

"Maybe we should work out how we're going to move what we need," I said.

"That's just code for pack less," said Alex.

"Well, yes," I said. "Whatever we take from here, we've got to haul ourselves."

"I want to see what's happened to my place," said Claire.

"Let's do that then head to mine. Best case it's fine and we only have to carry everything a few kilometres."

"So, why don't we pack as much as we can carry there. If we can get stuff to Claire's we can figure it out then?"

I sighed. "It'd be easier to cull it now."

"It's too hard!" said Alex. "How the hell am I supposed to know what I'll need, and what Jacob will need? Look at it out there. Once we leave, what are the chances of me ever coming back? So, what, you just expect me to discard photos of Kendrick?"

"I don't know Alex. All I know is I've looked outside and we've got a big day ahead. I'm just saying the more culling you do now the better."

"Fine!" said Alex, as she opened one of the suitcases in front of her and started another more vigorous edit.

I took a deep breath then turned my attention to Claire, who nodded her approval.

"How did you go with the radio?" I said.

"Nothing. I've got one at mine if we can get in. You've got one too, right?"

"Yeah, but the sooner we find out what's going on the better."

*

Billy sat on the joist and kicked his foot down. It passed through the gyprock and he leaned in to see where the hole led.

He looked up through the tiles they'd removed to the girls above him. "So close, next one over."

He tried to ignore his shivering as he readjusted his position on the beam and removed the insulation before kicking in the gyprock on the other side. Once successful, he looked through the newly created hole. "Bingo!"

He removed another few squares of insulation then widened the hole so he could fit through.

Once he was satisfied, he rolled over so his stomach was on the beam, before sliding himself over the edge. He gripped the beam in both hands as he dangled beneath it, hoping his feet would come into contact with the kitchen benchtop. When he realised he was just short of the feat, he took one more look at what lay beneath before letting go and dropping the small distance to his landing.

The benchtop let out a noise of complaint but stayed together.

"You good?" said Liv from above.

"Yep! Come down."

Soon the three of them were back in the kitchen, staring over the space.

"Oh, fuck," said Liv, as she looked at the body tangled in the sliding door frame.

It was that of an older male, as best she could tell. That was based mostly on the hair. The bloated, pasty body could have belonged to anyone. While it definitely was not Ashley it was completely disturbing regardless. She shuddered as she thought about having to fight her way free of its limbs the night before.

Silence reigned as the realisation dawned that the next body they were likely to see would be Ashley's. It was enough to kill any conversation. Attention now turned to the rest of their apartment. The carpet was sodden, squelching under their feet. The furniture had been upturned and rearranged. There were holes in the wall and broken crockery and strewn items of clothing everywhere.

"It stinks," said Em.

"It's pretty grim," added Liv.

"Let's just grab what we can and get out of here."

"Fuck!" said Billy, as he frisked himself. "Where's my phone?"

"Where are we heading?" said Em.

"Towards the hills," said Liv. "However far it takes to get past the tsunami damage."

"Focus you two," said Billy. "Have either of you seen my phone?"

"How big must it have been to make it all the way up here?" said Em.

"Scary big," said Liv.

"Current model Apple, white, little scratch on the front."

"When did you last have it?" asked Liv.

"I definitely had it in here as the water was rising, then I…" started Billy. "Shit it was in my pocket when we hit the balcony. This is a disaster."

"Dude!" said Liv, as she held out her phone and shook it in his face. "Look – completely fucked. Em?"

Em fished her phone from her pocket. The screen was smashed to the point where circuitry showed underneath. "Same."

"How are you both so calm right now? This is completely fucked," said Billy.

Liv was well experienced in not giving Billy's immediate needs full attention when it felt unwarranted. She threw her phone on the warped kitchen counter and turned her back on him to search the lounge for anything that might be useful. Em followed suit and Billy retreated to his bedroom with a huff.

*

The salvage operation continued in silence. Each dealing with the shock of survival and everything they witnessed in getting there, as well as the devastation of seeing what little remained of their possessions.

Em found herself staring at the body again. "How many people do you reckon ended up like him? Like Ashley."

"I don't think I want to know," said Liv. "C'mon, you both look around my size. I'll see what clothes are still in my room; you guys can help yourselves to whatever you need."

"Oh, thank fuck!" came the call from Billy in the other room. "My master stash!"

Liv sighed. She and Em started packing a sodden backpack with whatever saturated clothes they could get their hands on. It was grim and laborious work.

Eventually, Billy popped his head around the door and looked at Liv. "So, how much do you love me?"

She rolled her eyes and stared at him in judgement at the levity.

From behind the door frame he slowly revealed a boot. "I found this bad boy in the sink."

THE PARADE: APOCALYPSE SURVIVORS

"Not much I can do with one boot."

"Which is why I kept looking until I found this near your new mate."

Billy brought the second boot together with the first.

"My Docs!"

He bowed. "You're welcome."

*

Thunk, thunk, thunk.

The sound of suitcases dropping over concrete steps had been a constant for more minutes than we'd probably care to remember.

"Last flight!" I said, as I led the caravan around the final stairwell landing.

I had a backpack on and a suitcase in tow, same as Claire, who followed in my wake. Alex had Jacob in a sling on her chest, while she too pulled a suitcase with a compacted pusher strapped to its side.

"Oh thank fuck for that," said Alex, as she caught sight of the exit door.

Hints of light danced around the door's frame. When I pulled the handle, it flooded into the stairwell, temporarily blinding us. I held the door open to allow the others to pass through. Once outside, I held the guard rail as I descended the last half a dozen steps to street level.

While I'd already had a look at the damage from ground level, it was fresh for the others. I took in my surroundings, but was equally into the reaction from Claire and Alex.

Cars were piled up against buildings, flipped on their roofs or balancing on some bizarre angle in piles of unrecognisable muck. The building next to the apartment tower was now an unrecognisable frame and brick pile, Greenhill Rd itself was a complete disaster and the majority of trees in the parklands had toppled.

"Holy fuck!" said Alex, when she touched down at street level. "Why didn't you say it was this bad?"

"That's exactly what I did," I said.

"But I didn't think you meant *this* bad!"

There was a couple across the road and another woman on the median strip. Alex recognised both of them as residents of the apartment building. Aside from that, the area was completely devoid of human activity.

"We're never going to get all of this to the city and then the Parade," said Alex.

I managed to resist an eye roll, while I stretched my muscles out from the recent stairwell descent. "Why don't we make a start and see how we go?"

*

Even as they stepped onto their street the feeling of impending bad news was almost overwhelming. Silence had taken over from observations about the damage and what they should do next should the house be in the state they feared. With each block they passed the destruction got worse. Their surroundings told the monumental story as they descended into the mire. This close to the city, nearly half the houses had been wiped out of existence.

Yamato reached out his hand. Sara took it.

The street was deserted as they crossed the last cross street before their house.

Soon, what remained of it came into view. Some remnants of the heritage stonework facade and a pile of stonework that stretched from the back corner of the house into what would've been the neighbour's place, had there been any signs of it.

Yamato burst into tears. Sara, too.

They stepped onto their grounds and made their approach.

When he reached the front wall, Yamato touched the stone, triggering another bout of tears. Memories of times gone past flooded back from a world that would never be again. Sara moved in to pat his shoulder.

"I miss her too," she said.

Without making eye contact, he nodded and moved his hand onto hers until he collected himself enough to focus on the task ahead. "Clothes, food and photos."

Sara nodded and the two made their way into the space that used to be their house.

*

Liv, Billy and Em marched three abreast up the Parade. They headed east, each step a little uphill, surrounded by a little less destruction and a little closer to something more normal. There was no traffic and the streets were quiet.

The quartet were all still shivering from their wet clothes and the lack of sleep. Now, dust clung to their clothes, causing each step to scratch their skin.

It was everywhere, limiting visibility and casting a gloomy hue over everything.

"This is super creepy," said Em. "Like, we're in some horror film or something."

Among the carnage of broken buildings they spotted occasional bodies in the street. Some were impossibly twisted in their final resting place, some were missing limbs and some appeared as if there was nothing wrong with them.

"Should we bury them or something?" said Liv.

"Have you been counting?" said Billy. "I've got 27 right now – that would take us days."

She nodded. "Just doesn't seem right though, does it?"

"Maybe once we get to safe ground there will be someone with a plan. Like, police or something," said Billy. "We can tell them what we've seen."

Liv nodded again.

They continued on the trek Liv and Billy had taken dozens of times before. Seeing their stomping ground grimly reimagined was too surreal to process.

Soon, they were soon passing Norwood Oval, home of the Redlegs. It was from that point on the Parade evolved into a cosmopolitan strip of shops, restaurants and fashion houses, almost as if the oval sat in guard of the heart of the precinct.

"Is this the first block we've passed with no damaged buildings?" said Billy. "I'm pretty sure it is."

"We must be getting close to where the waters came up to," said Liv.

It was at that point they started to hear a crowd.

"Boom!" said Billy, as he stepped up his pace.

"Sounds like it's coming from near work," said Liv, as she and the others matched his enthusiasm.

"We did it!" said Billy.

*

"Why would we head to the Parade?" said Hayley.

She rolled her suitcase over the bumpy footpath behind her.

"We're not exactly flush with options right now and everyone I know who could improve our current situation is connected there somehow."

"What about my parents? Erindale is not that far away."

"I'm not walking to Erindale. Besides, we have to make decisions around what is the best move for our survival."

"Wouldn't that be surrounding yourself with family?"

"I'm talking about the basics. What about food? You said they weren't part of the hoarding crowd, which means they will only have what's in their fridge and pantry. Let's assume they still have power for the fridge, how long is that going to last for two people, let alone four?" said Patrick.

"We need to—"

"I don't think I need a lecture on what we need to do from the person who would've had us all drowned in a tsunami if she got her way."

Hayley stared at him in stunned silence.

22r

"The only way we're getting through this in the best shape is to keep the heartbeat of this area alive. I'd been talking to people before as we were preparing for things to go down. There's a lot happening behind the scenes and it would be moronic to give up being part of that to go and slowly starve in Erindale."

With Patrick's follow-up look, the decision was made in the way it always was when it came to conflict. Hayley nodded, defeated.

"The Parade is only a couple of blocks away now."

They continued their march in silence.

###

###

CHAPTER 13:

BROKEN CITY

"If we head that way for about 30m we should be past the worst of it," I said. I was standing on a pile of rubble nearly 3m high, a mix of fallen building debris and whatever dregs the tsunami had washed into it.

"We could probably head to Pulteney St. It's not too far out of the way," said Claire.

We were only a block into the city grid of streets and already the scale of the damage there was becoming clear. Smoke was everywhere. We knew there were at least three buildings on fire from observations at Alex's apartment, but perhaps there were more. Between the smell of that and the overwhelming stink of whatever contributed to the post-tsunami muck, it was almost too much to handle. Each of us now wore one of Alex's tops as a face covering to try to limit the assault on our olfactory senses.

We hadn't passed a building yet that had not been obviously damaged by the waters – most had been significantly impacted. Bodies, or parts of bodies, were already a common sight and we hadn't seen a living soul since passing through the parklands into the CBD.

"Do you think anyone in the city survived last night?" said Claire.

I made my way back to the others and we resumed our trek to her apartment. "Maybe, if they were in one of the highrise apartments," I said. "Given what we saw last night, I don't think anyone else had a chance."

Claire nodded. "It'd be good to see someone, you know, alive."

Conversation went quiet after that. I guess everyone sat with those words and how it hit them. We focused ourselves on the walk and it needed our attention. We dodged rubble and snags, avoided bodies and took in the scale of destruction. We didn't share our findings. Somehow our recent observations had been enough and there's only so much momentum constant references to destruction of one kind or another can give a conversation. I think we had found our limit that morning and quiet reflection seemed to be the unspoken cure.

Not that it bothered Alex. She hadn't said much since we crossed into the parklands. A fact difficult not to notice from a person whose mouth was normally sharp and unafraid.

We had soon reached Hurtle Square and Carrington St beckoned.

"Where's my favourite sign?" said Claire.

"What sign?" I said.

"The forest of dreams."

I gave her a blank look.

"Do you not remember the big lettering saying exactly that? It was right here – *the forest of dreams* – it circled this intersection?"

"Ah yeah, that's right, naw I liked that."

"It's a sign," said Claire.

"Sign?" I said.

"Omen perhaps. I mean dreams, think about it. I used to connect to that sign and that word. Now they're, well, wiped away."

I was trying to get a read on how invested she was in this train of thought. And where her head was at in general, given everything. "Maybe it's just a sign that a massive tsunami rolled through here."

She smiled thinly. "Probably."

"Stay positive, huh?"

"I'm trying, but it's hard with, you know, literally everything we keep seeing."

With that, we made the final metres to our destination. Claire tried, unsuccessfully, to settle her heart rate as she narrowed the ground to Carrington St. She could make out the row of terrace housing before she fully reached the street. Or, to be more accurate, where the terraces used to stand.

She stopped in her tracks, content to observe the destruction from a distance. Tears flowed. Soon, we were by her side, offering our condolences.

She settled herself and prepared to speak, but no words came.

I gave her a kiss on the forehead.

"This is just working out fantastically," said Claire, eventually.

"Hey, welcome to the homeless club," said Alex. "All the cool kids are doing it."

It was enough to elicit a small laugh and some eye contact.

"I knew it. Like, I felt it or something," said Claire.

"Adelaide's not the neighbourhood it used to be," said Alex.

"I know. I mean, it was just a rental and I'd been asking myself, what would I even want to keep if it was still there – and the answer was not much. I've got my phone, my memories, everything else is just stuff."

"Well, you've got my clothes now, so you've upgraded in a way," said Alex.

Claire smiled again. "Yeah, I'll get to look 25% more street worker at the end of the world."

Alex laughed at the speed of the return of serve. "Might come in handy now you're homeless."

It was the first time Alex had been, well, Alex, the entire day. That in itself was a release of tension for all of us. We laughed, standing across the broken row of terraces in the middle of the broken city.

Claire looked at me. "No pressure, but you'd better still have a house."

"I know. I guess there's only one way to find out."

"Well, no point hanging around here," said Claire, as she reached out for her suitcase handle. "Which way?"

"If we push along Pulteney to Pirie before heading east we can get a look at what it's like in the city centre."

"Sounds good to me," said Claire.

*

Liv, Billy and Em crossed over Osmond Tce and into the heart of the Parade. A crowd was gathered. It seemed to be centred on the pedestrian crossing between the two big food shops – Foodland and Coles. There was enough movement in the crowd and the odd scream to let them know tension was in the air.

"This is a surreal way to be near work again," said Em.

"What do you think's going on?" said Liv.

"Hard to tell," said Em.

"It doesn't look good," said Billy. "Maybe we should get in close enough to hear without getting too close, if that makes sense."

They continued forward until they slipped into the fringes of the crowd, then zigzagged their way forward until they could hear what was happening.

A police officer addressed the crowd. Tensions were clearly high. "Ladies and gentlemen, can you please stop pushing forward. It is not helping the situation."

"What's Steven doing there?" said Billy.

"Where?" said Liv.

"He's just behind the cop."

Liv looked at Billy and shrugged.

"Ladies and gentlemen, please stop pressing forward," repeated the cop. "We are awaiting word on how to handle the situation. We ask for your patience right now."

"My children are starving," yelled one lady.

"Where are we supposed to go?" said another.

Steven – Liv and Billy's manager at Foodland – stepped up next to the officer. "We are awaiting word on how to best handle the situation. But we'll need to have order before we open the doors."

"It's a shitshow," said Liv. "We should go see if we can help."

"You want to work? Now?" said Billy.

"I want to help. Don't you?"

Billy stared at her, mouth agape.

"If you're doing that, I'm heading to Coles," said Em.

"What, so, we're splitting up?" said Billy.

"Looks like it," said Liv.

"Em, didn't you say it seemed like we were in some horror film? Isn't rule No.1 of horror films don't split up?"

Em rolled her eyes.

Liv eyed him up and down. "Man up, Billy. Take a look around, we need to help."

"I'm manned. I'm fully manned! OK, fine, but can we at least organise a place to meet after we do all this help?"

Liv gave him another look. "Good idea. What about just down the street where it's a little less crazy – say Caffe Buogiorno?"

Em nodded. "Done."

"And stay safe," said BIlly.

*

They had been at it for well over an hour – sifting through the remains of their house – without luck.

"Dad, I'm hungry," said Sara.

"Me too," said Yamato. "But we're only going to get one shot at this."

"Everything's gone. Almost everything I've dug up hasn't even been ours. And look at my hands."

Yamato looked at the cuts, then back at the scene that confronted them. He exhaled deeply, while he pondered their next move. "True patience consists in bearing what is unbearable."

Normally one of his sayings would annoy Sara, but there was something about the determination in his eyes and thoughts of keeping alive memories of her mum that let it slide. She stood up, surveyed the damage and selected a new dig site. They'd been in the footprint of their former house the entire time. She decided to move her search to what would've been outside – to the east of where the house used to stand.

That's when she saw it. A small wooden corner barely peeking above the surface. Something about the shape or colour was familiar – one of their photo frames. She swooped on it immediately and gently dusted some of the debris away. She gave it a tug. Judging by the resistance that came back, the frame felt like it might be in one piece.

"Dad!"

Yamato was over in seconds. She looked at him, he looked at the frame and was soon on his knees next to her digging it out of the dirt.

Once they felt it start to wiggle in its tomb, they gently shook and pulled until the frame came free. They turned it over to reveal a picture of their family in better times – a holiday in Fiji. The glass was broken and there was dirt on the actual photo, but it didn't matter.

Yamato removed the remaining shards of broken glass before removing the photo and wiping it as clean as he could manage. Then he cried.

Sara followed suit.

They held hands once more.

They had something. They had everything.

*

With each passing block the buildings got taller, as did the scale of destruction. We'd seen two office towers on fire and another completely razed to the ground. It was all cocooned in the eerie silence of the dusty, smoky greys that had taken hold of the city.

Claire coughed. "I think I've seen about enough."

"I hear you," said Alex. "I can barely breathe."

"Pirie St is next anyway," I said. "That'll take us through to home. If there is a home."

"There will be," said Claire.

Before she knew what was happening, I had my arm in front of her – a warning sign to stop walking. She obeyed, then chased where my eyes were leading.

At the intersection ahead, two people were crossing, dragging suitcases and heading east. They were too far away to make out any details, other than if a gait could tell a story, this one would say broken spirit. The mystery duo didn't notice they were being watched.

"Jesus," said Alex.

"Must've been from one of the apartment buildings," I said.

"Yep, no one else in the city was surviving all that," said Claire.

"Looks like they're headed east too," said Alex.

"I'm not really sure there are many other options," I said.

Once the mystery walkers disappeared out of sight, we continued on. We reached the intersection a little over a minute later. As we did, another person was walking through from the west.

It must've been a combination of the situation and the conditions but, all of a sudden, having another human in our orbit filled us with doubt and insecurity. I could sense it coming from the others just as I was feeling it. The accidental crossing of paths almost felt like a threat. We found ourselves too close not to acknowledge the person, since they would soon be headed in the same direction down the same street.

I nodded at the stranger. He was wearing a dark hoodie, black jeans and shoes. Between that and his dark skin, he cut a perfect silhouette into the dusty destruction behind him.

"Hey," the man said.

There was something about his tone that eased the tension. It was enough for me to feel comfortable enough to ask a question.

"Where did you come from?"

The stranger stared at me. "Sudan."

"What? No, I didn't mean that kind of where."

He laughed at himself. "Sorry, habit. Near Light Square – apartment block. You?"

"Erm, Greenhill Rd," I said.

"What are you doing in the city?"

"I live... lived here," said Claire. "Wanted to check on my place."

"It was completely fucked," added Alex.

"Where you headed?" said the man.

"East," I said.

"Me too," said the man. "Someone said the Parade was the place to go. Didn't get drowned last night."

I felt the relief wash over me at the information. Maybe my place was still OK after all.

The man approached and held out his hand. "Asim."

I shook his hand and introduced myself, followed by the others.

"So, what exactly did you hear about the Parade?" I said.

"Not much other than it's still there," said Asim. "That was enough for me. I'm probably more heading away from the city than to the Parade. Everyone's headed east."

We nodded and Asim joined our pilgrimage east.

*

"Steven! Steven!" yelled Liv, over the din of noise coming from the crowd.

After several more attempts she managed to grab his attention. He signalled to a couple of the men around him and they parted the crowd to let her and Billy through.

"Thank God you're here, we could really use the help," he said, before eying them up and down. "What the hell happened to you two?"

"Bit of a run-in with the tsunami," said Billy.

"Jesus!" said Steven. "We've got spare uniforms in the office. Just give me a few minutes to sort this out and we can get you some dry clothes."

"What's happening?"

"We're about one shove short of a riot. A couple of cops are helping and most of these guys have just volunteered to keep everyone back. They'll loot the place if we don't sort something out. Oh, and the power just went out again."

"Why don't you just give them some food? Calm them down a bit."

"It's a bit of a clusterfuck. I was told I'd hear something from management this morning – nothing. The cop – Kyle – says he's not getting shit either. So, basically no one knows what's going on, like, anywhere. Anyway, Kyle reckons if we can't get calm out here it'll blow up once we open the doors."

There was more commotion at the front of the crowd.

"Kyle!" yelled the hefty man as he shoved people out of the way. "I need to get through. Kyle!"

Eventually, the policeman heard his name above the rest of the chaos. "Patrick?"

Kyle rushed over to let Patrick and Hayley through to safety.

"Slightly different circumstances than the fundraiser," said Patrick.

Kyle shook his head in disbelief. "What was that, two months ago?"

"Bang on. Got yourself a bit of a situation?" said Patrick, as they shook hands.

Kyle exhaled in a way that vented his frustrations. "You could say that. What are you doing here?"

"We lost the house."

"Shit, sorry mate." Kyle turned to Hayley. "I'm sorry. Good to see you again."

"So, how can I help?" said Patrick.

"Well, another body or two wouldn't go astray right now. We just need to knock this on the head before it gets out of hand or until some backup arrives."

"What backup?"

"I'm not sure what shape the force is in right now, but if they can send numbers they will. Before this all went down, we were hearing the army would be on standby to step up. So, hearing a lot of things but no actual live and current communication anywhere."

"So, a lot of maybes?" said Patrick. "What's Plan B?"

"Plan B?" said Kyle with a sarcastic laugh. "Right now all I can see is a couple of cops with pistols and a handful of helpers holding back several hundred hungry, confused and pissed-off people."

Patrick looked over the crowd in contemplation. "Can I make a suggestion?"

"I'm all ears."

"What if we start sorting these people into groups. Some of them are probably just here to stock up on extra food. But there are going to be a lot of people, like us, who don't have a home any more. They're probably the ones going hungry as well. If we can sort something out for them, like food – soon – then a way to get a roof over their heads tonight, that'll go a long way to calming the situation."

"Makes sense, but look at what I'm working with here. I've barely got enough people to guard the doors."

Patrick thought on the conundrum for a few seconds. "We need to work out who here still has a home. Maybe they have spare rooms they could offer. That might help. There's also a camping store down the street. If we could get access we could get tents and camping gear to set the rest up somewhere – just for a night or two until we figure something more permanent out."

"That could work. Where would they camp?" said Kyle.

"The oval. It's only a few hundred metres from here and surely it's big enough to handle, well, whoever we have left."

"And food?"

Patrick paused again in thought. "Do we have access to Foodland and Coles?"

"Steven over there is manager at the Foodland and we have senior staff here over at the Coles entrance."

"I'm sure if we put our heads together for a few minutes we can come up with a plan to give away enough food to get people through to dinner and make a start on the accommodation problem."

Kyle nodded, before grabbing the attention of a member of his newly formed volunteer group.

"Yes?" said the helper.

"Can you head over to Coles and get whoever's in charge to head this way to help come up with a plan of attack?"

"Yes sir," said the man, disappearing into the crowd.

"He called you sir?" said Patrick.

Kyle smiled for the first time in hours.

"Right, next stop is to calm the crowd," said Patrick.

"Good luck with that," said Kyle.

"If I could talk to them, show them we're planning how to deal with this, we'll–"

"Do they look like they're in a listening mood at the moment?"

"Perhaps we should put them in one?"

Kyle stared at him, confused.

Patrick nodded to Kyle's sidearm.

"Like you said," said Patrick. "We need to knock this on the head before it gets out of hand."

Kyle looked at his weapon, the numbers he was holding back and his support.

"What do they say? A stitch in time saves nine," said Patrick.

Kyle removed the weapon from his holster, released the safety, aimed it into the skies and pulled the trigger.

*

Claire, Alex, Jacob, Asim and I reached the foot of the Parade. Even east of the CBD, we were still surrounded by devastation. But the incline in the path ahead was now noticeable and with each block we passed, there were changes in the level of building carnage.

It was a cruel mix of hope and dread for me, knowing somewhere ahead was a line where the tsunami waters stopped and I didn't have the faintest idea which side of it my townhouse was on.

Soon after the intersection at Fullarton Rd, we reached the turnoff to head to my place.

I turned to Asim. "This is where we say goodbye."

"You sure you don't want company, just in case?"

I smiled at him. "I think we're good."

That's when we heard the gunshot. We looked at each other in shock.

"Still sure?"

I looked at the others before nodding to Asim.

He nodded his acceptance before shaking hands and wishing us all luck. "Maybe I'll see you at the Parade some time."

"Maybe," I said.

As we crisscrossed the side streets on our way to my townhouse it became apparent my home was not going to be east of the damage.

When we reached the door, it took several minutes to clear muck and debris from the doorstep so it could be opened. The smell, although different to that in the city, was still overwhelming. The high watermark of the tsunami was marked on the side of the house as a dark line. Everything below it was now a slightly grimmer colour than that above. Almost all of the ground floor windows were broken or cracked.

Eventually, we'd cleared enough space to open the door.

I breathed in deep and held up my crossed fingers for the others to see. "Well, here goes then."

###

###

CHAPTER 14:
GATHERING

One of my enduring memories of impact night was the way we viewed other people around us. It was as if the second everything went FUBAR, your trust in others went south. Trying to describe that feeling is hard. It was a sense hanging in the air surrounding everything. It was just intrinsic to every interaction with outsiders. You'd assume after going through a moment in history like that there would be a sense of support or kinship or connectivity. There wasn't. At all. Maybe it was the first time our survival instincts had really ever had to kick in. When you don't have a roof over your head, or any surety in food, or any of the basic survival needs, something changes inside of you.

Trust has a different meaning when you're there.

You could feel it in yourself, you could see it in those you knew when they reacted to others, and you could see it in the eyes of strangers when they saw you. It was something now woven into the fabric of every interaction with people you didn't know. And it was scary.

None of it was helped by people's actions between finding out about the comet and 12/4. That also triggered something distasteful in the collective us. Violence, vendettas, selfishness and greed – that's what came out in us the most. It was ugly. It was also ugly to know that – as a species – we were one collective piece of bad news away from being entirely darker versions of ourselves.

Like, who are we? Are we the people we pretend to be when everything is going well or the people who turn when everything is not?

I can't say I ever really asked myself that until writing this, but the thoughts that led to the question were everywhere in the days and weeks after 12/4. We'd just been through hell, lost, well, in some cases, everything and now we faced reinventing everything that was. We had to do this with people we didn't know, fresh off of seeing the lengths people would go to to serve themselves at the expense of others. Fuck!

When I think about it now, that could not be further from the headspace you'd have to collectively be in to successfully work together and thrive.

But that's where we were.

*

I scanned the scene in silence. Claire followed behind me, with Alex feeding Jacob bringing up the rear. The entire downstairs area of my place was a writeoff. The waters had ruined everything that hadn't floated away, while also dumping a foot-deep layer of grime and rubbish everywhere. The stairwell was intact, at least.

We climbed to the first floor, where the waters had barely made it. Perhaps peaking 10cm above the floorboards. But they were now buckled from the soaking, while most of the furniture had also been touched in one way or another.

I grabbed my backpack from the cupboard and went about filling it with a variety of clothes that hadn't been affected, as well as a couple of pieces of jewellery and some toiletries. Claire helped where she could.

I let thoughts of what my friends had lost act as perspective to what I was going through. Having more than the clothes on your back seemed a relative luxury.

Soon, we returned downstairs and waded through the goopy filth to the kitchen, where we gathered as much food and medicine as we could salvage.

"So, we're heading up to the Parade and we think a lot of people could be gathering there?" said Alex, breaking the silence.

"That's the plan," I said.

"And, what, we now have two bags of food as well as our clothes – it's a lot."

"We really don't have far to go."

Alex removed the bottle from Jacob's mouth and towelled around his lips and chin. "Yeah, I know. And we could totally do that. But, what if we stash the food and medicine here and just go and check things out first."

Claire and I looked at each other.

"I guess it can't hurt to see what's going on first," said Claire.

I looked around my place. "We can't stay here though."

"No," said Alex. "But do we even know what's going on up there? Would it hurt to have this place and a few supplies up our sleeve? You know, just in case."

I paused in thought for a moment. "I guess not. Maybe I could stash the food in the laundry?"

"Works for me," said Alex.

Claire nodded her approval.

We stowed the supplies then headed out for the last leg of our trip.

*

It was early afternoon when the power returned on the Parade. The grid had come back on before they could find a solution with the generators. There was a jubilant roar from the crowd. Things were evolving quickly. Order had temporarily been restored. Queues now formed at both the Coles and Foodland, where everyone was being offered enough food for a meal.

Those who were manning doors were now ushering crowds through the system. Once supplied, those who were without a home were prompted to the camping store, where tents and sleeping bags were issued. Those with places to go were encouraged to disperse. They were told there would be another gathering at dinner, where everyone would be fed and plans would be locked in for the next day.

It was the first sign of structure and process and there was a noticeable shift in the behaviour of the crowd. Hope can come in many forms and, in this moment, it was in following orders and queues.

Our long journey via the city had meant we'd missed the pre-lunch unrest, but we'd soon be joining the long queues and hearing about it from others.

*

Yamato and Sara left the Foodland queue with a sandwich and a juice and began to refuel as they made their way to the camping store.

"Look at that," said Yamato, as yet another lengthy queue stretched out in front of them.

The line was nearly 200m. Those leaving the store with supplies were being directed west to the oval.

"I hope they don't run out of stuff," said Sara.

Yamato studied the numbers ahead of him and tried to guesstimate what sort of stock the store might have. "Me too. I'm sure they'll think of something if they do."

"If not?"

"We'll figure something out."

"Excuse me," said Asim, as he joined them at the back of the line. "Do you know what's going on?"

Yamato studied him. "This line is for those who've lost their houses. They're giving out tents and everyone's headed to the oval to camp out."

"I'm in the right spot then. Asim," he said as he offered his hand.

"Yamato, and this is my daughter Sara."

Asim shook their hands in turn, then had a bite of his sandwich. "So, where are you guys from?"

"Rose Park – it's pretty much wiped out. You?"

"I was in the city. One of the lucky ones I think."

"The city? From what we saw last night we didn't think anyone there would make it."

"My apartment was 15 storeys up and the waters nearly reached me."

Yamato and Sara's expressions of disbelief were all the response they could muster. They then turned to what remained of the skyline, barely visible through the dusty afternoon sky. Plumes of smoke rose up from various points below their view – one from a highrise they could see.

"The place is a dead zone. Bodies everywhere, buildings on fire and falling. I'm just happy to be out."

Yamato nodded.

"I'm not sure too many did, but whoever did make it was headed this way it seems."

"You are not the only lucky one. Our house was completely destroyed, but fortunately we were at a friend's place last night. Saved our lives."

"Here's to luck," said Asim, as he opened his juice and offered the container out for a cheers.

"To luck," said Yamato, then Sara.

They clinked containers, not glasses.

*

That's when we came wandering past.

"Asim!" said Claire.

"Long time no see! How was your house?"

"Not great. Hence being here," I said.

"What's going on? What do we do?" said Alex.

"Head up to the zebra crossing. They'll direct you to the food line. Once you're done, head back to this line to get a tent."

"Alright!" said Claire.

"Are there going to be enough tents?" I said.

"Hi, I'm Yamato, this is Sara. We are concerned about this."

"Hi Yamato, I'm Zoe. This is Claire, Alex and Jacob. Any chance you could reserve one for us?"

"I… I will try."

*

By the time we had gotten to the pedestrian crossing where we were to be directed to the food the army rolled in. Well, when I say army, it was two soldiers in a dump truck – probably the only thing – short of a tank I guess – capable of surviving the roads without getting punctures.

It wasn't a huge showing of force, but it was the first sign some bigger organisation was at work and we were being looked after.

We saw them talking with those who were now in charge of what was happening at the Parade as we disappeared around the corner to join the main queue to Foodland.

If I can cherry pick a moment where hope was highest that, despite the hit we had taken as a city, there would be some sort of measured, coordinated and smooth response, this was it. It just felt like everyone was coming together as best they could and we would resolve it all in a civilised, supportive way.

The feeling was strong for the rest of this day. A sense of greater support which changed the level of trust we were feeling generally. We were all working together on this mutually beneficial solution – that was the vibe and it felt good.

In one way or another, it eroded or imploded in fractions large and small from that point on. Maybe it was never really there and I imagined it. Who knows. Regardless, I actually look back to that afternoon with fondness. Perhaps it was my belief in what was happening and what would follow, or my belief in people in general.

Instead, we have this book.

Whatever the case and as strange as it sounds, this speck of time stays with me.

*

It took at least an hour to get our food and make our way back to the camping store. We could already tell something was up by the time we were in earshot. Voices were raised and the neatly arranged queue had lost its shape, instead forming as a gathering around the camping store entrance.

We saw Asim, Yamato and Sara near the entrance and made a beeline for them.

"What's going on?" I said, despite the yelling around me already indicating they were out of tents.

"It is as we feared – no more tents," said Yamato.

"So, what do we do now?"

"They don't seem to know. One of them has gone to get one of the organisers."

"I was not OK with sleeping in a tent and I'm definitely not OK with not sleeping in one," said Alex.

"What's going on here?" said Patrick, as he marched into the commotion with two soldiers at his shoulders – Sergeant Jillian Goodwood and Lance Corporal Derby Manningham.

"We're out of tents, um, sir," said the woman, who seemed to be spokesperson for the group inside the camping store.

"How many more do you think we'll need?"

"Best guess, at least 250 more," said the woman. "But that could double if people keep coming in."

"Where can we get more from?" said Patrick.

"I… I don't know."

Patrick cleared his throat, ready to address the crowd. "Does anyone here have any idea where the closest camping store would be?"

"Rundle St in the city has a few, unless they've been destroyed," said a middle-aged woman.

Patrick turned to the soldiers. "Is there any way you can get your truck into the city to get the tents we need?"

"Yes, sir," said Sergeant Goodwood.

"I'm assuming you'll have no shortage of volunteers, should you need," said Patrick.

Goodwood nodded and a number of arms raised into the air. She and Lance Corporal Manningham soon selected four of the strongest in the crowd, including Asim, and they headed back to the truck for a supply run.

###

###

CHAPTER 15:

THE OVAL

Everyone still waiting for a tent migrated to the oval. A depressing haul, to say the least. We walked down with Yamato and Sara. There was a stillness in the air and, between that and the smoky skies, it was almost forcing everyone to introspect. As crazy as it sounds it really felt like the conditions were conspiring to force us to sit in the moment and contemplate how truly shit everything was.

Thankfully, the activity at the oval was the perfect antidote to overthinking. A tent city of refugees was evolving in front of our eyes. Maybe everyone was staying busy so as to not let the weather conditions force them to think. Seeing the tents go up was both comforting and confronting. It was comforting to know we'd (hopefully at that point) have a place to sleep that night, as well as knowing that whatever we were going through, we weren't doing it alone. Also feeling that sense that we were being helped kept a million negative thoughts at bay.

It was a small win but that was worth making the most of mentally. Even in these early moments it was hard not to see where things were heading and come to the realisation we were staring at a grim future. Anything that resembled even mild good news was worth being thankful for.

We killed time helping those with tents put them up. We also plotted out some space for ourselves, reserving a little pocket on the playing surface near the scoreboard. From there, we just sat around, watching the surreal repurposing of the football stadium happen in real time around us.

The next few hours were our first experience at something that would become another significant part of our life from that moment on – waiting. It's an acquired skill, waiting. Something our anything-on-demand world had not really prepared us for. Even a dull moment could be killed in the world that ended on 12/4. Could've been filled scrolling socials, putting on some music, binge watching or whatever hobby you chose to pass the hours. But here, the phone networks were down and no one had much more than the clothes on their back, so whatever their usual entertainment options, they were no longer available.

We settled for people-watching and small talk. Our main thoughts were preoccupied with Kendrick and other loved ones we couldn't get in touch with, as well as hoping the soldiers and volunteers would hit paydirt on their tent recon. Even the small talk seemed like it was there to pass the time and avoid the conversation getting into territory no one wanted to deal with at that moment.

It was a very long three hours until the scouting party returned with a bounty of camping equipment. There were cheers of wild celebration when they did. I know a tear came to my eye.

*

"This better be good," said Alex.

We were a small part of the tent city army, marching their way back up the Parade for dinner and a town hall meeting about what was going on.

"Cut them some slack," Asim said. "I think they've done well to get everything together today."

"Don't you want to find out what they've got planned?" I added.

"I'd much rather them hand me a bottle of red and tell me they'll fill me in tomorrow," said Alex. "Actually, two bottles of red."

"Maybe we'll ask about red in the meeting," I said, trying to keep her focused.

She nodded.

In truth, I didn't really want to talk, plan or problem-solve, I wanted to be in this moment as much as I could. As a few hundred people marched our way up the Parade, to a backdrop of the smoke from many distant fires, the hint of recent tsunami and death aroma and the general filth of a broken city, it felt like we were doing something, well, significant.

Part of me wanted to completely absorb what that moment was but, equally, part of me wanted to be absolutely ready to absorb everything that was said at the meeting. Not just the words, but anything and everything that might help give us a sense of what was going on around us and who was who. Maybe that was borne out of the trust thing, maybe it was trying to find something I felt I could control in a world where the choices I could actually make suddenly became very limited.

Asim was recalling some brag point moment from his tent salvage mission as we made our way to dinner. He walked with Yamato and Sara, with Claire, Alex, Jacob and myself right behind them. Claire was occasionally interrupting Asim to ask questions.

Soon, the smells of the end of the world were replaced by that of cooking meat.

"BBQ!" said Asim, interrupting his own story. "I am starving."

"Me too," said Claire.

As we crossed over Osborne Tce, we could see the crowd gathered around a strip of restaurants. Queues of people were getting served BBQ basics before finding some open space to eat. There was a sense of excitement and unity in the air, despite what most had gone through, or were going through. A buzz of chatter enveloped everything on that still night.

*

Billy bit into a sausage and onion sandwich, sauce exploding from where he gnawed in. "I seriously earned this."

Liv looked at the red marks on his chin and did her best to ignore them. She chewed while keeping her eyes on the crowd for Em.

"When do you think is a good time to talk to Steven about pay?" said Billy.

Liv rolled her eyes before spotting her target in the food line about to get served. "There she is."

"It just feels like a double-time situation," said Billy. "Maybe public holiday rates?"

"Can we just eat? We still need to get our tents set up. Plus there's that meeting."

"This is important."

Liv sighed. "Take a look around you Billy. What's really important?"

Billy was thrown by Liv's tone. "Chill, I was just asking."

"Heya," said Em, as she approached with food in hand. "Today was mental."

"Same," said Liv. "You heard about the meeting?"

"Yep, apparently there are too many people to fit in the town hall, so they're doing two sessions."

"Really?" said Liv. "We should head up there now then, make sure we're in the first group."

Em nodded and the three started migrating east towards the town hall. The late 19th century classical architecture was one of the jewels of the Parade. They passed under the eye of the clock tower less than a block from the restaurants, to round the corner onto George St, where the town hall entrance greeted them.

A lady at the door nodded them through. Em shoved the rest of her sandwich in her mouth and signalled to the others she was good to go.

*

"What do you mean two sessions?" I said, through chews.

"I just overheard two people saying there are too many people to fit in the hall – even with standing room, so they're doing two sessions," said Asim.

"Everyone got their food?" I said.

After a round of nods, I signalled for us to start moving towards the town hall.

"Wait, we've still got 30 minutes," said Alex.

"Yeah, and I assume once the session is full up we'll be waiting around for the second. So let's go and get a seat now."

Alex sighed, mostly at the inconvenience of having to plan and arrange her presence.

"I wonder what they're going to be telling us," said Claire.

"Anything would be a solid improvement," said Alex.

"They've probably got a plan," said Yamato.

"Hopefully," I said. "But If you've got any questions, ask them. I will be."

We walked in silence a while longer, shoving food in as we went. "Just, pay attention to everything. We can chat on the other side."

The lady controlling the entryway saw us approach and nodded us in.

"Thank god," I said.

###

###

CHAPTER 16:

QUADE

"You are such a nerd," said Alex.

She was staring at me in a way that said my alleged nerdom had sickened her all the way to her core.

"We've been here for 25 minutes and still there are seats available! We could've just walked in now and had the same experience."

"They're not as good as these seats though, are they?"

"I have no words for you," said Alex.

There was movement on the stage, followed by an ear-piercing microphone feedback scream.

"Sorry," said Patrick. "Ladies and gentlemen, we'll begin in a couple of minutes. We're just ushering some more people up from the festivities."

I could feel Alex's eyes on me but didn't take mine from the stage.

"Must be the free wine down there," said Patrick. "Perhaps we should've waited until after."

His attempt at humour received a couple of token laughs, but not enough to encourage new material. Instead, he left the lectern and consulted with someone else near the side of the stage.

"Wine?" said Alex, her eyes now boring a hole in the side of my face.

I looked at her but knew no facial expression was going to make up for nearly half an hour of unnecessary sitting and missing out on wine.

Patrick was soon back on stage. A number of other people filled the chairs positioned behind him.

"Thank you all for your patience over the course of the day. As you well know, things are a little, well, chaotic right now. We are doing everything we can to get as much relevant information as to what's going on as we can, but the truth is, it has been very limited at this stage—"

"I've been asking for hours and I still don't have anywhere to sleep tonight!" said an older man in the crowd.

This triggered a number of questions from the crowd. Patrick just held his hand up to the audience until they stopped.

"There will be plenty of time for questions soon," he said, before looking at the older man. "I understand how hard it's been. We still have people wandering in and we will do our best to make sure everyone has a tent or room tonight.

"I just realised I forgot to introduce myself. For those who don't know me, my name is Patrick Quade. Yes, the Quade Real Estate Quade. I'm also on the board of the Redlegs for those who like their footy."

He was trying to keep the mood light, but his attempts were not meeting crowd expectations. He took a second hint with an awkward cleaning of the throat and a shift in his tone.

"Behind me are just some of the people trying to navigate our way through this. Sergeant Jillian Goodwood from the armed forces, Senior Constable Kyle Jenkins from Norwood police and Percy Peterson, who many of you may recognise from his years on the local council."

Patrick paused for applause but none came. He cleared his throat again and continued.

"We've been informed there is an effort to get the phone lines back up and running, which will be massive from a communication point of view. We have representatives from the army here and they are developing a broader response which will roll out over the next few days.

"So, we may have to ride out a tough few days, but we're hoping things will start to come together in a more coordinated way shortly.

"In the meantime, the local government and business community are joining forces to ensure we can make the next few days as comfortable as possible, starting with the basics of food and shelter for everyone.

"Tomorrow morning, we'll be looking for volunteers. If you're capable of helping in any way, please put your hand up when asked."

He looked around the crowd. We were silent, trying to absorb every detail we could.

"Look, I know this is a lot. Too much perhaps. I'm sure everyone here is dealing with... far more than they'd wish to. All we can do is work for each other to ride out this next little period.

"I'll be back to answer your questions shortly but, first, I want you to hear a few words from the people behind me. I'd like to call Sergeant Jillian Goodwood to the microphone. The army is putting together a survivor register and we'll begin taking your names in the morning. It will help inform them on the larger support response they are planning to deliver in the days and weeks to come." He turned and gave her a nod of invitation. "Sergeant."

*

It didn't take long once we filed out of the hall for Alex to track down the wine supplies. Soon there was a small group gathered around discussing, well, everything.

"If someone gave them the keys to the liquor store, why didn't they raid the top shelf," said Alex as she gave her plastic cup a betrayed look.

Having known her for as long as I had, I knew to expect random jokes, criticisms and general outlandish comments as her way of coping with Kendrick and everything else that was happening. She'd open up eventually, I figured. "It'll be good to have the phones back," I said.

"Hells yes it will," said Claire. "I'm not a fan of relying on others for our information. That includes Quade from Quade Real Estate and the board of the football club."

"What a knob," said Alex. "Can I just reel out of all the reasons why I'm buddy buddy with everyone and entitled as fuck to assume leadership with no actual credentials?"

"Once we get that and the army help, things will change fast," said Asim. "Hopefully some credentialled leadership."

I smiled at him. His positivity was definitely a welcome guest at that moment.

"Would've been nice if they could've answered a few more questions," said Alex. "I'm not sure I'm any wiser now than before I went in."

"Must be tough. Hopefully, things start to come together over the next few days," I said.

"Question of the night went to you," said Asim, as he looked at Alex. "Why is there only one woman on stage?"

There were more than a few sniggers from our group.

"That stumped him more than a question of when the mobile signal coming back online!" Claire added.

"Well, screw him," said Alex. "They introduced us to, what, ten people? And the only woman was the army outsider!"

"Does this in any way surprise you?" said Claire.

"No, yet another cock forest does not surprise me," said Alex. "I guess the long, long history of men sorting things out perfectly every time means it must be the right thing to do."

Alex chugged her wine, dropped the glass on a nearby table and revealed the second glass she'd been hiding at her side by taking a swig. "All I could see on that stage was wrinkly, podgy, balding, grey haired entitlement. And Patrick is the dux of the class. Chief fat man or porky silverback or something."

I sniggered. "We'll have to work on that ratio."

The conversation fell away after that as we all pondered her words or worked them out of our mind.

Eventually Yamato raised his glass. "To the future," he said.

We all took a drink in solidarity. Or hope. Or belief. We stood around and chatted for well over another hour. Everyone was guessing what tomorrow would bring and how, with a few days of hard work ahead, things would change for the better. There was definitely a buzz in the air that night while surrounded by hundreds of people in the same situation.

It was eerie when I think back on it. Not for how wrong we were about the outcomes we were expecting as such, maybe for the bubble of a moment we were in. The company was great and there was more than a hint of hope that this thing would be temporary – a blip.

It seems so stupid and naive I'm almost embarrassed when I think about it now.

But that's what the moment gave us.

Who knows, maybe it was the best thing for us. There was already too much to absorb with what we'd seen, heard and knew. And what we'd seen, heard and knew was the tiniest fraction of what had happened. I don't think we were capable of ingesting any more of it on that night. We had already reached some type of critical mass of horror memories. And there would be more ahead. Yeah, maybe a couple of drinks and talking bullshit about what was to come in a little cocoon of hope was the perfect antidote for it all.

The magic spell didn't last long though. We were soon on the march back to the tent city. It was almost as if the moment we started that journey, shit got real again. The talking faded to nothing and thoughts turned to all the things we didn't talk about when we were sharing a drink. Mine did, that's for sure.

None of which was helped by the moon. It probably seems a weird thing to mention with everything else going on that day, but you couldn't help but be consumed by its creepy red hue that evening. It was almost like there was a lunar eclipse, but there wasn't. It looked too heavy to stay in the sky, but it did. Between its ominous red gaze, the scattered pillars of smoke and the smell of general apocalyptic waste, we had a real-time reminder of how surreal our reality had become.

I'm not sure anyone escaped that or the thoughts that started to surface with it. I'm not sure how it would've been possible. Thoughts of family and friends and the reality that so many were no longer here, the unknowns around every aspect of life, the loss, the change in everything. It might not have been a topic for first night conversations, but it was weaved into everything said and done. Every thought, every action we were taking – all a result of the things we didn't talk about. But that was to be our new reality and there was no escaping it for too long.

Nothing made that more clear than reaching the oval and seeing the rows of tents in the park out the front. The fact that the numbers of homeless were now spilling outside of the stadium made it seem bigger – more real.

By that time, there was no speaking at all within our group. We were all physically and mentally shot. We managed our goodnights then disappeared in silence to our tents. By that time, Alex was a mess. She hit the sleeping bag spooning a sound asleep Jacob, then just burst into tears. They didn't stop. I reached out and held her hand in the darkness until sleep took me.

###

###

CHAPTER 17:

SYSTEMS

"Muffin?"

I had barely prised my eyes open and stepped outside the tent before I was tempted by a food offering. The guy making the offering looked like he'd be more at home driving B-Double trucks across the Nullabor. Well-greyed goatee, unkempt hair and a frame that looked like it'd digested many a pie with ample beer chasers.

He smiled at me as he leaned the tray in closer.

"Big day ahead, you'll need the energy," he said. "C'mon, I don't bite."

I smiled back and took one. At that point Claire popped her head out of the tent and the tray was offered in her direction. She also took one.

"Alex, wake up! Come grab a muffin," she said.

"Where'd you get these?" I asked.

"The bakery just up the street. Was up early and thought I'd have a wander to see what was happening. Anyway, they'd taken a bit of flood damage. Thought they'd bake up what they could rather than let it go to waste. I think they're going to drop a lot down here, but they gave me a tray full so I thought what better way to meet my new neighbours."

His name was Terry Cole. He'd soon offered muffins to Yamato, Sara and Asim, whose tents were next to ours. Then we met Liv, Billy and Em as well as Keira Narangga — an Aboriginal artist — and her teenage son Charlie, who were in the tent that separated us from the teens.

As we introduced ourselves and ate, we heard stories of how everyone came to be in a tent on the oval.

It turns out Terry looked like a truck driver because he was. He'd been running goods from interstate when the news dropped, managed to get his way back to Adelaide then was one of many truckies helping ensure the stores stayed stocked in the lead-up to 12/4. He'd stayed in accommodation out north when everything went down so he was ready to help move whatever.

Keira and her boy had been living on the wrong side of Osborne Tce when the tsunami rolled in. Their place was only a couple of streets from mine actually. Not far enough west to be destroyed, but far enough for her place not to be livable any more.

What Yamato and Sara saw from the foothills, as well as the view Claire, Alex and I had, really gave everyone a new perspective on the level of the damage Adelaide had suffered. But it was Liv, Billy and Em's story that had everyone speechless. Their fight for survival, the loss of their friend – incredible.

Turns out Billy knew Charlie from a junior representative footy squad they'd both made a couple of years ago and Sara had gone to school with Em, although they were a year apart and didn't know each other very well. So completely Adelaide.

It's hard to fully describe the connections we made in those moments. While we didn't realise what it was going to amount to at the time, we did share this monumental event that had led us all to the same few feet of turf on the Parade at the end of days. There was something powerful in that.

*

Queues. That's my memory of that day. First breakfast – the muffin was definitely not enough. They'd opened up a few of the cafes and restaurants along the strip and were serving all sorts. Word had come out that it had been decided all the businesses would write off all their stocks to the situation, so for the next few days food didn't have a price. Whereas the day before I think they were all grappling with how to handle things from a profit and loss perspective. It was a sign a new reality was hitting home. We weren't on a three-day blip away from normal life resuming – we were on the slow descent into some entirely different way of existence. Money just didn't seem right, at least not until we found a meaningful way to reinvent its purpose, perhaps.There was also the fact there was no connection to the banking system, so unless you had cash there was no way to transact for goods – and there was not much cash going around.

Pretty shameful, really, but in the end, the right outcome transpired for the getting-through-it short term. But, Norwood being Norwood, there would be a generous spread of the locals who would prefer to hang onto the money system.

After a refuel came the queue for the survival register – the longest of the day. A second army team had rolled in at dawn. Three large trucks packed with supplies. Once we eventually reached the desk, we had to fill out a form with basic details – name, date of birth, address etc.

The contact details section made me and the girls laugh. Address – no longer exists, phone – not accessible, email, not accessible. Not one way to reach me was actually available at that point in time.

Anyway, the survival register was part of the long game, part of building hope. A plan to stay connected to something bigger in whatever world would form out the other end of what we were diving into.

Hope also came in the form of a care package for everyone who filled out the register. We each received two boxes of basics – canned food, flour, long-life milk, preserved fruit, biscuits, pickled onions, a can opener, torch and batteries.

There was also an information pack. All the remaining shopping centres across the city were now known as survivor centres or hubs. They would be used as points for distribution of supplies and information.

We felt pretty lucky to be in close proximity to the Parade – or Norwood Hub – at that moment. It was comforting to know we had a medical centre, two large grocery stores and just about every other major service nearby.

"Would you like to donate it to the collective?" asked a woman as we passed out of the line with our goodies.

The path had taken us near the entrance to the shopping centre. There was a large pile of boxes gathered behind the woman, with teenagers running their contents back into Foodland.

"What?" said Alex. "Why?"

"If we gather our supplies, we'll be in a better position to cope with the next few days."

I exchanged glances with Claire and Alex, who both shrugged their indifference at the request. I shrugged myself before handing over my package. "It's not like we can cook it anyway," I said.

"Thank you," said the woman. "Can I please grab your names?"

"Wait, why didn't the army just give everything to you in the first place?" said Alex as she handed over her boxes.

"That wasn't their instruction. They're doing the same thing everywhere. But our situation at Norwood might be a little different than everywhere else. We have lots of refugees."

"Oh my god, we're refugees," said Claire.

"Wait," said Alex. "What are the people in the houses doing? Are they handing their boxes over?"

"The only people heading back this way are people like you from the tents. Hopefully those with homes will have enough supplies to get through and we can focus on keeping you all fed before further help comes."

Once again the three of us exchanged glances. There were some confused looks about what had taken place. But there seemed like too many other bigger things to worry about.

With that, we headed to the queue at the volunteer station.

*

It proved a long day before the three of us began the trek back to the tents. We had all offered our services to Foodland, where we spent the day doing a stocktake of the store room. There was a lot out there but, then again, there were a lot of people. We wondered how long it would last if no new food stocks arrived.

Tent city, as it was now being dubbed, had grown again during the day. There were now four more rows of tents for other new refugees on the grassed area outside the stadium. The spot was teeming with new arrivals.

"Have a look at them," said Alex, clearly not as quietly as she'd imagined.

A couple of mums looked up at us as we passed. Around them, five children whined about their hunger. The expressions on their faces really hit home for me – a mixture of confusion and brokenness. I nodded, smiled and received a nod back.

"That was us yesterday, you know," I said.

"True that," said Alex. "But look at us today, we're checkout chicks."

"Living the dream," I added.

"Let's be real, we were stocktakers," corrected Claire. "But if we play our cards right, we might get a promotion one day."

"Nothing wrong with checkout chicks," said Liv, as her, Billy and Em caught up with us on their return to tent city.

They were each carrying large packages of sausages.

"Hope you like snags. BBQ tonight?" said Billy.

"Argghh," said Alex. "Could we get any lowerbrow? Besides, there's nowhere to cook them anyway."

"Yes there is," said Billy. "Plenty of places in the members area."

"Snags!" she said before making a vomit noise.

Claire and I offered apologies to the teens.

"Anyone else see the phallic symbolism from our all-male leadership heroes?" said Alex.

Claire scoffed. "You don't actually think they sent sausages as a message?"

"Look at it. May as well be saying eat me."

I looked at Liv and her posse, unsure how to react. "Ignore her. Looks like a good feed."

*

It was just after dinner when the sounds of a distant explosion ripped through the air above us. So fierce and full was the noise it was hard to fully tell which direction it came from. There was something in the signature of the soundwaves that spoke of it coming from a long way away and being unimaginably big.

We eventually settled on north as its direction but without any certainty.

It was an unsettling moment for many reasons. Firstly, we had no idea what caused it. Our best guesses were just that – guesses. We didn't know if it was natural or man made, if it would affect us or not, would it come back again? Would it be closer? Was it safe?

Nothing.

This completely goes against your human instinct to know and understand. We did not know what it was then and, given there was no way of news getting passed around, there was a fair chance we might not ever know what happened. Eventually we just had to accept it for what it was – a distant and epic-sounding explosion that may or may not have ramifications for us then or in the future.

By now, even something as simple as being informed what was happening around you seemed like an aspirational dream. There were no news crews. Maybe it was a job we'd underestimated in our lifetime for a thousand different reasons, but the core of journalism was about keeping people informed.

Now we knew nothing. War could have broken out a ten-minute drive from us and we'd have had absolutely no idea.

It's not great for navigating a path of survival for thousands of people.

It also added to the isolation. There was a channel still broadcasting news reports – ABC. Despite the main transmission towers at Mt Lofty being destroyed by the Melbourne blastwave, someone had managed to get a signal out. It was intermittently clear enough to be received at the Parade, not that any of us at tent city knew about it.

Regardless, it was reporting limited information from local, national and international signals. There was probably nothing new past the night everything changed, but perhaps that didn't matter – someone was trying to keep the system going. Outside of what was happening along the Parade, someone else was trying to bring connectedness and normality by providing a news service.

It was a similar thing with electricity at that point. We had lost power then had it restored several times over the first few days. We didn't know the whys of the outages any more then we understood the reasons it managed to get restored. All we knew was that out there – somewhere in wider Adelaide – people were trying to restore order.

*

Life without anything resembling a modern convenience was starting to hit us at the oval. During the day we interacted with each other around whatever necessity presented itself. At night it was a completely different story. It was unwind time, forget the realities of the universe time, but that was easier said than done.

Some wanted time to themselves, which was totally understandable. But for the rest of us who wanted a distraction or escape, things proved a lot harder. Entertainment wasn't something you could stream or download. It could only exist now if you created it or sought it out. Aside from food and water, there weren't many things as vital as keeping sane. And a big part of that was feeling connected with your world. It was clear very early on that if we didn't go out and create that ourselves we could find ourselves drifting.

I did not want to drift.

"So, tell me about your paintings," said Claire.

"I'm not actually a painter," said Keira. "I make films."

"Ahh... yeah... sorry , I just—"

Keira laughed as she took another bite of her sausage sandwich. "Don't worry about it. Happened more times than I could count."

"Tell us about your movies then," I said. That's when I saw the guitar case with her belongings. "Oh and you play guitar."

We had gathered between our tents, sitting in two rows facing each other and shooting the breeze while we ate. The teens had finished their food and were kicking the footy on the nearby terraces. Alex was putting Jacob down, while we consumed her gift for the night. She'd somehow managed to scam a few bottles of wine, which we were enjoying from plastic cups.

"Honestly, they're nothing special. Arthouse shorts, if you were finding a polite way to describe them," said Keira. "And the guitar's just something I've always done. Keeps me sane."

"I'm sure they're great," said Claire.

Keira smiled. "Thanks."

"We might be able to use your music here at night," I said. "Doesn't look flush with things to do."

Keira laughed. "I'm not sure I'd inflict you with that."

We smiled back and I was more curious than before about what she sounded like.

"How long do you think it'll be until they find us a house?" said Yamato. "That's the plan right?"

"I don't mind the tent life, but if there are rooms available, I want one," said Terry. "Does anyone else feel like a second-class citizen giving our food up while the home owners kept theirs?"

"Yes!" said Alex as she emerged from the tent. "That was some sort of bullshit."

"I really don't think that's what they're doing," I said. "I think they're just hoping to give those who already have pantries full of stuff enough that they don't have to rely on the shops until things get better."

"Why do you always have to be the teacher's pet on this shit?" said Alex.

Despite knowing her playbook of ways to put her friends in uncomfortable positions around strangers, it didn't always equate to handling with aplomb. "I'm not!" I defended.

She smiled at me in the way that said she knew she'd gotten to me. I narrowed my eyes in begrudging approval, then she raised her glass at me.

"Alex, say what you want about the dick symbolism, but since they started cooking the BBQ, it's been the first time I haven't been overpowered by the smell around here," said Claire.

Good to know she had my back. Tackling the conversation in hitting Alex on a different bow.

The others looked at us, confused.

"Alex thinks the sausages were sent from our leaders to symbolise their appendages," I clarified.

Yamato opened his mouth in shock and Terry gave a bemused look while Keira started laughing out loud.

"See," said Alex, gesturing towards Keira. "She gets it."

"Hey, you're the one that asked that question yesterday," said Keira. "Respect. Also, there is definitely too much decision-making dick."

Alex raised her arms out to the sides in triumph as if someone had finally gotten her message. Then she picked up the remaining morsel of her second sausage, pincered it between her fingers and flopped it back and forward.

By this point, Yamato didn't know where to look, while Terry, Claire and I had joined in the laughter. Although my version involved a facepalm.

That was the start of another night of getting to know our expanding group of survivor buddies. Soon the conversation would turn to how the world was reshaping around us, the Parade and what we thought would happen next. Again, the deeper thoughts about worry for friends and relatives or general fear went left unsaid. It was almost becoming an unspoken pact at this point. We had gathered together as survivors, or refugees, and our role was to support each other forward. That was the line connecting us. It was our purpose as a group.

While our evening played out, the red moon hovered overhead again. Keira had her camera gear out at some point and filmed it, before taking some general shots around the camp. It was a sight we would become used to.

The moon wasn't as spectacular on this night. In fact, it was barely visible through the thick haze that had developed in the upper atmosphere. The haze wasn't normal cloud. This was the beginning of an ash cloud. It had been discussed quite a bit in the lead-up to the strike, so it was something almost every survivor was aware might happen. The way it had subtly rolled in as the evening progressed made it feel so insignificant. It was virtually ignored, apart from a brief talking point every now and then.

How wrong we were. It could be argued that what was starting to spread out high in the skies above us in that moment would be more impactful than every effect the comet strike had had until that point.

We just didn't know it yet as we talked pie-in-the-sky futures surrounded by a sea of tents.

Before long we returned to those tents. As we did, our darker thoughts returned to us. That was the lock-it-in guarantee of alone time in the apocalypse. They were as unstoppable as the ash cloud.

###

###

CHAPTER 18:
ASH

The next morning it didn't take long to realise the dust would become more than just a distant atmospheric observation in our lives. We were greeted with it when we left our tents at first light. I hadn't even noticed the tent roof sagging in before I made my way out, too overwhelmed by the new and grimmer-than-previous-grim smell.

"What the fuck?" I said as the shadowy silhouette outside made unzipping the door a challenge.

"What?" said Alex, in her annoyed morning voice.

"Something's... wrong."

"With the zip?"

"Kind of. There's something blocking it or something."

Soon Claire and Alex were investigating, then helping me get the tent open. We toyed with the zip until it started to do its job and the entrance opened up.

"What the fuck?" said Alex.

The three of us and Jacob made our way outside. We took in the sight of tent city, looking completely different than it had when we closed the door on it the night before. The surface of an alien planet would not have been an exaggeration. Ash, perhaps a few centimetres deep, lay over everything. It was browny grey in colour and somehow managed to steal all the colour from the landscape around it.

It wasn't just on the ground, either. You could see flakes of it snowing down from the sky. There must've been much finer particles of it as well, as the visibility had lowered to the point we could barely see the grandstand across the other side of the oval.

Our entire field of vision had become a soft, grey brown haze. The only hints of remaining colour came from the tents themselves, but all the vibrance of their hues had been sucked away.

We could see some of the other early-risers shuffling about through the substance, looking every bit as confused and astonished as we were. Not that you could tell that from facial expressions, unless they were within 20m or so. But there's a certain way a human silhouette moves that lets you into their thoughts.

Jacob starting sneezing.

"I'm going to take him back inside," said Alex. "What are we going to do now?"

Claire and I looked at each other and shrugged.

"Well, figure something out," said Alex.

"I'm not sure I'm going to be able to today," she added as she closed the zipper.

Claire and I just looked at each other as the realities of this new situation washed over us. It was all too overwhelming to speak. Maybe the demons that came to Alex at night were keeping her there today. It was hard to know how to react, aside from an understanding nod and some space.

I shared a look of concern with Claire. It said a lot about her that, despite her own loss, she was dialled into what her friend was going through in that moment.

"Well, that's just fucking great," said Terry from behind us.

We turned to see him zipping up his tent before returning his gaze to the ash show. He didn't have anything else to contribute to the conversation.

Within minutes, Yamato and Sara had joined us, followed shortly after by Keira and Charlie. It seemed speaking wasn't within anyone's grasp at that moment. If they were anything like me, they were trying to work out how we'd start again. Again.

*

By the time the tent full of teenagers finally woke up, we had formed a posse and were heading up the Parade to find a way to get our accommodation upgraded. Yamato and Sara had strips of cloth covering their mouths and I wished I'd been smart enough to think of that too. We hadn't even halved the ground on our short walk when my lungs started screaming at me.

I was coughing, too. A lot of people were, both in our group and the many, many others who were migrating east along the Parade.

It was a strange experience to be part of, being one of the shadows in the dusty fog. The ash on the ground meant you could barely hear the footsteps. In fact, the ash in the air seemed to swallow the sound as much as it did the colour. The bottom line was that both sight and sound senses were significantly hampered. So, not only were we walking through a phenomenon that probably hadn't been seen on the planet at this scale for millions of years, we were doing it at a vastly reduced capacity.

The grime was getting everywhere fast. By the time we reached the cover of Norwood Place, I could feel a thick layer of ash over every part of my exposed skin. Not only that, I could feel it up my sleeves, down my top, just about everywhere you wouldn't want ash to gather.

As we turned into the arcade that led to the shops, the absence of army trucks didn't go unnoticed.

There were a handful of skeleton volunteers busying themselves inside the centre by the time we reached the double doors. Someone knocked and it took a couple of minutes for someone inside to sort the keys out and open up.

Whether it was our ash filthiness and the threat it made to the respectively sterile shops inside, or the intimidating numbers, or the lack of organisation, it was clear they weren't overly keen to let us in.

Four of the volunteers blocked the doorway.

I eyed the one who looked like they were in charge. "Can you please let us in?"

"Can you give us a few minutes to get organised? Mr Quade's been notified," she said.

"Why should he need to know?" said Terry. "We have every right to be here."

Behind us, a number of others roared their approval.

"We understand it's been a rough couple of days but—"

"Take a look at us," said Terry. "Just let us in for Christ's sake."

With everything we said the crowd let their thoughts be known, either cheering or adding comments along the same general vibe. We had found ourselves as the mouthpieces of the crowd.

The woman in control of the door opened her mouth but no response came forward. We must have looked an intimidating sight.

"Look, I don't know if you've seen what's going on out here, but it's bad," I said.

"And getting worse," said someone behind me.

Soon, someone started repeating the chant "Let us in." Within seconds it had been adopted by the majority behind us, the words echoing up and down the arcade.

Someone came running over to the volunteers from further inside the shopping centre and whispered something into the ear of the lady in charge. She nodded her acceptance to the message then went to speak, only to be drowned out by the chanting. She put her hand up to indicate to the crowd she had something to say, but it was having no effect.

Then Terry put his fingers into his mouth and let out a whistle that had the potential to burst eardrums. It did the job, with the chants fading to nothing within a few seconds. "Let her speak," he said, to override the straggling chanters.

The woman was quite rattled at this point. She cleared her throat. "Mr Quade is preparing the town hall to address you all shortly. If you can make your way up there, they'll be able to take care of you."

It was a plan that seemed to confuse the group around us. I think they'd had their attention so fixated on getting into the centre, they seemed to forget why we were even there in the first place.

Terry whistled again. "Alright, you heard the woman, let's see what this fancy Mr Quade has to say."

The crowd laughed, then Terry made a hand gesture to indicate everyone should about-turn and head to the town hall. I mimicked the signal to those gathered on the other side who may have missed his. Soon we were on the move again.

*

"Thank you ladies and gentlemen for your patience. I know it hasn't been the most ideal of mornings," said Patrick Quade as he addressed the crowd. "Obviously, this has hit us all quicker and more intensely than we expected."

There were several hundred of us gathered in the town hall by that point. Perhaps half the population of tent city, with more trickling in all the time. By the sides of the stage were a number of volunteers, facing the crowd. There were maybe 15 of them, some of whom I recognised from the shops a few minutes earlier. Like with the tent city crowd, more volunteers filtered in. It was tense, no doubt about it.

"Where are we going to sleep tonight?" someone called out from the crowd.

Patrick nodded at the woman. "Good question. Our initial plans were to foster people into rooms in houses where the residents have volunteered them. Between that and the vacant houses in the area, we're pretty confident we could have everyone relocated within a couple of weeks. But for—"

"Are you fucking kidding me," yelled out Terrry. "A couple of weeks?"

"I'm not going back to tent city!" yelled another man.

Patrick nodded and raised his hands in concession. "I understand, I understand.

"Look I'm not saying that is entirely necessary, I'm just giving you the background on what was happening before today. We've been working tirelessly

111

to get all of you relocated as quickly and seamlessly as possible. Things have now changed, so we have to change."

"Who is making these decisions?" I said.

The words flew out before my brain could intercept them. Pre-12/4 my brain would have definitely intercepted them. But as soon as I asked the question I was glad I did, even if it created a few seconds where he looked a little rattled and had to collect himself before answering.

Patrick cleared his throat, then held my gaze for a few seconds before delivering a relaxed smile. "I introduced you to most of the team two nights ago. They are people in business, the forces, government and industry – a very capable group."

"...who seem to have shat the bed with tent city," said Terry.

The crowd laughed.

By the side of the stage I saw the police officer move in next to the volunteers with another cop at his side. He and Patrick exchanged nods.

"Like I said, today has caught us off-guard," said Patrick.

"Where are you sleeping?" said Terry.

If my question had made Patrick uncomfortable, this one trumped it with ease.

"My wife and I have been put up by friends," he said after collecting himself. This sent a wave of whispers through the crowd.

"Just as you will be," he added soon after.

"Have you actually seen what's happening down at the oval?" said Terry.

Patrick glared at him. Clearly he had not. When he opened his mouth to respond Terry just talked right over him. "The ash is already about 4cm thick and it can't have started coming down until the early hours of today. If it keeps going like this we won't be able to get into our tents tonight."

Whatever tension was there at the beginning was starting to go to the next level. The sort of level where I think everyone involved realised if things weren't calmed it could soon get out of hand. It was Patrick's move to make. I watched his facial expressions as his brain ticked over while he pondered his next response.

"Look, clearly we need to pivot quickly around this situation as it changes. If you need to take some time away from your volunteering duties to move this morning or this afternoon, just do so.

"Perhaps, it would be best to get a committee of voices from tent city to help with the response. We have already located a few empty houses and between that, the retail space not being used, the cinema and this hall, we'll be able to find enough space so nobody is left in the weather tonight."

He had played the moment well. The crowd were less restless and he now had an attentive audience once again.

"I suggest you, you and… you," said Patrick as he pointed to Terry, myself and one of the other men who spoke up during the meeting.

Terry and I looked at each other. The morning had taken another interesting turn.

###

###

CHAPTER 19:
STORAGE

I remember the moment as if it was yesterday. It still makes me feel as sick now as it did then. The powers-that-now-seemed-to-be were preparing to head down to the oval for a tour of conditions. It seemed like half of Norwood had gathered for the moment, the outcome of which would have a significant effect on how those with and without properties coexisted.

"Get the fuck out of town," said Claire.

"What?" I said, searching the throng for whatever had caught her attention.

No luck. I looked back at her and the expression seemed like a Picasso of worrying emotions.

"What?" I said again. But even before the word had fully formed in my mouth I had my answer.

Not more than 50m from where I was standing I saw him. Craig. He was holding hands with the woman I recognised from social media as Anita, chatting to another couple on the outskirts of Patrick's main group, all gathered and waiting for their leader to return.

"What in the actual fuck is he doing here?" said Claire.

I tried for words but my mind and mouth weren't working together in the moment.

Still, the collective power of two sets of eyeballs didn't take long to grab his attention. He looked up before being washed over with mouth agape, shocked. He just stood frozen in position and facial expression, staring back at us.

Way too many seconds passed before he turned his back and walked away from us, nudging his new partner to follow after him.

"The fuck?" said Claire. "He lives – lived – in Bowden! He should be…"

"Dead," I said.

*

"Charlie!" yelled Keira as she passed through the last of the crowd waiting for Patrick to head down to the oval.

She lost track of him in all the commotion, but she knew in all likelihood where he had gone and what he was doing. She headed back to the oval.

A few minutes later she was through the main entrance and wandering into the heart of tent city. It didn't take long to spot Charlie through the tents. He had his back up against the boundary line fence at the far side of the ground, football in hand. He took a couple of steps towards the nearby goals, laid the football across his boot and sent it curling towards its target, only to have it rocket into the behind post short.

The post rattled and the ball squished into the ash below. Keira could hear him swear from the other end of the ground as he kicked the ash in frustration.

"Charlie!" she said as she closed the ground between them.

He ignored her as he retrieved the ball and headed back to the boundary to take another shot. Before he did, he kicked away the offending ash.

"Oi," said Keira as he lined up again.

Once again he ignored her as he took his kick. This time the toe of his boot caught the ash and the ball dribbled forward a few metres before coming to rest well short of the goals. "Fuck!"

"What was that?" said Keira.

"It's not me, it's this fucking ash!"

Charlie retrieved the ball before turning his back on her and heading back to the boundary line for another shot.

"Charlie! Stop right there, we need to talk."

"What's there to talk about?"

"You. Here. Alone. Now."

"What about it?"

"What's going on?"

Charlie looked at her for the first time. "Mum, there is literally nothing going on, like, at all! That's the fucking point."

She looked at him, letting her silence conjure out more of his words.

"My entire life is fucked," he added eventually.

"How is it fucked? You're alive, that's more than most of the population from a week ago can say."

"What's the point in being alive if... if... if you can't live?"

He spun the football in his hands as he stared at her, demanding her wisdom.

"Every breath you're living, you just need to—"

"That's easy for you to say."

"It's not easy for me to say at all. I don't need to tell you what we've lost in recent days."

He conceded eye contact as he thought about his extended family. "I don't mean that. I mean, what do you do with your time? You film shit or you play guitar and sing. They're your things. You can still do your things. You can still be you."

He spun the football in his hand again to let it grab her attention. He pushed the ball into the oval deck. Pre-12/4 the underbelly of the ball would've connected with the surface and bounced back into his hands. Now it just died in the ash, the substance smothering all the life out of the move. "I can't do my thing," he said. "I can't be me."

She nodded her understanding and closed the ground to give him a hug. "I can only begin to imagine how you feel about that."

They embraced, a move only allowed by Charlie given the oval was all but deserted, with everyone at the meeting.

"I know it's hard to see it right now, but this is all temporary. No matter how overwhelming it all gets, it's only temporary."

"But it isn't really, is it?" he said. "It's not like the mess will be cleaned up in a few months and we'll go back to the way we were."

Keira squeezed her eyes shut, hoping to prevent the tears from falling. It failed to work.

"I was 14 days too young for the draft last year. Fourteen fucking days. I could have been on an AFL list. Now there are no lists, no AFL, no fucking anything football. I have spent my entire life preparing to be good at a thing that no longer exists."

Keira squeezed tighter. "I know, I know," she soothed. "Maybe that thing you love doesn't come back the way it was before, but it will come back."

She pushed herself far enough away so eye contact could be had once more. "Look at me," she added, when he tried to avoid her gaze. "This thing you love. This thing a lot of people love. This thing you're extremely talented at. It will be back. And it will be one of the most important things there is once again.

"When people have stopped surviving and want to start living again, they are going to want to escape again. They are going to want to be entertained again. They are going to want sport again… and movies and music. And they are definitely going to want football again."

Charlie's eyes were now moist as well. He nodded as he broke eye contact.

"What you do is special," said Keira. "And it has a place in our future. Perhaps a more important one than ever before."

"That could be years away."

"Maybe, I don't know. In the meantime you didn't learn to just kick a ball though. You've learnt leadership, discipline, teamwork, public speaking, helping other people in your community, just to name a few skills. That's what the world needs from you now."

Charlie thought on her words, eventually nodding and squeezing her hand in appreciation before stepping back into his own space. He exhaled deep and slow.

"Charlie!" said Billy from the terraces as he headed in their direction. "I've been looking for you everywhere."

Keira looked at her son and gave a small smile. "You've got this."

Charlie picked up the footy and handballed it to the approaching Billy.

"You're a hard man to find," said Billy as he grabbed the ball. "Just about everyone in the Parade is headed this way. So, me and the others are going to find a place to hang as far away from all that as possible. Want to come?"

He handballed the ball back to Charlie.

Charlie nodded then handed the footy to his mum.

"Can we bring that?" said Billy. "I'm dying for a kick."

*

Olivia lightly wrapped on the door. "Got a big crowd out there."

The door was ajar, giving a little with her knock. After a few seconds of silence she entered the room. "You ready, babe?"

She knew a bit of body contact and praise could get Patrick focused if he was facing a big moment and this was a big moment. One look at him stopped her in her tracks. He already had his game face on and something about his expression struck her as new.

"Things would be so much easier around here if we could just get rid of them," he said.

"Rid of them?"

"Sure. Move them on somewhere else. Why does it all have to fall on us to deal with?"

"I guess it's just how things have unfolded."

"That's what I'm saying. We're in the position of power here. They've come into our area and asked for our help. I guess we'll give what we can while we can but, at some point, maybe we just have to reconsider how accommodating we are."

Olivia nodded. "I'm sure you'll make the right decisions when the moment is right."

She pressed her body into his and gave him a peck on the cheek. "That's for good luck. Hoping for more later."

"I should have a window before I have to go home."

*

"It's open!" said Billy as he pulled on the sliding door.

The entryway to the industrial-sized storage facility moved briefly before the ash tampered with the sliding wheels and brought its momentum to a halt.

"Give us a hand, would you?" he said.

Soon Charlie, Liv, Em and Sara were also leaning their weight into the door until it gave in to the force and opened far enough for the five to enter. They were greeted by an open space leading to a number of corridors lined with individual storage spaces.

"Oh, that's what I'm talking about," said Billy as he lowered his backpack to the ground, grabbed Charlie's footy, then ran across the concrete until he had adequate kicking distance between them. He turned, nodded at Charlie, then kicked the footy back to him.

Charlie clutched the mark, spun the ball in his hands then bulleted a pass back.

"Holy crap!" said Billy after the ball slapped his hands. "Lethal!"

He loaded up his best return pass and let fire. Not as pacey nor as accurate, but Charlie covered the ground and caught it in one hand. He shot Billy a grin as he spun the ball in his hand then kicked back.

"Showoff!" said Billy as he took the next mark. "Liv check my backpack."

"Jesus! What the hell you got in here?" she said as she lifted it.

Then she heard the clinking of glass. She reached in and removed a bottle of gin, then a couple of bottles of tonic.

"Made a deal with the guy at the booze shop," said Billy. "Consider this a starter pack."

"What deal?" said Liv.

"It was one of those mind-your-own-business type deals," he said, dropping his most Liv-annoying smile for emphasis. "There'll be a kitchen somewhere, you should be able to grab some glasses."

"Who died and made you king?"

"The gin says I am king!"

Em looked at Sara, who nodded. "We can go."

Liv rolled her eyes, even before Billy winked at her. She focused her energy on removing the goods from the bag.

"I've got my stash in the little section at the back," said Billy. "Oh, and some tunes."

Liv stared at the haul, then at Billy in disbelief.

"I think the words you're looking for are, you're welcome," said Billy.

"But how?"

"Survival is all about priorities," he said, before catching and kicking the ball once more.

"Got glasses," said Em. "They even had some snacks in there – chips and nuts."

"Oh, boom!" said Billy.

He ran back to the rest of the group, handballing the footy to Charlie as he did. "Only two hours until work starts, so drink irresponsibly."

Liv nodded.

"Yes please," said Em.

"Maybe not for me," said Sara.

Billy gave her a confused but accepting nod. "More for the rest of us," he said as he lined up four glasses.

"I might give it a miss too," said Charlie.

"What?" said Billy. "Ah, don't tell me, you're both more your stoner types? I respect that," he said as he slid a plastic bag over towards Charlie.

Charlie slid it back. "I think I'm good, actually."

Billy shrugged, trying to show indifference, but some of his disappointment shone through. He offered it to Sara with less expectation.

Sara giggled nervously as she shook her head. "My dad would kill me. Besides, I can barely breathe as it is."

"Go on then," said Em. "Someone's got to stand in solidarity."

She reached out as Billy passed her the spliff before she took a toke then handed it back.

"What sort of tunes you got?" said Charlie.

Billy smiled. "Now we're talking."

He leaned over and passed Charlie a device, then turned on the speaker. "There's no password. Just go to the music folder – it's packed with all sorts of shit."

Charlie smiled and dived in.

Billy returned the smile before handing out drinks to Liv and Em, then turning his attention to the plastic bag.

"Seriously, where the fuck are you getting all this shit?" said Liv.

"We work at the supermarket," said Billy. "We're sitting on a gold mine. All I'm doing is connecting people."

"What people?"

"People who have something and want something else."

Liv gave him a look that demanded more answers.

"Basically anything you want really. Except for what's in this bag. I still haven't found a new source for what's in this bag."

Em reached over and passed him the joint. He flicked his lighter into life then inhaled until he coughed.

"Still, early days. There'll be someone," he said, once he recovered.

The speaker burst into life, reggae beats filling the wide open storage space.

Billy burst into laughter. "Good call Charlie. On message. Bob Marley?"

Charlie nodded as he dropped his head into the beats.

"Don't know the song though," said Billy.

"*Sun is shining*," said Charlie. "Underrated vibes."

"Fuck I miss the sun," said Liv.

"Me too," said Sara.

"Hence the audio therapy," said Charlie.

They all sat and listened as the song played through the first two verses and chorus.

"This place is amazing," said Billy. "We need to make this our official getaway retreat."

"Agreed," said Em.

"I'm not sure I want to admit how much you've nailed it," said Liv.

Billy feigned a shocked face before he stood up to address the group. "Humans of the storage facility, it is my duty to indoctrinate you into the club. It is a club that seems to have no real purpose… other than to not be with the old people… and as such it shall be called… erm… from henceforth and stuff…"

"This started so much better than it's currently going," said Liv.

"…because I'm trying to think of a name on the fly…"

"OK, stop now."

"…if I keep doing this, something genius is bound to come up..."

"We really don't need a name."

"…and then I'll stop talking and the name will just be in my head… now!"

Everyone looked at him.

"Didn't work," said Billy as he took another toke.

They all laughed. Even Billy.

*

THE PARADE: APOCALYPSE SURVIVORS

"Jesus," said Patrick as we made our way out onto what used to be the oval's playing surface.

It had been the first time he'd spoken in our walk down from the town hall. "I... I had no idea."

We were leading a crowd of tent city people who had been at the town hall. The commotion of our arrival saw the remainder of the population head over. They either saw what was going on through the ashy mist or heard about it from afar.

I tried not to roll my eyes at Patrick's performance – and it was a performance. He was putting on a show for everyone who was at the town hall. This was his empathetic good guy. He was like a politician. I swear, if there were any babies nearby he would've kissed them.

Thankfully that wasn't something we'd have to endure.

I exchanged a few looks with Terry, which let me know we were on the same page about Patrick.

Next thing I knew we were investigating the depth of the ash. Terry buried his hand in, then cupped it full of the stuff. Patrick was soon rolling his sleeves up to investigate.

"That's got to be at least 7cm," said Patrick when he pressed his fingers deep into the ashy surface.

"At least," said Terry. "And I don't think we had any before 2am."

Patrick nodded.

"Night owl," added Terry.

"So, if it keeps up at this rate, what are we talking about?"

"We're not far under a centimetre an hour. At least 20cm a day," I said.

"At least," said Terry. "It's coming down heavier than it was at dawn."

Patrick looked up at the sky, while his mind ticked over. "So, if we're looking at 2-3 days of this, this entire facility will be uninhabitable."

"If it's not uninhabitable tonight, it will be by dawn," said Terry.

Terry and I both looked into the ever-darkening sky. It was not long past 9am and the sun was just a hazy light point in the endless browny grey.

"And 2-3 days," I added. "I think what we're looking at here is going to last a lot longer than 2-3 days. Could be weeks."

"I heard some of the experts say months," added Terry. "There were a lot of varied opinions on that, like everything, but I definitely heard multiple people say months."

Patrick rubbed the ash between his fingers and let it slip out of his hands towards the ground again while he thought. "Well, this becomes mission critical for today. I'm going to head back and chase up the unoccupied housing situation. While I do, I suggest you go on a recon of the cinema and town hall and any other unused space you can find.

"How many people do you think we're dealing with, approximately?"

"I wouldn't be surprised if there's 1000," said Terry. "We'll do our best to get a headcount."

"Jesus Christ," said Patrick.

"We should also get a measure of the footprint of the tents," I added. "That's how much floorspace we'll need."

Patrick nodded at me. "Sounds like a plan. When you need me, come to George House. It's about 100m east of the cinemas on the Parade – can't miss it."

###

###

CHAPTER 20:
MIGRATION

"C'mon Alex, let's get some breakfast," said Claire. "Everyone's about to head back up."

Alex remained silent, lying in her sleeping bag in the foetal position. By her side Jacob played with a toy keyboard, hammering out a mishmash of sounds accompanied by bright lights.

"The fresh air will help," said Claire.

"What fucking fresh air," said Alex, eventually. Her voice was muffled by the sleeping bag.

"Good point. But you can't stay here all day. It's not healthy."

"Watch me."

"What about this? I take junior for a walk and we'll bring you back something to eat?"

Alex grunted in frustration, but the tone was also a conceding of position.

"OK, good," said Claire. "Hey Jacob, want some breakfast? We can also get your mummy something to eat."

*

By the time we had marched our way up the Parade for a late breakfast, we already had more volunteers than we needed. We divided them into twelve teams and, after our feed, we set out on our first recon mission.

In the end we were looking for nearly 18,000sqm of floorspace. It was a daunting number to think about, but as drilled down into what was available it became apparent we would reach our quota with ease. It wasn't so much the amount of space available, it was factors like the quality and what we could gain access to that would determine who would end up where.

It also became pretty clear the transition was going to take way longer than a day to complete. Way, way longer.

Firstly, some of the business spaces that would be prime locations for living were locked, with no signs of how we'd gain access. Some were even boarded up the way owners would have left them on 12/4. This became one of the many things that would be a problem for another day.

With so many people to move with limited daylight and time, we decided to go for the big hits. The lower level of the Webbe St car park behind Norwood Place and the car park underneath the Parade Central complex, home to the cinemas, would do a lot of the heavy lifting for space. As would the entry walkway to the cinemas, the cinemas themselves and the town hall. Every inch of ground space was utilised.

It wasn't great, especially for those in the car parks, but it was better than being exposed to the conditions and it was only temporary.

Once the plans were cemented, the oval became a sea of activity as hundreds of tents came down and more than 1000 people began migrating up the Parade to their third home in quick succession.

It was an eerie sight in the low visibility. As far as you could see into the distance, there were silhouettes of survivors hauling everything they now owned, as well as the tents that would house them for another night. Some moved with purpose, some fighting their mental exhaustion and all of them moving based on the plans I had been a part of making.

That hit a spot in me. Whatever the outcome of this migration, I had a responsibility. I felt way too many emotions as I watched the action unfold.

*

Asim knocked on the door for a third time. He waited a few seconds before shaking his head to the two others behind him.

A man named Graham stepped forward and went about releasing the lock – a skill he'd mastered years ago as a locksmith. He toyed with the mechanism for a few seconds until it gave him a satisfying click, then turned the handle.

Graham, Asim and a woman named Katelyn headed into the house.

"Anyone home?" said Graham as they waited in the entryway.

After another short wait he nodded again and they made their way further into the property. They split up and swept through the house room by room until they were sure it was vacant.

Soon they were gathered in the kitchen. "All clear?" said Graham.

"All clear," said the others.

"I found these," added Asim.

He held up a set of keys. Graham took them, rifled through the choices, selected the one he was most interested in and returned to the front door. He slid it in and turned the lock.

"Perfect!" he said as he made a note of the address on a piece of paper and put it with the keys in a plastic bag, which he pocketed.

"Right then, let's go shopping."

*

"We're back!" said Claire.

Alex sighed under the sleeping bag.

Claire sighed. "C'mon Jacob, what say we give your mum her breakfast?"

Alex stuck her hand out from under the covers and Claire helped Jacob pass her an avocado roll.

She started crying.

"There's coffee as well," said Claire. "You told me you can't morning without one."

After a few seconds, the sounds of crying subsided. Alex huffed again before making her way to a sitting position, still inside the sleeping bag. The sounds of chewing could be heard within.

"It's not going to stay hot for long," said Claire, now holding out the coffee.

Alex huffed again and, after wrestling with the zipper for a few seconds, lowered the sleeping bag around her waist. "I know how it feels," she said as she took the offering.

Claire and Jacob watched her consume in silence for a few seconds, hoping more words would come. They did not.

"We should probably start to pack up once you're done. You should see it out there, people everywhere," said Claire, pausing for a response that never came. "They're converting one of the furniture stores into a creche."

She stared at Alex, hoping the look would be returned at some point and break the tension. It didn't. She looked at Jacob who was smiling at her.

"Anyway, it could be just what Jacob... and you... need during the days."

Chewing and silence.

"Maybe we could even volunteer to help them out?"

Alex choked on her avocado and went into a coughing fit.

"You OK?" said Claire.

Eventually the coughing settled and Alex washed it all back with a large swig of coffee. "Me? In a creche? I'm struggling to deal with one kid right now."

"Well, maybe just Jacob then."

*

125

"The committee will see you now," said Olivia.

I was waiting at George House with the others in the tent city relocation team, as we really didn't want to call ourselves. Archie – the third member of our team – had been an architect before things went south. He had good ideas and the three of us seemed to get along well enough with the task at hand.

I looked at the pair of them as we rose to our feet and prepared to follow Olivia upstairs and into whatever this committee situation was.

We were ushered into a room where nine people sat around a boardroom table – Patrick at the head. There was a round of introductions as we met the police officer named Kyle, a councilman and a number of business leaders. There were too many names to absorb them all. Regardless, it was clear this was where the decisions were being made.

Soon we had introduced ourselves and were reporting on the day.

"The job was too big for an afternoon, so we've relocated tent city to the lower level of the Webbe St car park, the car park under the cinema, the cinema itself and the town hall," said Terry. "Everyone will have some sort of roof over their head tonight."

"Excellent," said Patrick. "I assume you have other locations in mind."

"We do," I said. "We have a list. I've only brought one extra copy because I didn't realise we'd be presenting to so many…"

I passed the second copy of my handwritten notes to Patrick. He perused the list while I continued.

"Many of these businesses are locked with no signs of anyone opening them soon. If we did manage to get access, I think there'd be enough space for perhaps a third of us. Ideally we'd move the people in the car parks first, get them in a fully enclosed space. Assuming we can continue using the cinema space and the town hall, I'd say we'd have more than enough, especially with whatever unused housing you find."

"We're going to need to remove the church from your list," he said.

"But that's a huge space and—"

"We've had to make a few tough calls today. In case things don't get better as fast as we're hoping, we're going to need everyone contained within the suburb of Norwood, so anything east of Portrush Rd is no-go, I'm afraid," said Patrick.

"There are a number of spots on the list east of Portrush," I said.

"I understand, but the logistics of spreading people out so far may come back to bite us. We also have a number of spots not on your list. Once we merge everything together, I'm confident we'll have space for everyone. Even the 83 new arrivals today."

I opened my mouth to respond but I really didn't know what to say. After sharing a look with Terry and Archie, I left it at that.

"Well, nice work team. We'll need more of that tomorrow," said Patrick, gesturing towards the door.

We exchanged nods then headed out.

"Make sure everyone knows I'll be giving an update after dinner tonight."

"Will do," said Terry.

*

"I don't think I can go on any more," said Billy.

Liv rolled her eyes as he retracted his hands from his pocket.

"I must reach for my phone every five minutes. It's instinct. Probably some stage of grief."

"Denial," said an uninterested Liv, returning her attention to closing down the store for the day. "Unless you're still high."

"Fuck!" said Billy. "Anything but my phone. I mean the normal world was barely tolerable without a phone but this is something else. Argh!"

"Anger."

"Please, God, if you're there, and that's a whole different conversation, just bring my phone back, OK?"

"Bargaining," said Liv. "You know you don't have to go through all the stages of grief in the same breakdown. Feel free to spread them out a bit."

Billy stared at her. "How are you not feeling this? No phone, man. No all-the-things-the-phone-can-do. No connectivity. Ever again."

He pierced a contemplative stare into the distance, then sighed heavily and dropped his head and half cried, half mad laughed to himself.

"Depression," said Liv, this time not even looking up from her tasks. "You know, there are other people you can talk to about this."

"Yeah?"

"You can figure that out. Just saying it's a bit much to hear a different version of the same conversation every five minutes. Newsflash: The phones are fucked and they are just not going to be a thing any time soon."

Billy went to respond but Liv's stare stopped him in his tracks.

"Dude, with everything going on – I mean everything – how is this your focus?" said Liv.

Billy nodded for several seconds, half in agreement, half lost in his own thoughts. Eventually he stopped and inhaled heavily. "OK. You're right. This is happening. I can do this. I can and will live without my phone."

"There it is. Acceptance."

"I'll just say my goodbyes and make peace with it as best I can."

"There you go," said Liv as she shut the security door at the front of the store.

"Maybe I should have a funeral?" said Billy as he connected the lock and clicked the gate shut.

"You're an idiot."

*

"My chest hurts," said Sara.

She had finished helping out at the Coles store for the day. Yamato was waiting for her to show her to their new camp site. He gave her a hug. "Asthma? Have you taken your puffer?"

"Twice since last night. It's this ash. I can't breathe properly."

"Are you going to be fine to walk home?"

Sara nodded and the pair headed down the arcade to the Parade. "I'm saving some for tonight. It was bad last night."

"Let's get you set up in the tent, we'll grab some dinner and I'll see if I can find a doctor."

*

Patrick eyed the crowd and collected his thoughts. "Thank you all for joining me once again."

You could feel the tension. The crowd's growing expectations and the pressure on Patrick to placate them with his words. There was something in the tone of the murmuring that spoke its own language of dissatisfaction.

Patrick cleared his throat. "Before I begin, some housekeeping."

I hated the term housekeeping almost as much as when he cleared his throat.

"Congratulations to everyone involved with the migration. Tonight everyone will be sleeping under one form of cover or another. Including our new additions today."

He paused for a round of applause that never came, then cleared his throat again. "Just remember, this is still a temporary solution. From tomorrow we'll be rolling out more permanent accommodation solutions in both abandoned houses and the many selected retail spaces that can be converted for comfortable living.

"This is a massive undertaking and we appreciate everyone's patience in the circumstances."

Again, the crowd weren't giving much in terms of approval or appreciation. There were pockets of applause at best and they quickly dissipated without the support of the greater group.

I could sense Patrick's mood in the moment as he cleared his throat again. He was rattled. I knew he had gotten to the end of the good news and he'd obviously planned to enter the next phase of his speech with the crowd won over. I enjoyed that facial expression.

"We've also been working hard behind the scenes to make sure we are as best placed as we can to continue to transition into this new world.

"I would like to break down some numbers for you so you can get a sense of the logistics around what we're dealing with. Hopefully it will give you some perspective around some of the decisions we've made."

As soon as he said that, any last murmur or note of approval from the crowd disappeared into the still ashy evening. It could not have been more quiet. Aside from the more than occasional cough that is. There were plenty of those since the ash rolled in.

"Firstly, the latest headcount of our suburb, including refugees, is 4938. This is both good news and bad. Good because it's less than pre-impact numbers, which means, once all is said and done, there will be a bed for everyone here. It's also bad because that is a lot of mouths to feed.

"That's not a problem for today, or next week, but it will be soon. Given the stocks in both grocery stores, as well as what currently remains on all the private properties, we estimate we have about 10 weeks' worth.

"If the ash continues to fall, as it looks like it will, transport will be almost impossible, which completely hampers our ability to source additional resources.

"While we have a few weeks to think of solutions around food, there's no point sugar coating things – it's going to get tight.

"If we ration diligently, we can extend that period perhaps another 3-4 weeks and we are working on a plan around that as we speak. If we all work together and can survive what may be a tough winter, we can position ourselves for what we can only hope will be more favourable conditions in the spring.

"You need to hear this. We need everything to go in our favour – and pray – if we're going to get out the other end of this thing. Part of that means making other tough choices. And some of them are really going to seem tough. Hopefully the choices we make now will help all of us in the long term."

Patrick glanced at the people standing to the side of the stage. All of the important people. All of them connected to George House in one way or another.

"Firstly, we are shutting the borders to our suburb, effective at midnight tonight."

You could hear the gasps in the crowd. One of them came from me.

"You can't do that," someone yelled from the crowd.

"We are already at our capacity to survive and we have to draw the line somewhere. We've already taken an influx of survivors from the city. Think of where we are positioned; we have probably taken on more than any other location. Where does it stop? And when those in surrounding suburbs run out of their own supplies, where do you think they're going to come?

"Another 500 people, for example, is ten days less food for everyone. It could be a lot more than that, far more."

"My parents are just across Portrush Rd, are you banning them?" said someone else from the crowd.

"They have until midnight to make a decision. If you feel they are better served here, then I suggest you convince them tonight."

"How is this fair?" said the same person.

"No one is saying it's fair," said Patrick, emphasising the word fair with air quotes - another pet peeve of mine. "This is about drawing the line for survival. We have to have a realistic look at how we can achieve that, and with everything changing so fast, we have to draw a line in the sand somewhere."

By this point there were overlapping voices coming from the crowd and the scene was descending into chaos.

"What about people from Norwood returning home?"

Patrick went to respond but stumbled on his words.

"What if they return and someone is living in their house?"

Patrick went to respond but was again overwhelmed by dozens of overlapping questions.

"OK, everyone, slow down," he said as he raised his hand.

It failed to have the desired result and more questions and commotion came from the crowd. It took over a minute of working the microphone and hand gestures to pacify the situation enough to speak. "Should any of those things arise, we'll deal with it. A resident of Norwood will be welcomed back to Norwood."

His eyes worked their way around the crowd as a tense standoff balanced on a knife edge between control and chaos.

"We are in a key moment here. Have a look at the ash already. It doesn't look like it's stopping anytime soon. Have a think of what life might be like in a week. A month. Three months when the food's run out. If we don't act swiftly, our situation will get away from us before we realise it."

Patrick's words were strong enough to have the crowd on the back foot. The threats closing in on us were not to be taken lightly.

"Who was consulted in the decision-making around this plan?" said Terry over the low murmurs of the crowd.

"The same team of people I introduced you to a couple of nights ago. We have our best people on it," said Patrick, summoning his best reassuring tones.

"And who here voted you in to represent us?" said Terry. "And how do you quantify best people?"

His comment was supported by some yeahs in the crowd.

Patrick shifted uncomfortably as he prepared a response.

"Last I checked, this country was a democracy."

This ushered in more support from the crowd.

"We're in an emergency situation right now," said Patrick. "All of us value our democracy, but we're in a period where we need to get through as best we can."

"So, just do what you guys say?" said Terry.

Patrick glared at him. "The last thing we need right now is internal friction. If food does start running low, there's going to be enough pressure. Not just *us* here – but everywhere. Again, it doesn't take much to project what that could turn to in a few weeks."

Patrick gave a nod to his group gathered to the side of the stage, then eyed the crowd. "Things could turn ugly. If we don't have our shit together that could spell trouble for us."

"They are two separate issues!" said Terry.

"That's easy for you to s—"

A crack of gunfire echoed around us. It was distant, but not too distant.

It was enough to stop everyone in their tracks. A hush came over the crowd just as a second shot rang out, then a third. After a few seconds of silence, a short barrage of fire burst out before the evening went deadly quiet.

Patrick nodded to the side of stage and the cop – Kyle – was next to him in seconds. The two whispered asides to each other and pointed in the general direction the sounds seemed to come from, before Kyle gathered the other officer and a couple of others and they headed out in pursuit.

Once again Patrick looked over the crowd. The shift in tone could not be more stark in the moments since the gunfire. "Ladies and gentlemen, I recommend you make your way back to your houses or shelter, while we investigate whatever that was.

###

###

CHAPTER 21:
SIDES

While the food stocks on the Parade were good for approximately 10 weeks, it was a different story with alcohol. The suburb of Norwood had more bars, pubs and bottle shops than almost anywhere in Adelaide. Even if the survivors were all heavy drinkers, it still may have taken more than 10 months to diminish the stocks.

The community dinners would stretch well into the evening as people established themselves, forgot about their problems or found an easy way to avoid the sheer lack of exterior entertainment. Not saying they were great, there was just literally nothing else to do.

Once the events of the meeting had settled down, many stayed along the Parade strip drinking and talking. We would normally stay far longer than we did on this night, but Craig was there again. Being aware he was in the area made me very alert to his presence.

It had to have been a similar situation for him, as I looked up on a few occasions to see him staring at me. Of course she was there as well, pretending not to notice me or the byplay between Craig and I.

In the end I didn't know what to do.

When I left with Claire, Terry was in the thick of the action, with many of the refugees making their agreement with his stance known. While it was not a place to talk in depth, given eyes and ears were everywhere, it was a place to bond and let allegiances be known.

It was almost the moment everyone became aware that there were sides and, whether you wanted it known or not, you should definitely have one.

*

Terry said his goodbyes and began the short stumble back to his new tent location. I'd managed to get us all in a small area once more. Our tents lined the back wall of the undercover parking near the cinema. Not the best spot, but at least we didn't look like we were just looking after ourselves in the lot allocation.

"Terry! You got a second?"

It was Patrick.

Terry looked at him for a moment before continuing his walk.

"A little birdy told me I might find you here," said Patrick

"What do you want?"

"A chance to clear the air."

Terry sighed and stopped in his tracks to allow Patrick to approach. "Well. Clear away."

Patrick smiled. "You know, we're not that dissimilar, you and I."

"How exactly? You own a large real estate company and I drive trucks," said Terry.

"Sure, there are some differences, but we're from the same vintage. And I like to think we both have a good idea how people tick. And we'd both do anything to survive."

Patrick reached into his jacket pocket and pulled out a hip flask. From another pocket he retrieved two shot glasses. "Nightcap?"

Terry responded with a nod.

Patrick smiled, before pouring a scotch and handing it to Terry. Then a second for himself.

Terry brought the glass to his lips before hesitating and locking in a glare on Patrick.

Patrick rolled his eyes, then raised his glass at Terry and threw the drink down the back of his throat.

Terry followed suit, giving a small wince at the liquor burn.

"I can't help but think how beneficial it would be for us to work together," said Patrick.

"Look, I'm not sure what you're selling here, but I'm pretty sure I'm not interested."

"I meant what I said today," said Patrick. "Things very much have the potential to get ugly. When that food starts running low people are going to come to where they know more exists. Hungry, desperate people. We can handle that one at a time. Perhaps even 10, maybe more. But we may have to be prepared for something far more than that."

Terry looked at him without responding.

"We could really use someone with your strength of character. And your leadership. It's not gone unnoticed that a lot of the refugees are gravitating towards you and that Zoe woman."

"Perhaps because we are helping them?"

"We have made you part of our community. Is that not help?"

"Look, Patrick, you have no more ownership of this community than me. Entitled shit. And if things are heading as south as it looks like they might, well, we'll all be the same."

Patrick scoffed. "What do you mean, the same."

"There won't be any businesses, or government, or police, or council or anything. Land ownership… pfft. There will just be people. People residing here to survive, who used to do something else before the world was fucked up."

A flash of fear passed Patrick's eyes before he controlled it with a smile. "Perhaps. We really will be similar then."

"We will never be similar," said Terry.

He handed back his shot glass then continued the walk to his tent.

"Sleep on it," said Patrick. "Maybe you'll feel different in the morning."

As Patrick headed back up the Parade, a group of men were watching from the shadows. As he passed them, he nodded and they headed into the darkness after Terry.

*

"Zoe."

I heard Terry's voice, immediately knowing something was not right. I could hear the pain in his tone as he whispered my name outside our tent. Claire was also woken. It must have been well after midnight.

We could see him slumped against his tent, his face bruised and bloodied.

"What the hell happened?" I whispered.

"I got pounced. Four of them."

"What? Who?" I said as I examined him with all the skills I didn't have.

He winced as I ran my hand over his ribs. "Patrick's men."

"Jesus! Are you sure?"

"Positive. He came to see me. Made me an offer. I refused. He left. Then this happened."

"Fuck!" I said.

"This is bad," added Claire.

"Do you need a doctor?" I added.

"No – no doctors. I just need some time… and sleep."

"OK," I said.

Claire tended to him, while I opened his tent and prepared the space so it was as easy as possible for him to crawl into his sleeping bag. He nodded his appreciation then winced as he made his way in. Claire and I offered support as best as we could from in front and behind.

He rolled delicately onto his sleeping bag and we zipped it up around him.

"You OK?" I said.

"I'll be fine."

"Can we get you anything?"

"Some painkillers. Maybe some plasters," he said. "Wait 'til mid morning and don't draw any attention to yourself."

"This is fucked. I'm worried," said Claire.

"He's making a statement of me," said Terry. "We just need to not let it show. Don't say a thing to anyone. Just go about your day tomorrow as normal."

"Then what?" I said.

"We'll get the group together when things quieten down tomorrow evening and come up with a plan."

"What plan?"

"I'm going to make a statement of him."

*

We spread the word around everyone as to what had happened and the fact we needed to lay as low as possible. We'd go about our day like it was just another day in the apocalypse. Except it wasn't. I mean, no day was normal at that point, this one especially so. The night had revealed just what people were prepared to do. Perhaps more accurately, it was a sneak peek. It had everyone on edge.

I know I looked at everyone differently that day. We were all on the same side, at one level, as we cleaned up office space to make it habitable for living. But we weren't. Sides were developing. Cracks were forming. And survival in a group came with conditions. I remember being sickened by that thought alone, doubly so when I thought of Terry.

The rest of us decided to not show ourselves gathering together in public too much, so we stuck with our roles.

While I was creating liveable spaces for the refugees, I cast my mind to where our group would end up. Safety and security took on new meaning as I did. Did we need a place to stay together, or dwellings close by each other? Definitely something with multiple exits, and something with a good vantage point on the goings-on along the Parade. Before last night I was happy to roll along, sorting out the other refugees' accommodation needs before tending to those of me and those around me. Now things seemed far more urgent for us.

No matter what thoughts I had, or what actions I took, my overwhelming thought was that a new benchmark had been set for life at the end of the world and there was no turning away from it now.

*

"Now that's what I'm talking about," said Graham.

Asim's jaw dropped and Katelyn gasped as they shuffled into the space after him. Another house raid had them in the open redesigned back area of a property many times above their pay grade in the 12/4 world.

"I think I just found my new place," said Graham as he picked up a vase that was probably worth a small fortune before the world went pear shaped. "Probably could do without this," he said as he dropped it.

"Dude!" said Katelyn.

That was enough for Asim. He'd grown very tired of Graham and the lure of a house scout was the perfect getaway – there were plenty of potentials here for a good find.

"What? Nobody gives a fuck about a pot," said Graham with an indifferent shrug. "What's your guess? Mine: old fuckers – he's a doctor – gyno – and she still gave gobbies right up to the end."

"If I could go a lifetime without hearing another one of your views about women, that would be ideal timing for me," said Katelyn.

"Relax, honey, it's just a game."

"This is one of those times I literally don't know if you're trying to bait me or you genuinely have no fucking clue."

He gave her a grin that aimed for annoying, successfully hitting the target.

"Just," continued Katelyn. "Don't talk to me."

She turned her attention to picking through the kitchen, searching for food, drinks and medicines. Graham took a few large strides and jumped into the leather couch. "Oh, that is amazing!"

The others ignored him from other rooms but well within earshot.

"I'm seriously thinking about tagging this place as mine."

"I don't think that's a thing," said Katelyn.

"Maybe not for you. But I happen to have a unique and handy skill set, and this world seems to keep giving. Bossman tells me I can have my pick."

"Bullshit."

"Deadset legit," said Graham. "Play your cards right and you could come and join me."

Katelyn made a vomit noise.

"What was that?" said Graham.

"You don't think you're actually going to get this place, do you?"

"Know it. Just got to say the word – from Patrick himself."

"That's bullshit."

"What? Has someone got their panties in a bunch because their personal assistant skills don't have a value in the new world."

"I'm a lawyer, dickhead," said Katelyn. "And as a lawyer I advise myself to cease conversing with the moron."

Silence reclaimed the house as Katelyn and Asim went about their scavenging work. Eventually Asim made his way back out into the main living area with a container.

"What you got?" said Graham as he reached his arm out to take hold of the find.

"A bunch of meds, that's about it."

Graham rifled through the stash. "Not bad, Asim. What do you reckon, me in this place? Could be the perfect match. There's spare rooms if you're keen to hang in style."

"Umm, perhaps."

"What do you mean, perhaps? You'd say no to this luxury?" said Graham. "Your loss then. Probably not a bad thing given you're hanging out with Patrick's No.1 person of interest."

Asim went to respond but the shift in conversation moved faster than his brain. It left him in mouth-open silence.

"Probably wouldn't be good for my life expectancy if Terry the truckie decided to visit."

Graham gave a toothy grin and settled back into the couch.

*

The Norwood medical centre was eerily quiet yet busy. People sat dotted across every third seat in the large waiting area. The odd cough punched through the stillness, as volunteers received new arrivals and gave them a queue number.

Sara's symptoms became more real to her while she sat waiting. Her knee twitched as she waited for her number to be called. Yamato offered the occasional soothing word or gentle touch, but none of it helped. Her symptoms had led her to get medical attention and that thought alone played on her mind.

Eventually, Dr Ratherford stepped into the sitting area. "Sara."

She exchanged a nod with her dad and the pair followed the doctor back to his consulting room.

"Thank you," said Yamato as he passed through the door and sat where directed. "Busy morning?"

"Indeed. More than enough to keep three GPs on their toes," said Dr Ratherford.

He turned his attention to Sara. "What seems to be the problem?"

"It's my asthma, I've never had it this bad."

"Hmm," said Dr Ratherford as he leaned in to perform some cursory examinations. "Yes, the ash seems to be playing havoc with quite a few people. Do you have a puffer?"

"Yes, and I've used my four doses every day since it started. But my chest is still tight almost all day long. I haven't felt normal for days and yesterday was the worst so far."

"Hmm. Are you wearing something over your mouth and nose when you're outside?"

"Always," said Sara as she gestured to the scarf around her neck. "I never leave the tent without it."

"Very good," said Dr Ratherford, before continuing his analysis.

Sara gave Yamato a look of doubt, which he returned with a nod of confidence.

Eventually Dr Ratherford stepped back and studied the pair. "We're in new territory here. I'll write you a script up for something heavier to use day-to-day as well as something should your symptoms escalate. If that happens and no other measures we've discussed seem to ease the symptoms, you are to return here immediately, understand?"

Although overwhelmed, Sara let out a small smile and nodded.

"You should know you're not the only one going through this. I have recommended my other patients keep a diary of their symptoms when it's worse, how you're sleeping as well as how heavy the ash is."

Sara and Yamato both nodded.

"Beyond that, I suggest you stay out of the conditions as much as possible."

"Yes, I will."

"Hopefully the ash will dissipate soon enough, but I'm afraid to say for the short term you're going to have to get used to living with it."

*

"Knock, knock," said Claire as she stood outside the tent with Jacob. There was no answer. "Alex?"

"What?"

"We're back. Creche was fun. Jacob made something for you."

Claire heard an audible sigh before a shuffling of sleeping bags preceded the sound of a zipper coming down. Seconds later Alex was staring at her without emotion.

"How are you today?" said Claire.

No response.

"OK, I've got a few things to do before we all meet this evening," said Claire, giving plenty of air for a response to come. It didn't. "Are you going to be alright with Jacob? I think he missed his mummy."

Something hit Alex in the moment with Jacob reaching out to her. Perhaps it was a merger of grief for a life lost and a rejection of the life she was being thrust into. She broke down in tears, reaching out for her son.

Claire handed Jacob over and Alex squeezed tight. Claire hugged her and kissed her on the head.

They held the pose in silence while the tears fell hard.

Just as suddenly as they had started, Alex turned the tap off with a sniff, then a deep exhale. "Fuck, what is wrong with me?"

"You're going through a lot. Cut yourself some slack."

Alex gave her a defeated but appreciative smile. "I need to get over myself."

"It's OK. We're here."

"No, I've been a shit. Thanks for looking after Jacob when I couldn't look after myself."

"Any time," said Claire, the moment causing a tear to well in her eye as well. "So, does that mean you're good for tonight?"

"Yeah bitch, I'm back."

###

###

CHAPTER 22:
TARGET

"Come in," said Terry, as Yamato and Sara joined our group.

"Sorry we're late, we had to get something for Sara's asthma," said Yamato.

"Nobody followed you?" said Terry.

Yamato shook his head before making a nod of apology to everyone else back at the oval. It was our original group – me, Claire, Alex and Jacob, Liv, Billy and Emma, Keira, Charlie, Asim and Terry.

Terry stood on a knee that looked ginger, shuffling occasionally with a grimace. His face was bruised purple around both eyes, with a number of scratch marks not covered by plasters. His expression was determined and focused. "Thanks for taking the time to meet. Zoe and I thought—"

He paused as the sounds of a vehicle could be heard on the Parade. We all turned to watch the glow of headlights in the ash as it drove past. Secondary lights danced around from the windows where torches pried into dark corners. The patrols had started the night before and been a constant since.

"Horseshit patrols," said Terry. "Patrick's just putting on a show for the residents."

"What makes you think that?" said Asim.

"Because it was them in the first place."

Asim scrunched up his face. "What was?"

"The shots last night."

"That makes no sense," said Billy.

"It makes total sense," said Terry. "He had lost the crowd and did not like my line of questioning asking for transparency. Easiest solution: create a distraction. Not only did he create one, it was in the exact area of conversation he was talking about seconds earlier. What did he say directly before the shots? Things could get ugly."

"But why?" said Liv. "What is the gain?"

"Scared people obey," said Billy.

"He's right," I said. "That shifted everything. And I don't know if anyone else saw the look on his face when it all played out, but he looked like he was playing shocked more than actually shocked. I was looking right at him. It creeped me out."

"And that smarmy grin on his face afterward made me want to throw up in my mouth," said Claire.

Yamato cleared his throat. "I can see it is possible they might be using manipulation tactics to get the crowd in line. And I understand why we're all here. I just don't see how we can do anything about it. And with all due respect Terry, you look awful. I have a sick daughter and I don't want to end up like that."

"What even happened?" said Alex.

"I got the shit kicked out of me after I wouldn't take an offer to team up with Patrick."

"This is already getting out of hand," said Keira.

"Yeah, I really don't like this," said Liv.

"So, what are we going to do about it?" said Terry.

A long bout of silence followed his question.

Terry eyed them all in turn. "If he's like this now, what is he going to be like in a week? A month?"

"I understand what you're saying," said Yamato. "And I can't imagine what you experienced last night. But let's look at the situation. They have the power and the weapons. They have created the system that people are clinging to to stay alive. That's more than we can deal with."

"And they protect themselves at George House, away from everyone," added Claire. "There are many layers to this."

Yamato nodded. "Even if we raised 1000 voices in dissent, we are still in no position to do anything about it."

He turned to his daughter, who was coughing again. "Perhaps we should let some things be and concentrate on what we can do for our survival."

"Fuck that," said Alex.

Yamato stared at her, mouth agape.

"Not the you and your daughter thing, I get that. Fuck going back to cock forest leadership model. These dicks have all the money and power. They're only out for themselves and one way or another we'll be fucked by it. I'm not going through a global catastrophe to just watch on while the same shit starts all over again."

"Well, what exactly can we do about it?" said Liv.

"We could run for a position on the council or board or whatever you'd call it?" said Claire. "Perhaps a voice in decision making is a good start."

"Fuck that – token shit," said Terry. "Nothing would change. Not only that, we'd be endorsing their made-up system that seems to be treating them very well. You're right when you said there are many layers to this, but if we don't make a significant impact, we'll make no impact at all."

Everyone paused on the statement.

"And we're still living in fucking tents," added Terry, grimacing at his ribs.

"Tonight's the last night, I promise," I said. "I've lined something up. Very secure. Hopefully tomorrow."

"Just playing devil's advocate here," said Claire. "But some of these things are just going to take time."

"Maybe," said Terry. "But some things could take no time at all."

"What does that mean?" said Asim.

"It means we have options."

Terry studied our faces in the silence that followed his statement. "We could change the game like that," he said with a click of his fingers.

Again, a long silence followed.

"What, exactly, are you saying?" said Billy.

"I'm saying we could change the management of this place in a day."

Billy looked around the group, then back at Terry. "Dude, I'm not exactly sure what you're talking about, but it's freaking me out."

"I'm talking about taking back some control of our lives here. Look at my face. That's what being an outsider looks like here. That's what being different looks like here. Take a look around us. What do you think they think when they look at us? Underclass? Workers? Employees? Cannon fodder? Pawns?

"We're certainly not equals. And my face tells you how different opinions are valued. When do you think that is going to change?"

Silence.

"The further into this thing we get the harder it will be to change the way things are."

"Can we take this back a notch?" I said, feeling the tension in the air. "Maybe you should tell us what you had in mind and then we can see who here might be interested?"

I didn't like the looks on people's faces I saw in that moment. "I'll start. I really don't like what's happening on the Parade, but the thought of doing something about it scares the shit out of me. I can't see us taking over without weapons and manpower and, even if we got both, I don't think I'd want anything to do with actually using a weapon in anger."

Terry nodded. "You're right, we can't do this without weapons and manpower."

I gave him a look that invited more details.

"We have all the people we would need just waiting to sign up – that won't be a problem. You've seen the looks on people's faces. We are just the tip of the iceberg for regime change."

"And the guns?" said Liv.

Terry looked at the group in turn. "I know where we can get them. Far more firepower than the cop and his little deputies have."

"I think I'm going to have to tap out," said Keira. "Charlie, you too."

"You don't even want to hear the plan first?" said Terry.

Keira looked at the group while she thought on her words. "I've heard guns and that was enough for me. Guns don't work out well for people like me."

Terry gave her a confused look.

"If we come in the vicinity of Patrick with weapons, here's what's going to happen," said Keira before looking at Terry. "They're going to kill you."

By this stage the conversation had gotten bigger than anyone had imagined. I remembered looking at the scared faces of some of the teens.

"And once they're done, they'll kill Asim," said Keira. "Then Charlie and then me. That's what's going to happen."

Everyone knew the implications of her words yet no one could make a reasonable case against them. I was watching Terry's reaction. He was nodding with his expression but something less understanding lay underneath.

"I don't think this is something Sara or myself would be involved in," said Yamato.

He nodded to Terry. "I am sorry."

Terry looked at Liv, Billy and Em. "What about you kids?"

Billy opened his mouth but no words came out.

Liv cleared her throat. "I'm all for doing something to change things, but not this."

"What she said," said Em.

Billy shrugged and nodded.

Terry locked eyes with me. "So, that leaves me and the women."

I looked at Claire and knew there was no way she wanted any part of this. I turned to Alex who was visibly shaking her head.

I took a deep breath. "Look, Terry, perhaps this is all just too much. I mean, who knows how things are going to change in the future, but for right now maybe our best bet is to just get through the next few weeks."

Terry laughed to himself, shaking his head in disbelief. "Are you all forgetting everything that's happened and blocking out all the red flags you're seeing?"

"There's too much going on right now," said Asim. "The world is changing every day. We can't predict what's going to come next."

"All the more reason to take care of us first," said Terry. "No one else is going to do that for us."

His words went unresponded. Many were now avoiding eye contact for fear of being dragged further into the conversation.

"OK, have it your way," he conceded. "But if we're not going to act, can we at least plan?"

"Plan what?" I asked.

"The guns," he said. "We need to secure the guns."

"What guns?" I said.

"I'll tell you once you tell me you're in."

Again he faced silence.

"Look, I get it. What I was proposing was scary shit. But so is what's happening at George House. Shouldn't we at least have a contingency plan if things get worse? Some way to control what we can control?

"Because, if we don't, someone else is going to do the controlling for us. And I don't know about you but I don't fucking trust those doing the controlling."

This drew everyone back into the conversation.

"So, what are you even suggesting?" I said, hoping to reach a point where we were all at least somewhat on the same page.

"There's a place I know of, not far from here. Potentially more weapons than we'd know what to do with."

"Potentially?" said Asim.

"What place?" I added.

"Nothing's guaranteed here, but if it pays off it's a massive game changer."

Terry eyed the group again, seeing more interested eyes facing back at him now. "It's easily walkable if we can get there before the ash gets too high. It's below the tsunami line so I doubt it's on Patrick's radar yet with everything else going on.

"All we need to do is go on a recon. If this stash is there, we just relocate it. Somewhere safe. Somewhere only we know about.

"Think about it," Terry continued. "We have a little intel on a big find. We have a window of opportunity before the ash buries it completely to put something in our favour. To have a safety net to use if we ever need it."

"Wait," said Billy. "Are you talking about the firearms place on Magill Rd?"

"Bingo! Someone give the kid a prize!"

Liv stared at Billy in a how-the-fuck-do-you-know-that way.

"What? There's a dinky little sign up near Fullarton Rd. I didn't even think of it until we started talking about guns."

Terry looked at the group again. The tide was turning.

"See, it's hardly a secret. It's there and people will know about it. Now it might take a while for their needs to catch up with the part of their minds that remembers this place exists, but at some point in time very soon, someone is going to have exactly the same thought. Someone hungry who would do anything for food perhaps? Patrick and his lackeys? A group that has a problem with Norwood shutting their borders?

"All of those are very shit outcomes for us."

"Wouldn't it be far better to control that situation and secure what will probably be the biggest – perhaps only – cache of weapons in what remains of the city?"

"I'm in," said Asim.

Everyone looked at him.

"If it means keeping them out of the hands of Patrick and his crew that is a very good thing."

"Me too," said Liv. "Getting guns out of the way – definitely in."

"In," said Alex.

The commitments to the cause fell like dominoes after that. I couldn't have been happier. Not only with the plan and the reasons why, but the fact that we were all getting back on the same page again on something that had threatened to run away from us. "I'm in," I said.

"Brilliant,' continued Terry. "We just need a place to stash them. Ideally something under the tsunami line that would be easy to—"

"My place," I said. "I've got the perfect spot, depending on how many weapons."

"Me too," said Keira. "We're kind of neighbours."

Terry smiled and we shared a nod. "What's everyone doing at dawn tomorrow? How does moving the weapons then setting up our new digs sound?"

###

###

CHAPTER 23:
NETWORKS

"What's going on up there?" said Billy.

He was walking back from the meeting at the oval with Liv and Em. The groups had separated and taken different paths home, the teens getting the dream run up the Parade. Ahead, a large group of people had gathered around a store front in their dozens. There was a lot of yelling and movement as the sounds of glass breaking could be heard.

"Is that the bank?" said Liv.

"Maybe," said Em. "But what's the point of breaking into a bank?"

"Seriously," said Billy. "Take all you want, it's useless."

"Wait, that's the phone store," said Liv as they got closer.

"Phones are about as useless as money," said Billy.

Soon they were at the outer edge of the commotion. A teenager pushed his way through the crowd with a small white box, coming face-to-face with the gang.

"What's going on?" said Billy.

"The network's back!" said the girl before running off into the ashy dusk.

Billy's jaw dropped. He gave the others a quick glance before heading into the fray.

"Billy!" yelled Liv.

She looked at Em. "For fuck's sake. He has the impulse control of a child."

"I want a phone too," said Em.

They were soon chasing him into the throng.

*

"And you absolutely promise it's the last night in the tent?" said Alex as she unzipped it, then ushered Jacob in, before climbing in herself. Two bottles of red clinked in her grasp.

"We couldn't get you out of it for days and now you never want to see it again?"

The words escaped my mouth as playful banter before I could process how offensively Alex could have taken them. She must've seen the look of doubt on my face and burst out laughing.

"Fuck that. That tent now reminds me of all the things that led me to not want to leave it. When I come out tomorrow morning, I'm going to leave all of it in the tent. Well, as much as I can. It can stay there."

Alex looked around at the structure that had housed her for nearly three days. "You hear that tent, it's all yours."

She accentuated her point with a chin flick before returning her attention to Claire and I. "I'm sorry."

Then to Jacob. "And I'm so sorry to you. You'll get the best of your mum now, OK?"

We all shared smiles. It was a massive weight lifted to know Alex was back in a good spot again. I shared a look with Claire at some point that expressed just that. Life was never a straight smooth line in Alex's orbit. Her highs were exhilarating and her lows all-consuming. Being her friend was never dull, that's for sure. But the extremes of this new world had Claire and I scared she'd gone to a place she might not come back from.

So, it was more than a relief for our friend in that moment, it was also relief for us. The wine came out and so did the laughs – including more than a few self-deprecating jokes from Alex. It was a rare nice moment of celebration. Then the conversation turned to tomorrow – excitement of a new adventure, a more permanent home and a few more layers discovered in the people we were spending our time with.

*

For a few hours that evening we had a mobile network signal. Like the electricity coming and going, it felt like someone had been working behind the scenes to make sure we were connected once more. Also like the electricity grid, it wasn't destined to last. And while our reconnection with the phone network was a brief one-off, it was utterly significant in so many ways.

Rumours ripped through the community that phones were live once more as was the internet through the mobile network. Every phone owner had a charger on their phones almost immediately. Everyone else was ripping the plastic open on a new phone box.

For several hours there was no other purpose for existence. For the first and only time for many months from that point on, our phones were more than fancy torches and game consoles.

I still had my phone, though not the charge.

Claire, Alex and I took Jacob and our devices to a nearby abandoned store. We all had chargers and just needed access to a power point.

We were plugged and waiting in no time. Soon enough, beeps and alerts challenged us to look. And it was a challenge, just the very act of looking. As a collective, we had developed the only coping mechanism we could to get through those early days – we buried everything.

Every loss, every emotional scar, every feeling about the past – all of it had had been compartmentalised in a newly created and fuck-off-large part of our brains manifested by necessity to take all the damage and hide it away from our day-to-day operating system. Our consciousnesses didn't have any hope at that point in time of coping with it all. Perhaps they weren't even capable of operating at all.

Just holding my phone – my live, active phone – hit me with a complete awareness of all of the above.

I was holding information. I was holding danger. Unlocking and absorbing it would change me and tamper with the temporary coping mechanism I had formed to get through the past few days.

But you couldn't not look, you just couldn't.

This feeling was shared across the Parade. I shared it with Claire and Alex. We looked at each other with phones aloft.

"Ready?" I said.

"Ready," came the response.

And we were in.

*

"Fuck, I can't remember a single password," said Billy. "I literally can not get on to any one of my social platforms. This is worse than having no phone."

"Dude, go to a news site and just start reading about what's happened like the rest of us," said Liv. "And stop talking!"

"Says here the ash cloud has all but covered the southern hemisphere and will be completely global within days," said Em.

"There's riots in the US," said Charlie. "Shit, looks like just about every city. Police fighting back – getting ugly."

"Global flight ban," said Sara. "Expected to last for months."

"Global food shortages, billions face a bleak future," said Liv. "Fuck."

It was a conversation that continued as long as the network lasted. While we were ahead of the curve in terms of destruction and social breakdown, it looked like no one would escape the inevitable.

As painful as being smashed in the face with 12/4 was, perhaps it was better than seeing your dire fate presented to you weeks in advance. Maybe that was a new kind of torture. The telegraphed final chapter to the destruction.

*

Alex breathed in deep before she opened the message thread with Kendrick. She consumed the words then doubled over in tears. Claire and I touched her from either side, letting her know it was OK.

As we did, we browsed through our own messages from a world that used to be.

Eventually she straightened her back and lifted her phone up once more. "'Something big just swooped us. Sky lit up like day. Scary shit. Still here tho x'.

"Then a couple of minutes later. 'Love you and see you soon xx'.

"Then that's it."

We all fell quiet as we let Alex process the moment.

After a few minutes of silence it became apparent she wasn't yet ready to talk about it.

Claire cleared her throat. "'Hi hon, thanks for tonight. Really appreciate you and Zoe taking time to be with us. Wish Alex and Jacob all the best too x. See you on the other side'.

"Then: 'Did you see that? Huge. Your dad says if that didn't take us down we should all be fine xx'.

"That's it," she said as tears overwhelmed her.

I did my best to console the pair of them. I didn't understand family like them. Dad had left before I started school and Mum basically raised me until I was 18 then chased some guy to Thailand and we'd pretty much never talked since.

I've probably got issues around that but, really, in a moment like this it's just the inability to fully understand what your friends are going through. You see it and feel it, you just don't understand it.

We got past our moment and dived into the latest news from around the globe. It was a relief to feel informed and out of the Parade fishbowl for the first time since 12/4, but it was probably just as much of a relief to distract ourselves from last-conversation-ever moments.

Things would've stayed that way for the rest of the night had my phone not bleeped.

Everyone looked at me. Our phones had caught up with all the notification beeps a couple of hours before.

"It's from Craig," I said.

"What the actual fuck?" said Alex.

"What does it say?" said Claire.

All of a sudden my palms felt sweaty as I jumped into my messages. "Hey. I'm guessing I'm sorry won't cut it but I want you to know I am sorry. Just don't want it to get too awkward when we see each other okay."

"Is that it?" said Alex. "After all he did, that's all he can say?"

"And he's only trying to save face in public. He doesn't seem to give two fucks about you at all," said Claire.

"Are you going to say anything back?" said Alex.

I collected myself and took a deep breath. "Fuck that," I said. "Fuck him."

*

Within a few hours our time connecting to the broader world was gone. Of course, we didn't know it was the end but we didn't know anything.

It was like going through the emotional wringer. Ghost from the past, the broken world and how distant we actually were from it, both literally and through tech.

Maybe it provided a few people with closure, perhaps it helped others cope in different ways, but there was an overarching global message that resonated that evening – no one was coming to help Adelaide any time soon. On the Parade, we were in this thing alone, together.

###

###

CHAPTER 24:
GUNS

Before dawn took hold we snuck out of the camp in our usual groups, each taking a different path to our prearranged rendezvous point at the oval. The ash had proven a hindrance in even getting there. There was a permanent channel carved in it from the people coming and going along the Parade but the overnight dump had all but filled that in.

Where the ash lay undisturbed from the moment it started, it was nearly at knee level. With the channel no longer much shallower, it took a lot of energy to plough through it, the ridiculously high leg lifts sapping morning energy fast.

It was impossible to use the pusher for Jacob, so the three of us took turns in piggy backing him, which added another degree of difficulty. The ash was so deep now it had started reclaiming the Mateship and Memory sign out front of the oval.

It soon dawned on us how significant the ash would be in our mission.

"How are we going to cover our tracks?" said Yamato, as we gathered near the side gates on Woods St.

Everyone turned back to see the freshly carved channel our caravan had made and the scale of the problem became clear.

"Shit," said Terry as he shuffled a duffle bag into a more comfortable position over his shoulder.

Although the ash was falling steadily that morning, it would still take several hours to cover that channel completely. In the meantime our movements would be completely exposed.

"Maybe we should reconsider going?" said Keira.

"If we don't do this today, the ash will be too deep to do it at all," said Terry.

"Maybe we can have someone at the back filling in the tracks as we go?" said Asim. "It doesn't have to be perfect, just enough so the ash can cover it again quickly."

"Doing that all day will take forever," said Billy.

There was a moment of silence as everyone pondered the problem.

"Maybe not," said Claire. "If we head straight down Teresa St, it's only maybe 150m until we reach Sydenham Rd. That's so off grid under the tsunami line no one's going to be looking or wandering there."

She looked at everyone like she had delivered the answer, but got a lot of confused faces looking back.

"So, all we have to do is cover our tracks from the fresh ones at the oval until we reach Sydenham, then we'll be off grid."

"Brilliant!" said Terry.

We searched around until we found a couple of flat lengths of timber. And set about retracing our steps and levelling the ground we'd been through. Then we began the slow slog up Teresa St. One person breaking new ground at the front, one carrying Jacob and two people at the rear smoothing out any trace of a large group of humans moving through the ash. The roles were rotated every 20m or so to keep people fresh.

We hit the corner of Sydenham Rd and continued to delete our tracks for a few metres beyond. At the rate the ash was falling, any trace of our movement would be covered by the time breakfast was served on the Parade.

It had taken nearly 40 minutes to travel just over 150m. We celebrated with high-fives at the other end. But our trawling through the ash was only just beginning and, although the task was made slightly easier without having to cover our tracks, it was set to be a heavy slog. Particularly when it was your turn on point. The virgin ash was a bitch to get though. Each step was tough and the pace was slow. After a stint up front, you would step to the side and let everyone pass until you joined the peloton again at the rear, where the steps were easiest. Once you reached the middle, you had a stint carrying Jacob and before you knew it you were back at the front, slogging away with stupidly high knee lifts.

We passed the storage facility – blissfully unaware the teens were exchanging looks – we passed small businesses, we passed houses. Everything familiar to most of us took on a new look in the ash and the circumstances of the moment.

It was an eerie journey that seemed to go forever.

In truth it probably took us an hour to make a journey that was probably just under a kilometre.

We didn't cross another set of footprints along the way, which included a stint along Magill Rd. Had anyone else been still fleeing the city for the safety of the east, you would have thought Magill Rd would be a common exit route.

Soon we were entering the car park that led to the gun store.

Guns were just not part of the city culture in Adelaide. No one carried. Hell, no one even used the term 'carried' back then. Short of walking into a bikie clubhouse you would have zero suspicion or expectation there was someone nearby with a gun.

There were a couple of gun stores/rifle ranges in the CBD and maybe a handful of others – at most – in the west, north and south combined. That was it. And most, if not all of those, were under the tsunami line. This place was unique in the east and therefore unique in what had survived of Adelaide.

The only street side marker of its existence was a little sign that said firearms – one word. I can remember passing that many a time pre-12/4 and wondering, who would ever want to buy firearms in Adelaide's east?

Regardless, it did exist. And now I was there. In circumstances I would have considered extremely unlikely until just over a week ago. My heart was racing with the excitement and danger of it all.

"Someone's been having a go at this," said Terry as he examined the staff entry door at the side of the store.

You could see where someone had been trying to jimmy open the door, perhaps with a crowbar and hammer.

"Fuckers better not have damaged the mechanism," said Terry, as he extracted a pair of glasses and a notepad from a side compartment in his duffle bag.

He turned and smiled at the group before tapping a code into the keypad. A mechanism released inside the unit with a polite click. Everyone stood around dumbfounded at how he'd managed to obtain the number. "Well, what are you waiting for?" he said as he opened the door for others to pass.

I was at the back of the pack and had a quick study of the exit points to the car park. Even though there weren't any fresh tracks or indication of other people's movements, it didn't seem in keeping with what we were doing to just turn a collective blind eye to any potential dangers that might be closing in.

Our quarry would have been highly desirable, given what it represented and the stakes at play both in Norwood and beyond. We were taking risks on a scale we didn't fully appreciate at the time. Maybe part of me knew and that's what called me to circle the perimeter.

My heart kept galloping along. This moment was big.

Magill Rd was clear in both directions, but even a short walk showed me there were a number of ways to approach our location. Not only that, I couldn't help but feel a presence close by. Maybe it was my proximity to what could be a large arsenal of weapons that played with my mind, maybe not.

I was soon inside, just as Terry made a sound of celebration and passed by me on the way to the back of the store, everyone else in his wake.

We were soon standing in front of a safe door. Terry used the key he'd just found in the office to turn the lock part of the mechanism. Then he consulted his notepad again and typed a five-digit number into the keypad.

He turned to face his bewildered audience, gave us a wink, then turned the handle. It opened.

A round of cheers broke out. I shushed them. Terry was beaming, enjoying his moment by the door before he nodded to me then made his way inside. All eyes were on the quarry that waited.

"Billy, Liv, Charlie, Em, Sara," I said. "I need you guys to hold back and keep an eye on things outside. Perhaps one group – say three of you – keeping an eye east and west on Magill Rd. The other two can position themselves down the other end of the car park, which opens up to a side street.

"If you see anything dodgy – anything – send one of the group back to tell us. Got it?"

"Who do you want in each group?" said Billy.

"What? I don't know," I said. "I'm sure you can figure that out all by yourselves."

I could see he was hurt by my abruptness. "I mean I trust you guys to be able to sort it out," I said, touching his arm.

I looked up to a round of determined nods, then turned my focus to the safe as they left the store.

I could hear the astonished excitement even before I laid my eyes on a weapon inside the safe. When I did, I remembered summing up my thoughts in two words. "Oh fuck."

I really didn't have a chance to process the potential enormity of the moment beyond that as Terry threw a couple of bags at me.

"Fill those up. Guns first, then fill the gaps with accessories and ammo. If there's one thing we don't leave without every last piece of, it's the ammo."

"Wait," I said. "How did you do all that?"

"Got lucky," he said.

"No seriously."

He looked me in the eye. "There are a lot of people aligned with us. Some are able to help in different ways."

It was vague but time wasn't our friend at that moment. I just nodded acceptance before the focus turned to a weapon shopping spree. Fill a bag to the brim, zip it up and drop it outside the side door ready for relocation. Repeat.

Picking up the first was a strange sensation. Despite being in a rush, I couldn't help but hold it in my hands, feeling how the weight sat with me. I brought it up to my eye and aimed down the barrel at some poster on the far wall. I felt the power. More accurately, I tried to imagine the power that I held. How much it would kick if I fired it, what sort of person I would turn into holding it, what damage I could do with it. It was an intimidating moment.

"Where did you position the kids?" said Terry.

"One group on Magill Rd, one on the back entrance to the car park."

"Can we cut that back to one person on each mark? We are going to need all hands on deck if we're any chance of getting this done in a good time."

By the time Liv, Charlie and Billy had joined me back at the entrance, we were ready to run our first load to my place.

Terry wiped the sweat from his forehead as everyone gathered around. "Nice work everyone. Looks like we'll probably need three loads to get this all done."

He turned to me. "How far away is your place?"

"Maybe four blocks from here," I said.

"Good. Yamato – you stay with me to get round two ready. Alex, you can stay here with Jacob and help out where you can. The rest of you load up and follow Zoe. Bonus points if you can manage two bags."

"First load will be the hardest with the ash," I said. "It'll get easier after that."

With that, we were off. To say the extra weight we carried made forging a path through the ash tougher was a massive understatement. It was a complete slog. We used the same travel pattern, with someone taking point in the virgin ash for ten metres or so, before they stepped aside and let everyone else pass and joined up again at the rear.

To make the journey more manageable, we broke up some nearby storage palettes to use as skis underneath the gun bags. They spread the weight out so we could slide the bags over the ash next to the trench.

Despite the timesaver, it took us well over 40 minutes to travel what must have been no more than 300m.

Once there, I opened up and led everyone to where I'd planned to dump the cache. We dropped off the gear and headed back for another load. It took less than ten minutes to get back – no extra weight bogging us down and a trench carved in the ash.

Despite the chill in the air, we were saturated with sweat. And round two was waiting for us when we returned. This time Keira led the way to her place. We were able to use the trench for all but the last 80m or so. It took half the time of the first trip.

The loading team had the rest of the stock ready to roll by the time we returned. We took a few minutes to recover and double check we'd swiped everything dangerous, then gathered everyone to make the final run. Terry had found a permanent marker in the office and wrote 'Don't be stupid enough to follow the people with all the guns' on the outside of the door.

We hauled ass from the scene, exhilarated by what we'd achieved. Enough to stop the burning pain of muscles from slowing us down too much. We split up at the fork in the trench and half went to Keira's, while the other half followed me back to mine.

We reconvened at Keira's, which was closer to the Parade, and shared hi-fives before starting the silent journey back to the Parade. A few loaded handguns joined us for the journey, as well as some concealed rifles on those with longer jackets.

It wasn't long before we were headed towards Sydenham Rd again. The plan was to cross back the way we came up Teresa St, covering our tracks as we made our way back into the stadium, then we'd split into our smaller groups and head back to the Parade, where we'd begin moving into the place I'd found for us.

I was on point as we neared Sydenham Rd. I could hear voices up ahead. A rush of adrenaline hit me as I turned to signal everyone to stop.

###

###

CHAPTER 25:
ESCALATION

"Fuck, fuck, fuck," I whispered to myself.

I signalled the rest of the team to stay put and silent while I got a closer look at who had wandered right into our footprints.

The voices were loud, so it gave me a little confidence I could sneak my way into hearing range without being noticed. I entered the driveway of the house on the corner of Sydenham and inched my way through the carport to the backyard, paying attention to the ash underfoot as I went.

The group had stopped. Our tracks in the ash had their full attention.

"Who the fuck is moving along here and why?" said one man.

"It's not one of ours, that's for sure," said another.

"Looks like they were headed north, judging by the markings."

"I'm going to phone it in."

There was a momentary pause in conversation. "Delta to base, come in base, over."

"Base receiving, over."

"We've got fresh tracks in the ash down Sydenham Rd. Heading north by the looks of it. Looks like more than a few people, judging by the marks. Maybe ten, perhaps more, it's hard to tell. Please advise."

"Standby, over," came the voice through the two-way.

"Fuck," said the man with the two-way. "This is really not good."

"Hopefully they were just passing through," came the voice of a woman.

"Hopefully," said the two-way man.

"Delta, this is Alpha." It was Patrick's voice over the two-way. "Can you repeat what you told base?"

"We're approximately halfway to the target and have come across fresh tracks in the ash along Sydenham Rd. Headed north, we believe. We're guessing maybe a dozen based on how impacted the trench was, but it's really hard to tell. Just wondering if we should switch gears and follow where these tracks go, over."

"Acknowledged, Delta. Assume you're taking Sydenham to Magill Rd. Report back if you see anything. I'll remain online for updates. But don't deviate from the mission. This may be our only window to secure the firearms before they get ashed in. And you're the only one with the skills to break in. So, stay on plan, understood?"

I felt sick hearing those words. Everything changed in a second. They were heading to where we'd been. Our tracks would point them directly to my place and Keira's and the stash of weapons.

"Understood, Alpha."

"You're armed, correct?"

"We have a pistol."

"I'll send a second team your way. Keep the updates coming, over."

"Over."

*

I was shaking in the wake of the communication with Patrick. They were now on a collision course with everything we wanted to keep hidden. After a little more small talk between their team, they began moving out. Once they'd travelled a few metres further away from me I returned to where the others were waiting.

I shared everything I had heard and saw expressions change from apprehension to sickened. It was a sharp fall from the elation of a couple of minutes earlier.

"Sounds like it was Graham," said Asim. "He's the guy I raided the abandoned houses with. He can break into anything. Total dick though."

I nodded in appreciation. "So, what do we do now? The only thing going in our favour right now is they intercepted our tracks from Beulah Rd, so they have no idea that we're local. They think we're outsiders passing through."

"With a secondary team headed our way, that might not last. They cannot see what we've done," said Terry. "We're going to have to think of something big and fast."

"I can't see how we can do this without giving ourselves away," said Yamato.

"If we can cover up the trail out the back entrance of the car park, we can at least stop them from tracing things back to where the weapons are," I said. "If they can't connect the break-in to Keira's or my house, we may still be able to lay low and sneak back."

"That's not going to work," said Terry. "They'll be walking through our trench from Beulah. They'll be there in 15. I'm not sure if we can even get back there much before they do now, let alone fill a trench approximately 80m long to the point where they don't even notice it."

Silence followed Terry's words. The only clean solution wasn't even possible. It was a horrible feeling.

"If anyone's got any ideas, now's the time," said Terry. "But make it quick and make it good."

Silence.

"OK, here's how I see it. We're fucked if they find the stash. We're fucked if they connect it to us. We're fucked if we're spotted. Any plan that avoids those things happening is a good plan as far as I'm concerned. We have numbers and weapons advantage and perhaps the element of surprise, although they'll be twitchy, for sure."

"We have to shoot them," said Alex.

I just stared at her with my mouth open. "What?" I said, eventually.

"You saw what they did to Terry when he asked a few valid questions. What do you think Patrick is going to do if he finds out we were pulling something like this?"

No one was rushing in to respond, but the idea terrified all of us.

"Exactly," said Alex, in response to the silence. "I don't want to do it. I just can't think of one scenario where we are not fucked if we don't do it."

"Neither can I," seconded Terry. "Anyone else?"

Again, no one spoke.

"OK, it's settled then," said Terry.

He waited a few seconds for anyone to correct him that their silence wasn't agreement, but no one did. That moment – maybe five seconds of passive silence that everyone knew the implications of – I think about a lot. I always will.

"I'm going to need three volunteers to stay with me. The rest of you need to sneak back with Zoe as best you can and get visible setting up the new accom. Game faces on – nothing is happening. Understand?"

I'd been volunteered for the easy job as team leader. I didn't know how to feel. I nodded.

"Three hands up, people," said Terry.

Claire was the first to raise her hand. I felt my stomach churn.

"Excellent."

Asim's hand was raised soon after. Keira looked at him, shaking her head.

"I know Graham," he said. "I think I have to be there."

Terry nodded at him. "One more."

I saw Liv go to raise her hand, only to have Billy pull it back and raise his.

Liv then raised her other hand and looked at Terry. "Ignore him. I moved first. I'll go."

Billy stared at her, betrayal and disbelief in his eyes. I realised this may have been the same expression I gave Claire.

"Done," said Terry.

He looked at me. "Who was carrying the gun?"

"I think it was that Graham guy."

He turned to Asim. "That's the one you know, right?"

Asim nodded.

"Good. We're going to neutralise the problem, hopefully on the corner of Sydenham and Magill Rds. Then we'll set something up to scare any backup from heading down Magill Rd. Hopefully enough to stop them wanting to go anywhere near the gun place. We'll head back to cover our tracks from the rear entrance and hopefully the ash does its job and covers any evidence we were even there by the time the sun goes down.

"The rest of you, head back the way you came and for God's sake, cover your tracks down Teresa St. And split up on the other side of the oval. Remember, you have no idea anything is happening. If anyone asks for us, say you saw us a few minutes ago and you'll pass on a message or whatever you need to."

He looked at everyone in the party who was headed with me. "Poker faces everyone."

Then he turned to his crew. "Game time."

And with that, we parted ways. Each one of us knowing things would never be the same, presuming we saw each other again. I felt sick to my core. An idea that had made perfect sense and was designed to de-escalate how quick things were changing around Norwood was going to have the entire opposite effect. Each of us had played our part in a moment that everything to follow would trace back to.

I felt sick then, I still feel sick now.

I will never reconcile that moment.

None of those who still survive will.

###

###

CHAPTER 26:
SHOTS FIRED

I still remember the sense of silent dread and paranoia that flowed from our group as we made the open stretch of ground between Sydenham Rd and the oval. I was nervous, jumpy, scared and overwhelmed. Each step felt like it would be the last before we were busted. Each unexplained noise was without doubt one of Patrick's men with a gun about to open fire. All the while I couldn't escape the thoughts of the deadly shootout about to take place. Thoughts about the ramifications of the outcome. Thoughts about Claire.

If I felt I was alone in handling the situation in a far from optimal way, all I had to do was look at the others. You could see all the same thoughts in their expressions. We travelled in silence, communicated in silence and repaired the trench we'd made in the ash in silence.

I knew I was in a position of leadership in the moment, but the only way I could think to show it was to make sure I was aware of the group, making sure we were dotting Is and crossing Ts on every little detail as we made ground. It wasn't much, but it did keep things focused in the moment, I guess.

The covered trench in our wake was far from perfect, but we knew the falling ash would soon hide the last sign of us east of Sydenham. We would've been extremely unlucky if there were any visible trace of our passing through there within an hour, such was the rate at which the ash was falling. But there were no guarantees.

Once back inside the stadium, we circled off in different directions to meet up again at the other side of the oval. The idea was to have it appear like each track seemed to be that of a group moving around the oval with purpose, not headed to exit at the side gate. It would probably make no sense if someone spotted our tracks, but at least it would have them scratching their heads, rather than wanting to investigate the far side of the oval closer.

Soon we were back at the main entrance on the Parade side of the ground, hashing out a plan for who would take what pathway back. Since all the attention was now on the north-west side and would soon be further once the gunfire started, we decided to cross the Parade to the south side and circle around the back streets until we all slipped back into our day's tasks.

I led the group out from the oval in single file. I paused short of the footpath to make sure the coast was clear before I headed out into the open. I could see two of Patrick's men heading our way from Osmond Tce. I retracted my head from the corner and swore. I gave hand signals to the others that two people were headed our way. Then I withdrew the pistol from my belt.

I signalled the others to head back into the stadium. Most released their weapons as they did. Billy ignored me and stayed, and I was grateful for it. I remember watching the others retreat, praying Jacob would stay quiet and asking myself if it was possible for things to have gone any further wrong in the last few minutes.

I turned my attention back to the corner, where I found a sturdy position by a wall and eased myself far enough out that I could get another sneak peek at Patrick's inbound men. That moment helped me find one small positive in ash. Its movement as it fell from the skies distracted the eye from other motion. It gave an illusion that the whole environment had a flow, which made it so much more difficult to spot more subtle movements you would've noticed in almost any other daytime circumstance.

And in that moment, I needed that distraction.

There was enough time to retreat to a gazebo in the park behind us. It looked to offer enough cover that we might be able to avoid a confrontation if they were merely walking by. I was so focused on the plan I was confused when Billy grabbed my arm as I started heading across. He shook his head and looked to the tracks we'd already created in the ground.

I swore under my breath again. We then quickly made a plan B by retracing the tracks of our group and setting up at either side of the ticket booth a few metres in our wake. We found vantage points on either side of the small structure and sunk into the ash, prone. Now only the Mateship and Memory sign stood between us and the corner.

I just lay there building up the courage to pull the trigger should the moment come. And given it seemed that was highly likely, the only way that wasn't going to happen was if they passed without noticing our tracks.

Soon I could hear their footsteps. I tried to calm my runaway heart rate. Try as I might, the gun refused to hold steady in my shaking hands.

That's when the sound of gunshots came barreling through the air over our heads. I'll never forget it. First a solo shot, then a double, then another double, then a series of single shots – four if my memory serves me correctly.

It was so loud. So fucking loud. Maybe it was something to do with how the ash in the air combined with the stillness of the day, but it echoed over the skies of Norwood. There was no mistaking what it was.

The footsteps stopped. "What the fuck was that?" said one of them.

"What the fuck was that?" came Patrick's voice over the two-way one of the approaching men carried. "Delta report."

There was a long silence.

"Delta! Delta?"

"Graham? Anyone?"

Another long silence.

"Anyone closer pick that up? Was it gunfire? Confirm."

"Sounded like it, sir," said of those near us. "Pistols I think."

"Fuck!" said Patrick through the two-way. "Who is that?"

"Epsilon, sir. We're near the oval."

"Roger that. Gamma – press forward but stay under cover. Epsilon, everyone else, meet me at the corner of Osmond and the Parade. Bring your weapons, bring anything you can swing or throw."

"Yes, sir," said the nearby man.

It was followed by the sounds of a number of other confirmation comms coming through the two-way before it was replaced by the sounds of footsteps retreating up the Parade.

"Fuck," I said to myself as I exhaled some of the immediate tension, then waited for the sound of footsteps to recede so Billy and I could check the coast was clear and grab the others.

*

"I see them," said Terry.

He was leaning out from a pile of debris which was probably the result of something getting snagged in the tsunami and drawing other flotsam into it. A week and a few days of ash later, it provided an excellent vantage point to spy from – and a surprisingly unassuming spot to strike from.

"Remember, don't do anything unless you have to. I've got the element of surprise, should have them covered."

He gave a nod then signalled them away to their secondary location with a hand gesture.

Once in position, Claire, Liv and Asim took in their expanded view of Magill Rd. When Terry had doubled back and crossed Magill Rd, it had them doubting his decisions, but seeing the plan in situ made them see its genius.

"It's going to be like shooting fish in a barrel," whispered Claire.

Liv and Asim nodded and took in the enormity of what they might be witness to, even if they weren't required to be part of it.

Once the three enemy patrollers had neared within 80m of Terry's location, he slipped back into the belly of the ball of ash-covered debris, almost disappearing.

Once again the ash gave homeground advantage to those lying in weight. Obscuring subtle movements from the eye.

The enemy took each step slowly. They were wary. Very wary. At the same time, they were oblivious.

The first of them rounded the point where Claire, Liv and Asim knew Terry would have a line of sight. Terry didn't fire.

The soon-to-be barrel fish scanned left and right along the sights of his gun and was soon satisfied he was in no danger. After a signal, the others followed into the space with no weapons and less caution. The second man was the last to pass into Terry's trap.

Terry waited for Patrick's soldier to take a couple of steps past him before he fired a shot into the back of the man's head. He was dead before he began his fall to the ground and did it in such an ungraceful manner his head knocked his knee on the way down.

This caught the peripheral vision of the woman, who took a couple of seconds to connect all the inputs and realise the dire situation she was in. She was now in the reaction window where those watching on would expect her to scream, or run, or cry or attack or raise her hands. Instead, she just stared on, mouth agape, as Terry sent two bullets right past her and into the attacker with the gun – Graham.

Another awkwardly long period of assessing the situation followed. This time the woman decided to run. She hadn't even managed a step out of her turn before she was felled by two more bullets.

The shots hadn't killed her and a moaning, gurgling sound filled the air.

Terry took a moment to raise himself back to his feet, then brushed some of the ash off his clothes. He rotated his head around, releasing some unseen stiffness from his neck, before he stepped towards the injured woman.

He aimed the gun at her from close range and pulled the trigger. All was silent.

Then he took aim at his first victim and shot again, then at the gun wielder, then the woman again before he stowed his weapon and hand-signalled the others back to the location.

*

I had everyone lined up against the wall, leaving the oval to the Parade on the same stretch of trench we'd made minutes earlier. Everyone was rattled by the sound of the shots. Yamato was tending to Sara, who was breathing shallowly, perhaps hyperventilating. Everyone else looked like shit. Not so much their physical state, although they looked like they'd been doing hard yakka, but emotionally.

I signalled everyone to wait while I checked the coast was clear. Much better news this time around. It looked likely Patrick's crew had headed north on Osmond. Mostly likely headed down Beulah to Sydenham, where they'd connect to the trail via the trench.

"Looks like the coast is clear," I said on my return. "The better news is it looks like Patrick has taken most of his crew out after us – well, whoever they perceive us to be. That helps us sneak back in, but he's probably got eyes and ears everywhere.

"We're going to work our way back through the side streets on the other side of the Parade. Once we cross the road, split into your normal groups. Each group give the one before you 15 minutes before you head after them. Take a different path to everyone else. If you see fresh tracks, don't follow them. But as soon as you start circling back to the Parade, try and jump in on someone else's tracks.

"If we get back without raising eyebrows, or our tracks are too confusing, I think we'll be good. Remember, as soon as we—"

"Is Liv OK?" said Em.

I studied her for a moment. Her expression looked as broken as that of anyone. And judging by the looks of everyone else, it was not a subject I should've skipped past in the first place. I thought it was the easiest way to focus on the here and now.

"I'm no expert, but that sounded like the same weapon to me."

Em gave a nod and a thin smile.

"Sounded like that to me too," said Billy.

"Me too," said Charlie.

Soon it became the general consensus that the one-weapon theory was a truth. Not that I fully believed it. I was terrified something had happened to them. Particularly Claire, obviously. It was true enough for me to tell everyone else in the moment, but not one I fully believed.

"And we definitely fired it?" added Em.

"We had more weapons and we had the element of surprise. That was our weapon. I'm sure."

I looked around at the nods of agreement I was getting, then at Em. I tried to give her a reassuring smile but her reaction told me I may have missed the mark. Maybe she was buying my words as much as I was.

"Liv is fine. They all are," said Billy as he put his arm around her.

It was enough to seal the conversation up and refocus on getting back. We gathered in a circle, drew a little map in the ash and planned our pathways home.

*

"This. Is. Fucking. Heavy," said Liv.

She was dragging the body of the woman with Asim. They were walking backwards with one hand under an armpit and the other gripping onto the material around the neck hole of her garment. It looked ungainly and undignified for the victim. But this process was about time, not dignity.

"Not much further," said Asim. "At least you don't have to go back for another one."

"Serves yourself right for being half a foot taller than me."

The attempted distraction banter was left floating in the air. They struggled the last few metres, uttering nothing more than grunts. When they let the body slump into its final ashy resting place, they both looked at the woman.

"I think I'm going to be sick," said Claire.

"Try not to dwell on it," said Asim.

"You mean the…" started Claire before checking Terry and Liv were out of earshot. They were, but she lowered her voice to a whisper anyway. "The triple homicide? Or us tampering with the evidence? Or, you know, her, whoever she was."

Terry had to do that or else we were… well, it would not have been good."

"Yeah, maybe," said Claire.

Soon Terry and Liv had dragged the second body next to the corpse of the woman.

Terry looked at everyone. "Well done. I know it's not pleasant, but well done."

He took the few remaining steps to the corner of Magill and Sydenham Rds, and eased far enough around the building wall to see what might be headed their way.

"The coast is clear. For now."

He grabbed the marker he'd used to write on the door at the gun store and handed it to Claire. "Asim and I will go and grab the other one. I want one of you on lookout and the other one on marker duty."

"What's marker duty?" said Liv.

"Grab the pen and write a note as if it came from the killers. Say something like 'we have all the guns. Stay east of Sydenham Rd or this will happen to you.'"

"OK, but where should I write it so they see it."

"On the bodies."

"Glad I asked," said Liv.

"Gross," said Claire.

Then she saw the look on Liv's face. "I can do that if you're up for watch duty."

Liv nodded.

"Just up her arm perhaps," said Terry. "Make it look a little unhinged."

"How do I write unhinged? I don't know that font."

"Just... use your imagination. Maybe all caps. Or maybe that annoying thing the kids do and mix up caps and non caps in each word. Better still, maybe draw some symbol on their foreheads or something."

"What symbol?"

"I don't know. Something that makes us look dangerous. We just want to scare them away from ever coming here again."

"OK, got it. Unhinged font, dangerous symbols."

Terry gave her a look as if he was trying to work out if she was taking the mickey out of him. She was, but read the moment and gave her sweet-as-pie smile to defuse any potential situation.

With that, Terry and Asim headed back for the final body.

###

###

CHAPTER 27:
SCRAMBLE

"Fucking hell," whispered Alex. "What the fucking fuck did we do?"

She carried a sleeping Jacob as we wound our way back through the side streets to the Parade. We were the first group to leave. Not only were we tasked with testing the waters for everyone else, we had to get things started on the move to our new home.

There was a special kind of tension as we neared the Parade. I'm not sure my heart had settled from the potential close encounter near the oval, which hadn't settled from all the events that led us there in the first place. It was basically beating in a permanent looping overdrive.

Now we were doing our best to stay calm and look oblivious to events, should anyone see us.

I didn't know how to answer her question. "We can't blame ourselves for what's going on."

"We wanted to get rid of—"

My elbow gave her a little nudge and my eyes warned of the need for discretion.

She nodded. "A change of management," she whispered with discretion-delivered pride.

"We made a group decision," I said.

"Which we drove. And now people are… you know."

"I thought we were the voice of a middle ground. If it was up to Terry, it was going to be a war," I whispered.

"I'm not sure being slightly left of Terry's action strategy makes it OK."

This from the person who suggested shooting in the first place. I didn't know how to advance the conversation around her hypocrisy. My confused expression clearly enough for her to know what I was thinking.

"Yes, but…" said Alex. "Why the fuck would anyone listen to me? I clearly have my own issues and should not be having discussions around other people's fates."

"Can we focus on the fact everything could settle down after what could have been a very horrific situation."

"People are dead."

I elbowed her again. There wasn't anyone in our vicinity but we could now see people moving up and down the Parade, only 20m or so ahead of us.

"Can we talk about something else? We're getting close."

"OK, I can have conversations about alive people."

I elbowed her for a third time.

"You're no fun any more."

I'm not sure if it was unintended good timing or Alex genius, but it had us both stepping out onto the Parade sharing a smile. Seemingly without a care in the world.

The funny thing is no one seemed to notice us at all. All that build-up and it turned into a complete non-event. We kept the facade up long enough to get to the tent. The only challenge to our act was a couple of nods in passing along the way.

I let out the world's longest sigh as we made it back, while Alex buried her head into a pillow and released some squeal/scream/repressed tension.

After what seemed like an eternity, she retracted her face from the space. She wore a completely different expression. "Claire's going to be alright, right?"

"That is the only option I can contemplate right now," I said.

Alex went to say something but retracted it.

I didn't want to think about anything at that point. I just wanted to hide away and get stuck into the new project – our place. "OK, let's do this."

*

"We have all the guns. Stay east of Sydenham Rd or this will happen to you," said Terry as he read Claire's handwriting on the victim's arm. "I like what you did with the esses. They look a bit like the ones on the Kiss logo."

"Unhinged enough?"

Terry admired the work and nodded, as he swiped the two-way radio from one of the corpses. "Indeed. But not as good as the upside down pentangles on their foreheads."

"That was Liv's idea."

Terry gave her a nod and she returned it before turning her attention back to lookout duties.

"So, what's the plan now?" said Asim.

"I think this is where we say our goodbyes," said Terry.

Asim and Claire stared at him in confusion.

"I've been thinking about this," said Terry. "There's only one way to make our plan watertight and that's to have someone here – armed – should they decide to test the authenticity of our message."

"They're not going to ignore that," said Claire.

"Probably, but if they do, the entire game will be up if there's no one here to level up the threat. Tomorrow, the ash will have covered all our tracks and we'll be fine but someone needs to make sure no one comes along and fucks everything up this afternoon."

Claire and Asim thought through all the possibilities, eventually landing back at Terry's point.

"It's the only way," added Terry. "But before you go we need to cover the trench at the back of—"

"I see them," said Liv. "Looks like seven. No, eight."

Terry and the others hustled to the corner. Terry called Liv back and leant in for a look.

"We've got to go."

*

It took me a minute of fussing about with a set of keys to finally click the door open to our new digs. It didn't help that my hands were still shaking badly. Alex pretended to ignore the whole incident – something she would normally take great enjoyment out of embarrassing me over.

Perhaps it was the fact we had Yamato and Sara with us that tempered Alex's usual brashness. Sara was still a little overwhelmed by her breathing difficulties and all of us were emotionally exhausted. And everyone was hoping I'd chosen well in our accommodation upgrade.

So was I.

I entered the space and the others followed. Up until a few days ago it was one of the many fashion shops along the strip, but most of the contents had been either swiped by needy refugees or taken by Patrick's men and stored for future redistribution or trade.

"I figured we could keep the front half of the showroom as a lounge; we'll cover the windows for some privacy. There's space for another open area here, then a couple of small bedrooms back past the staff area through there."

I led them through, all the way to the rear access door, then back outside again. "The rear access was a huge selling point – and not many places have it.

Plus, of all the options, this one was one of the furthest from where Patrick and the others are set up at George House. Location, location, location."

I regretted my lame joke even before it didn't get a laugh. Nerves were no excuse. Back to business, I led them towards the stairwell.

"This is the bit that really sold me though," I said as I led them up. "Staff facilities, a little kitchen area, three offices – now bedrooms – and the main storage space which can be divided up into another three or four bedrooms easily. There's plenty of room for everyone.

"Oh, not only that, check this out."

I led them to the back of the space and its bay of windows. "Not only can we see what's coming or going out there, we have a little escape route across the rooftops if the front and back are blocked off."

They walked the space, taking it all in.

"Again, it's only temporary until we can sort out a proper house, but it's as good as I could find."

"You have done well," said Yamato.

"It's good," agreed Alex.

I nodded my appreciation and smiled. "Alright then. There's a lot to do, shall we get—"

There was a knock at the door downstairs. A wave of apprehension swept over us.

I took my time getting downstairs, hoping if it was someone other than one of ours, they would move on. Turns out I was just making Em and Billy wait.

"Sorry guys, come in," I said when I got to the entrance.

They looked worse than I felt. "How are you holding up?"

"I feel sick," said Em.

"What she said," added Billy. "Heard anything?"

"Not yet," I said, feeling a need to be the mature calmness in the situation, despite the doubts that screamed at me. "C'mon, I'll give you the grand tour."

Just as we were making our way into what would be the lounge area, a woman yelled out at the door. "Hello?"

I didn't recognise her voice until I saw her face. It was Olivia – Patrick's PA. A wave of additional nausea washed over me. I cleared my throat, collected myself and tried to put a spring in my step as I headed out to greet her.

"Hi, it's Olivia, right?"

"That's right," she said through a thin smile.

I wondered if the rumours of her and Patrick were true and, if so, what she saw in the situation that benefitted her. True or not, she was not someone I wanted snooping around at that moment.

"What can I do for you?" I said.

"Do you know where Terry is?"

"Terry? Is everything OK?"

"There's a couple of things going on today. I just wondered where Terry was."

I did my best to muster my most matter-of-fact voice. "He's been helping with the move, but I haven't seen him for perhaps an hour."

"Where was that?" said Olivia.

"He was here."

"Hmm," she said, not even trying to hide her suspicious tone.

"Look, is everything OK? He looks like he had the shit kicked out of him, but he's not telling us anything."

I thought it best to get back on the front foot with the conversation.

"I'm not sure about that," said Olivia, clearly lying. "Where would I find him at the moment?"

"I'm guessing he'd be back collecting his tent and belongings."

"Where was his tent?"

"What's going on and why do you need Terry?"

"That's not really information I can give out at this stage. I'm sure you'll find out more at the meeting tonight."

I gave her a look to sum up how unimpressed I was.

Olivia just glared at me, perhaps through me, as it felt like at the time. "I've wasted way too much time on this already. Just point me to where he is, please."

"One of the carparks. I think the one out the back of the shopping centre." Sure it was a lie, but at the very least all I had done was even the scorecard.

It was her turn to give me a look, before she sighed then marched back up the Parade, headed for the car park.

"Asshole," I whispered as I watched her leave.

"What was that all about?" said Keira.

She and Charlie had seen the exchange before they passed her, headed towards me.

"She was asking about Terry."

"Shit," said Keira.

"Yeah, not ideal."

"Anything Charlie and I can do?"

"I think we just need to stay focused on the move like we have no idea what's going on. Hopefully that'll be the last we see of her."

"Hopefully," agreed Keira. "She's a sour one."

"Yep," I said.

"Not sure the old used cock is agreeing with her."

"Mum!" said Charlie.

I laughed. "It does not appear so." I needed a dose of brutal takedown levity. I shared a nod of appreciation with Keira. Then I invited them through for the tour.

###

###

CHAPTER 28:

CHANGES

Terry wiped his brow, gave the others a nod of appreciation, then turned to see their handiwork. "Looks great. Another 30 minutes of ash fall and you wouldn't even know the trench was there in the first place."

They were standing a block away from the back entrance to the gun store car park, admiring the signs of human activity that had been swept away.

"I need to get back to Magill Rd to make sure we don't have any curious trespassers," he said as he pulled his gun out. "You'll need to work your way around to the Parade from the other side. Take Fullarton Rd until you pass it, then head up through the back streets. You know where the new place is?"

Liv nodded.

"Good. Just poker face your way through the next few hours and we'll be in the clear."

"You sure you don't want a hand?" said Asim.

"Thanks. But the less people involved with this the less suspicious."

Asim nodded.

"Good luck. If you hear gunshots, say a little prayer that they're mine."

"Will do and good luck," said Claire, as she and the others turned to leave.

"Oh, one more thing," said Terry.

They turned again to see him looking at Claire and gesturing to his elbow. She looked at her elbow to see a blood-stained patch on the jacket.

"Might want to get that cleaned up," he said. "Or just cover it in ash."

Claire nodded and this time they left.

Terry headed back to the gun store.

*

The tightness in my chest and throat didn't let up all afternoon. Sure, part of me relaxed a little more as the store started to look more and more like a house and everyone slowly found their space and set up their things.

But none of the little wins erased the big things from my mind. Something was happening/had happened a few blocks away and the outcome of those events would shape everything. Plus, I was now packing heat. I mean, come the fuck on. A gun? Me?

Worse still, there was a serious chance I might need to use it to defend myself. And soon.

And Olivia had been snooping around.

And Claire was still unaccounted for.

And I had a fuckoff payload of weapons at my old house.

So, yeah, I was taking the little wins, but there was no way my mind was going to relax until I saw the rest of the crew come in. Maybe it was like a Schrodinger's cat situation. There was an outcome that had happened that had life and death consequences but nobody knew the outcome until someone opened the door of events west of Sydenham Rd.

It was also a Chekhov's gun situation. How did we think bringing an arsenal of weapons into play was not going to result in someone getting hurt? It was 100 percent going to occur. It didn't matter how passive the initial intent was, the inevitable outcome only took hours to occur. Hours.

Hey fate, we have just recovered enough firepower to propel a government-toppling-sized militia into action, anything you want to do with that?

I think about that a lot. And I tell myself that if we hadn't done it, someone else would've for their own reasons and purpose. And rather than people who got killed as a result of our actions from that tip-of-the-iceberg moment, it would have been a completely different group of people getting killed for a completely different series of reasons and action from the hand of someone else. I convinced myself that was the case and that it was a truth I could live with because, reasons. And that helps me sleep slightly less shitty each night.

*

By late afternoon, the place was seriously taking shape. Everyone was making the best of their assigned sleeping place, adding what personal items they owned to make their little patch feel like home. It was a decent enough distraction.

Seeing what remained of some of the others' belongings, it felt like luxury having a case full of clothes. I just left them in the case, which I tried to hide under some bedding as I felt a little guilty owning, well, things. Besides, some of it was useless now. I had a dress in there. A dress! Seriously, what was I thinking?

To take my mind off the waiting, I rinsed out the clothes I'd been wearing. You didn't really get an appreciation for how all-consuming the ash was until you ran your clothes under a tap. Water went in one end transparent and came out the other end brown. Not a tea coloured tint of brown, a full immersive glug of brown. Like, the texture of the water was actually different.

I rinsed, I soaked, I drained, I repeated. By the third round, the material was starting to get back to normal again. But in the sort of way that was just a nod to the past brilliance of the garment. It would never be that again. Once something had been ashed, it wasn't ever being what it was again.

That statement applies to humans as much as it does jeans.

I hate laundry, by the way, like, a fucking lot. It was very depressing to realise how much more involved, manual and time-consuming the task would be for the foreseeable future.

*

I heard a buzz of activity downstairs as I was hanging out my things. They were back. I felt relief as I headed down. Hearing Claire's voice brought a tear to my eye.

"What do you mean, he's still out there?" said Keira.

This triggered a number of overlapping questions until someone shushed them. Things quietened down and Keira repeated her question as I joined them in the lounge.

"There was another crew heading in to investigate," said Claire, matching Keira's calmer tone. "We knew if they headed further west to the gun store, they would've found our path to where we'd stashed the weapons, then everything would be fucked.

"So, Terry's staying out there until he's sure the coast is clear for the night."

"By himself?" said Yamato.

"He's armed, he's got one of their two-ways and he's got the advantage of being able to bunker down. He says if they start wandering west past Sydenham, he'll fire some warning shots to keep them at bay. If we can hold them back 'til nightfall, the weapons stash will be untraceable after that," said Claire.

"He should be able to cause enough chaos to keep eight people back," added Asim.

"Patrick's headed down. He's got all of his people going down as well," I said.

"Fuck," said Claire.

"So, what, do we go back?" said Liv.

"We can't risk that," I said. "We've already got eyes on us."

"What about a smaller group?" said Claire.

"This is getting out of hand," said Keira. "I don't want to leave the guy facing that alone, but where do we draw the line? If any of us get caught going back, we're fucked. If Terry sees a group coming and doesn't immediately recognise them as, say, us, we could be dead. It seems to me the safest play is to let whatever happens happen. Terry sounds like he can handle himself."

"I agree," said Yamato. "The risks are too high."

"We can't just leave him there," said Asim. "He could be killed and we might lose the guns. Then we're completely fucked."

"That's the worst case," I said. "But at least we'll still be alive. They can't connect us to anything."

"Terry can definitely handle himself," said Claire.

Asim looked at the group in turn, seeing who he could appeal to for support. It wasn't hard from the facial expressions; it was going to be an uphill battle. "OK, what if I go? I can sneak back the way we came back."

"If you manage not to get spotted, how in the fuck are you going to be sure Terry recognises you before he starts shooting?" I said.

"I don't think there are too many 6 foot 4 black guys around here. Pretty sure he'll recognise me."

"I don't like it," said Keira. "It's super risky and if you're not killed you might get caught. If that happens, everyone is fucked."

"So, we're just going to leave him there?"

He was looking at me for answers. I was looking at everyone else not wanting a piece of his plan. Everyone was scared of how big everything was getting and I think if you had offered everyone a chance to turn back time, they would not have gone out and got the guns in the first place. "OK, let's put it to a vote. Group decides. Deal?"

Everyone nodded.

"Who's for going back to help Terry?"

Asim raised his hand.

"And who's for staying here, getting the place finished and not drawing any more attention to ourselves?"

Everyone else raised their hands.

Asim shook his head, but went along with the majority.

*

"They're coming," said Billy. "Patrick's there. Got a group of refugees behind them. They're asking questions."

He was on lookout at the front of the lounge room – we'd had eyes on the Parade all afternoon, waiting for this moment. Now the light was getting low and the hours had passed like days. The excitement passing by was too much to resist, as was our curiosity by that point. And blending in with a greater crowd seemed like as good a way as any to reintroduce ourselves into the population.

Patrick passed, accompanied by the cop and a few of his other important protectors. The rest of his foot soldiers either positioned themselves ahead to ensure nobody got up in Patrick's face or followed at the back of the troop. That's when I saw Craig. I couldn't tell if he was carrying a gun but he was definitely guarding Patrick.

"What happened?"

"Is everything OK?"

"Is everyone OK?"

People were hammering questions as the entourage passed.

Patrick stopped about 50m east of our digs and gestured to the crowd to quieten so he could talk. It seemed to have the opposite effect.

"Shut up," said one of his minions, equally effectively.

It was starting to get heated.

BANG!

The cop – Kyle Jenkins – fired his pistol into the air.

The crowd immediately fell into silence.

Except one.

"Don't shoot around here, ya dickhead," came a voice from somewhere within the throng.

Titters of laughter echoed out in pockets around the crowd.

"Enough!" yelled Patrick.

He circled around, trying to make eye contact with as many people as possible in the crowd.

"For fuck's sake, look at you all. Bunch of wild animals.

"Shit is getting very real around here. Full update at the town hall tonight. Attendance is mandatory. No further questions."

With that, he continued his march to George House, surrounded by his company and a very confused audience.

###

###

CHAPTER 29:
REALITY CHECK

"We've got to go," said Keira.

"Just give him five more minutes," I said.

After the eternal wait that afternoon the last thing we needed was more of the same in the evening. But that's what we got. Terry had not returned. Reading between the lines of what Patrick had said, and not seeing a stash, we felt he had not found the weapons. But we didn't know. We didn't actually know anything heading into the town hall.

The fact Patrick decided to make the meeting mandatory threw a whole new layer on top of everything else. Why would he do that? Was he going to pull something? Did he have his suspicions around Terry and was trying to catch him out for not being there? Was it something entirely different altogether? One thing we knew for sure was the word mandatory meant Patrick was assuming power at a whole new level and that scared the crap out of all of us.

*

The first thing I remember about the evening was seeing Terry talking to some other refugees over a feed as we approached. He had bypassed the new accommodation and gone straight to dinner. I didn't know what to make of it. He had perhaps a dozen people gathered around. They were all huddled in and whispering.

In the spot where Patrick and his most important cockwombles always gathered I saw Craig sharing a drink and conversation. Anita was by his side. The tone of every interaction that evening reflected the tense new world that was the Parade.

Our group got dinner and positioned ourselves close enough that Terry couldn't miss us. He looked up shortly after and gave me a smile and a subtle thumbs up. The gesture did put me at ease a little. I needed it, given I wasn't expecting him to return without touching base and certainly didn't expect him to be out having random conversations with other survivors.

There was tension everywhere in our group and beyond. Anticipation at what Patrick might say or do added an extra sickly feeling to it. It didn't help that Olivia and one of Patrick's men were watching the crowd. They tried to hide it, but I could tell the focus was Terry. Perhaps us as well, we sensed. With so much going on, you could almost hear the tension in the air around the crowd. The ashy dusk only added to the eeriness.

We stood around making small talk about the set-up of our new home. But really, we were just padding time with one eye on Terry and one eye out for Patrick. Not far below in importance was an awareness of Olivia's movements. We were also monitoring Craig.

We were just finishing up our feed when two soldiers walked in from the east. They were two of the group that were here in the first couple of days after 12/4. They looked exhausted and were covered in ash. Their arrival caused quite a stir, with many people gathering around them. We were too far away to get the gist of any conversation and the two were soon guided by a couple of the locals back east – we correctly guessed they were being taken to see Patrick.

Soon after, someone called everyone to gather at the town hall. We had already positioned ourselves close enough to be in the first of two groups to hear what Patrick had to say.

I was feeling sick by that point.

I made sure to pass close by Terry on our way in.

"Plenty of updates, I'll fill you in later," he said.

I nodded. In truth, I was just struggling to get through each moment. It took all of my energy and concentration just to keep my game face on.

It took forever to get seated – for those lucky enough to find a seat. They had set up a roll near the door and had a printout of everyone's name, ticking them off as they came in. Patrick was clearly serious about the mandatory attendance.

"The fuck's he going to do if someone doesn't show up?" said Alex as we moved in.

"Not sure," I said. "Glad we're not going to find out though."

We had been seated for nearly half an hour while the rest of the theatre filled up behind us. The eternity of that day ended when we saw Patrick and a few others file in from the left of stage.

He eyed the room. "Ladies and gentlemen, there's a lot to get through tonight, but first things first. Can I get you two to stand up?"

He gestured to the front row, where two soldiers stood up and turned to the crowd. "You may remember Sergeant Jillian Goodwood and Lance Corporal Derby Manningham from a few days ago."

He gave them a nod of appreciation and they took their seats again.

"They come with some pretty sobering news about the greater world right now," he said, before looking at them once again. "If I miss anything out or get anything wrong, please let me know.

"There was a gas pipe explosion near Edinburgh Air Force Base. No doubt this was the distant, yet seemingly massive, noise we heard a few days ago. Those several kilometres closer to ground zero have described it to me in two words – fucking epic. It's still burning now and, the reality is, will continue to do so until it burns out.

"The base had been all but lost already in the tsunami and the majority of the skeleton crew trying to recover some form of military were killed in the incident.

"It's not only the loss of life, including many personal friends of Jillian and Derby. It was also the only real chance for some of the former structure of our world to come back and hold things together. There is no defence force in our city any more.

"When you put it together with the other realities, it paints a pretty bleak picture. There is no police – Kyle may be one of the few remaining in what remains of the city. There is no government. There is no gas infrastructure. From what I've been told about the inconsistent electricity, we can expect that to end as well. We don't know who got the mobile network up and running briefly yesterday, but I would set expectations to not experience that again.

"If any of you did get a chance to search the internet, you'll probably share the same sinking feeling I did. The reality of what has happened to our world could not have been more horrifying. Everywhere is suffering – even those places that didn't take the brunt of the damage on 12/4.

"And the predictions are it will get worse. The experts are saying the ash may take many months – at the very least – to clear from the skies. Food production will be hit hard. Populations are scrambling to find ways to survive. Cities may not be viable. Flights will be grounded for the foreseeable future. It's a dire situation everywhere.

"Back in Australia, every coastal population has suffered as much as we have – worse in the cases of Melbourne and Perth."

He paused and looked at the two army folk, then over the crowd. "The reality is, Adelaide is on its own. We are on our own. And we're going to have to do it without, well, any help from anything mentioned above.

"As for the ash, we don't know how high it will get, we just know there's enough up there for the experts to be saying it will be a miracle if it's all rained down before the year is out. Eight months!

"That's the reality we face right now. I don't know how long that's going to take to sink in, but it's going to have to be soon, because the world has changed and if we don't change with it we're dead."

Once again he turned his attention to the two soldiers in the front row. "For us to have this information, these two people have travelled many, many kilometres on foot. They are not following orders – there are none to follow. They have taken it upon themselves to visit every shopping centre on the Adelaide plains to keep the people informed and in a position to make the best decisions.

"It was a mission they started in an army truck and, since the ash has gotten too high, now on foot. Many would've given up. But not these two. Tonight we shall house and feed them and tomorrow they will continue their mission south all the way to Noarlunga, with many stops along the way. It will take a few days.

"Just for some perspective, by the way, they've both said we are in as good a position as anywhere in terms of food and resources. So, two people who have crisscrossed the surviving parts of the city tell us we have it as good as it gets. That might be worth remembering when times and conditions get tough.

"I want to thank Jillian and Derby for their acts of bravery, wish them all the best and extend an invitation for them to join our group when they're done."

Patrick nodded and began applauding, before the crowd joined in.

He stepped out from behind the lectern to wander the stage a little, eyeing the crowd as he went. "I want to share another harsh reality with you. Yesterday afternoon, we investigated a site of interest. The gun store in Magill Rd."

My heart raced and I felt Claire squeeze my hand. There was gasping in sections of the crowd.

"Given how quickly the world is changing we believed securing the arms so they couldn't be used against us was a prudent strategy. It is a strong asset, within our lands and had rocketed up the priority list with each passing hour.

"The site itself is below the tsunami line and the recon team managed to locate it and see it had survived the tsunami in good condition. After a failed attempt to gain access, it was decided to return with a team capable of completing the job today.

"There were no signs of other human activity in the area."

Again he paused to look out over the crowd before clearing his throat.

"This morning, we sent a team back. Alan Jackson and Jane Whitehead, who knew the area well, as well as Graham Harding, our locksmith."

Patrick took a deep breath.

"Many of you would have heard the gunfire this morning, no doubt. I'm devastated to announce that was the murder of these three valued members of our community."

The murmuring in the crowd spread quickly – speckled with wailing – and Patrick let it take hold for what felt like a minute before he raised his hand to get everyone to quieten down.

"They were well known and liked members of this community and their loss will be observed in the coming days.

"But, if you haven't joined the dots on the situation yet, another group has entered our lands, stolen our guns and killed our people."

Again he paused. This time the silence spoke as much as his words.

"There could not be a more alarming situation for us to face. After the shots and receiving no response on the two-way, I gathered everyone who had been on active duty around the suburb to investigate what had happened.

"The killers had left a note on the bodies."

There was another bout of wails sounding out from a few spots in the crowd. I felt Claire grip my hand tight and turned to see tears welled up in her eyes.

"It was a threat to not cross west of Sydenham Rd or face more bullets. After much time and consultation, we decided not to head further west today. Three lives were enough.

"So, what does that mean for us? Firstly, somewhere out there is a group of people who completely outarm us. Relatively, our weapon situation is poor – just the pistols and tasers from the police station. Before this act, we were in a strong position. Now…"

Patrick collected himself. You could see his mind processing what the right combination of words might be to say next.

"We don't know these people, or their purpose. Based on the message, it seems if we stay clear of what they're claiming as their territory, we will be fine. But can we trust that? The area they've claimed is under the tsunami line with little in terms of stable shelter, food resources or any of the basics.

"You've already heard what's happening in the world around us. Whether they know this or not, they are not in a location that can sustain many people for very long.

"Perhaps they were passing through. Perhaps. If so, and even with a reasonably sized group, there is no way they'll be able to move the amount of firepower they have with them. If they're staying put, it's hard to come to any other conclusion than they will attempt to take our food resources at some point.

"Ladies and gentlemen, this was an act of war. Right now, we should consider ourselves at war. Maybe – *maybe* – they've moved on and left the weapons they couldn't carry with them. There aren't many other possibilities that will not lead to conflict.

"That is now our reality.

"Who knows, perhaps it was inevitable things would get like this. But we can't pretend we're not in this world we're in any more. We thought we were already making the tough decisions – we weren't even close. Now we know. We're smarter and more open eyed and we will be ensuring we don't get taken by surprise again.

"The first steps have already been taken. We are now pulling back our western border to Osmond Tce. It halves the area we have to defend – all of the land we're giving up is below the tsunami line. We have five lookout points along that new border, so no one is going to approach us unannounced.

"That leaves the area between Osmond Tce and Sydenham Rd as ours, but not active. Think of it as a demilitarised zone. We will be running missions to monitor for signs of enemy activity and planning around what we discover."

Patrick took a sip from a water bottle and studied the crowd again.

"I know this is a lot to take in. There is plenty more to come in terms of defence and protection strategies that will be rolled out over the next few days. We will keep you informed as we progress.

"If you take one thing out of everything that's been discussed tonight, let it be that the world has changed. And if we're going to survive as a group, we have to change with it. You have to change with it.

"We will be seeking more support on the front lines, so if you want to actively contribute to safety and security, there will be plenty of opportunity. Stay tuned tomorrow.

"Finally, it goes without saying that each one of you is a valued member of our ever-changing society. As such, you have a responsibility to this place and the people you're surrounded by. It goes without saying that should it come to light that any of our people were involved with recent incidents in any way, the punishment will be swift and brutal.

"Only together will we thrive. That is all."

A brief hush came over the crowd.

"Why didn't you secure the guns earlier?" said someone.

It triggered a flood of questions, all critical of decisions made by Patrick and his team. He tried to jump on top of the situation and answer, but was overwhelmed by the number of people speaking up in the crowd. I noticed many of those leading the voice of disillusion were those who were speaking to Terry before the meeting started.

Eventually Patrick lifted his arms and gestured the crowd to quieten down. It took another minute or so before the volume dulled to the point where he could talk over it. He lifted the microphone to his lips and the room quietened further.

"Unfortunately, there is no time for questions tonight as I still have the other group to present to, then we'll be planning our defences for tomorrow."

You could hear the murmur of discontent emanate over the crowd. That's when I spotted Terry, off to the side with a very contented smile. I wasn't the only one either. When I turned back to the stage Patrick was glaring at him.

"There'll be more time for questions tomorrow. Please make your way to the exits. Thank you," said Patrick as he placed the mic on the lectern and marched to the side of stage.

"Wanker!" someone yelled, before a large section of the crowd laughed.

I watched Patrick with everything I had. If things were tense before, they were at another level now. He tried to keep his cool, but as soon as he turned to face those supporting him from the exit he gave a look that even scared me.

###

###

CHAPTER 30:
PLANS, NO PLANS

We regathered at our usual meeting point in the dinner gathering area. It was a cool night, but the calmest we'd had since shit hit the fan. It could not have been more opposite than what was going on around us.

"Well, that was pretty fucked," said Alex, double checking Jacob was asleep on her shoulder after the words came out.

"I think we should head back home so we can talk about all the things," said Yamato.

"Agreed," I said. "We just need to wait for Terry."

I looked around the group. Everyone was exhausted, in all the ways. Not only had it been a massive day, we also carried a massive burden. And this thing we had done had gotten way too hot for all of us to handle. They were looking to me for solutions, but I had nothing. I needed Terry for the info, for a start. I could've screamed at that moment, at how out of control the situation was, let alone what was now brewing in the background.

That probably doesn't even fully sum up how far the dread had spread. I was looking at a bunch of people, most of whom I had only recently met, and now we had to trust each other on a scale I assume none of us had ever faced before.

In every direction lay unknowns. That scared me more than everything else the world was throwing at us in that moment.

I decided to focus on the one thing I could control. Starting with the teens, I went around the group and asked everyone how they were holding up. Claire and Alex picked up on my lead and worked their way between little sub groups, making small talk about some of the big worldview updates we'd just received.

"What did I miss?" said Terry as he stepped into the group.

"Where have you been?"

"Seeing a man about a dog."

It was an expression my dad used to use, which was a scrambled way of saying none of your business. Except with Terry, after everything the day and evening had brought, everything should have been my business – everyone's business.

It was the first time he had pissed me off and I knew the answer didn't cut it for anyone else standing there either.

"I think I want to know about that man and that dog, and all the other gaps. Let's get home."

The comment threw him for a second, but it had the desired result, and he nodded. His tone was suddenly far more agreeable. "Good call," he said, with far more humility than his last statement.

*

We soon found ourselves huddled in the main upstairs area of our new digs, coffee mugs from the staff room filled with scotch, or wine, or whatever people thought would give them the mental fortitude for the discussion that lay ahead.

We kept our voices low, not knowing who could be listening in, and Billy had taken the first guard shift downstairs. He was kicked back on a chair, blanket by his side concealing a rifle fixed on the door.

This was getting very real, very quickly.

I took a healthy dose of cab sav courage before looking at Terry. "So, let's start with this afternoon. What happened?"

"Went as good as can be expected," he said. "The message on the bodies did their job. Scared the shit out of Patrick and his cronies. They hung around for a few hours; everyone was there. Looked like some heated discussions before he put his tail between his legs and fucked off back to George House with all of his lackeys in tow."

"So, what, they headed back – what would that have been – just before 3pm?" I said.

"Pretty much bang on," said Terry.

"So what happened between then and when we saw you at seven?"

"Just because they left didn't mean I could."

The look I gave him must've said I needed more detail. He looked around the group, clearly sensing the anxiety he'd put us through while he disappeared. It was the first time I'd really experienced tension between him and I, and I think the group felt that too. That only added to the complete underlying dread that everything was headed towards a dark place and we had essentially put the wheels for that in motion.

"I couldn't leave," he continued, his tone softer. "What if they'd doubled-back another way? There was definitely a chance they sensed they were being watched and could have easily chosen that as a tactic. Or pulled the main group out but sent in scout parties. I couldn't take any chances.

"Dusk hit and I felt the coast was clear but I had to wait until nightfall to head back. I took the long way to avoid any watch points and once I was back in the community I slipped into the crowd gathering for the dinner, thinking that'd be better than leading people back to you guys if there was anyone watching on."

I nodded my approval at his reasons, trying hard to break through for a reconnect. "And the group you were talking to at dinner – what was that all about?"

Terry looked at the group in turn. Sure, we were discussing what happened, but this moment was also the entree to planning what we were going to do about it. "You all heard Patrick at the meeting. He's nearly at breaking point. He's lost a lot of people by not listening and he's about one bad decision away from breaking point. Don't tell me you can't feel that."

He pointed to the injuries on his face. "He did that over me having an alternative opinion. Could you imagine what he's capable of when shit gets real?"

He took a swig from his mug. "Shit is about to get very real. Some way, somehow this whole place is going to change. There is nothing surer. It just comes down to what that big change is and who makes it.

"Those people I was talking to are all observant people. They're like us. I was just doing some fishing to make sure they were on the same page."

"On the same page?" I said.

"Not fans of the current leadership or how they go about leading. Very, very open to change, to say the least."

"Wait?" I said, a sudden unnerving thought flowing in. "You didn't tell them about the guns, did you?"

"What? No," said Terry. "Nothing that obvious. But I know if we had a plan to take Patrick and his cronies down, they'd be on board."

"We decided we weren't going to use the guns."

"Yeah, this morning. But we already have used them. And Patrick has changed. I'm telling you, he's freaking the fuck out and he's going to snap at some point. I certainly don't want to wait around until he does."

The room went silent for a few moments.

"If you are talking about using guns to hurt other people, I don't want to play a part in that," said Yamato.

"I second that," said Keira. "And Charlie thirds it."

"What?" said Charlie.

His mum glared at him. "Fine, I third it then."

"Anyone else got any thoughts they'd like to share?" said Terry, trying his best – and failing – not to let his frustration bleed into his words.

"Shouldn't we just be laying low right now?" said Alex. "What we pulled off today was ridiculous. Like, pulled-it-out-our-asses ridiculous. We're back, safe and we have the weapons. It's fucking tense, don't add to it. People are dead. Patrick is pissed. Let's just get past this little bit of time, see what happens and reassess our options from there."

"What if we don't have time? What if he knows more about us than we think he does? What if he just suspects us and decides it's better for him and his people to act first? Waiting could get us killed," said Terry.

"Is that likely?" said Alex.

"You tell me," said Terry. "It just sounds like a bet I wouldn't want to take."

"So, what are you saying exactly?" said Asim. "To be sure they don't act on a worst-case scenario, we should take them out first? Just kill them all."

"I don't think we'd have to kill them all to be fair. Patrick, all the others who make decisions at George House, the cop and maybe anyone who looks like they're not going to accept the change – that should be all we need."

"That's at least ten people," said Alex.

"Ten people who are not us. That will make the world a much safer place for us."

"Jesus Christ," said Alex as she emptied her mug, then topped it up from the bottle. "That's a massacre."

"It's the surest way to keep us alive."

"By killing?" said Liv. "Sorry, I don't want to survive by killing."

Terry nodded at her. "I can respect that. This world might not, but I can." He took a moment to collect his thoughts. "Look, as far as I see it the path forward is a simple one. We have the ability to control the future to make our world a safer place, eliminating the clear threat."

"It's not just the killing," I said. "The thing I can't get past is if we do all of that and take control of Norwood, we'll be no better than who we replaced."

"I can guarantee we'd run this place better than the current management," said Terry.

"But taking control like that, it will just fire up some other group to get back at us."

"If we did do that, and targeted who I'm saying we target, I think what would remain would be a very amenable population."

"So, just take out everyone who has a different viewpoint than us?" I said.

"No, take out the failed leadership you already see as failing, who are a massive threat to our survival, that is all. Then start building this place in the way it should've been done in the first place."

"I'm out," said Liv. "This is way, way too much."

"Agreed," said Em.

"Out," said Billy.

"Well that's more than half of us already," I said. "Perhaps we should start focusing on another strategy."

I looked at Terry as he processed what was happening. You could feel him burning at our lack of want to be a part of his plan, but you could also see his need for us as a group. He went to speak a couple of times but no words came out. Perhaps they had been continuing arguments that were destined to fail now the group had shown their lack of appetite for his ideas. Eventually he stood up and drained the rest of his mug of scotch. "So the plan now is don't do anything and let whatever happens happen."

"I hope it works out for us," he said. Then he nodded his goodnight, nabbed the bottle and went to his bed.

Silence followed his exit as each of us pondered the enormity of the day, how things had escalated and how lucky we had been to not have triggered a civil war within the population. Each of us was completely out of our depth to handle whatever was happening in that moment and doubly so for any confrontation that may have lain ahead.

There should've been granules of good feelings after having played a part in avoiding conflict, but they weren't there. It was hard to think of anything other than it was coming regardless. Maybe Terry was right after all. But even if he was, we were not yet the people we needed to be to do anything about it. Maybe we didn't want to be those people – scrub that – definitely. That wasn't right or wrong, it just was what it was.

All we were left with was a sense of dread that Patrick was onto us and, even if he wasn't, shit was about to get a whole lot worse.

Words were few from that point onwards. Sound travelled efficiently in our new digs and no one wanted to voice any opinions that would travel to Terry. No one wanted to add any further conversation around what was happening and no one had much energy for small talk. It was just a shared state of mental and physical exhaustion, with our proximity to each other and the alcohol providing the only hint of respite.

What a way to spend the last night before things fell apart.

Seems not all of the plans were being made with our knowledge.

###

\#\#\#

CHAPTER 31:

GAME CHANGERS

Some of the details of this day are a little hazy still. Trying to pull all of the moments together in a timeline, based on those still around to recall them, is not easy. Most of the following is fact and some of it guestimation but the result is real.

*

We woke up to a hammering on the door at sunrise. The banging was relentless. "Let us in," said the voice on the other side.

"Hang on," yelled Asim from downstairs. He had retreated back from the lounge and was seeking cover behind the serving counter at the back of the former shop.

"Who is it?" I yelled and I searched around upstairs for my weapon and some clothes to throw on – easier said than done in an emergency. "Fuck!"

Claire saw my scramble and flicked a top my way. She picked up the gun next to her bed, hands shaking, gave me a nod and headed downstairs.

Billy and Liv headed past our door, armed and on their way downstairs.

"Who is it?" I yelled out.

"Patrick's men," said Asim. "Maybe a dozen of them. I see guns."

"Fuck," I said again as the scale of the moment hit home. "What do they want?"

"What do you want?" said Asim.

By that point I was headed down the stairs and signalling Billy and Liv to spread out to the far side of the room while Claire and I found cover near the staircase.

"Terry. Patrick wants to speak to him," said one.

At this point they couldn't see into our space. We were a thin privacy screen and a threatening moment away from being exposed as the gun thieves and murderers. I looked up the stairs just as Charlie and Em were headed down. I signalled them to stop. "Get Terry and check the back entrance," I whispered.

My heart was racing out of control.

"What does Patrick want with Terry?" I yelled.

"That's not your concern," the guy said.

"Last time he spoke to him he beat the shit out of him. Kind of makes it my concern."

"Look, lady, this is going to play out a whole lot better if you just cooperate."

There was something about being called lady that grated on me. Doubly so in that moment. But by that point I had bigger problems. Charlie and Em were back at the top of the stairs.

"Three men out the back, no sign of Terry," Charlie said, trying to make sure his voice didn't carry.

I just stared at him, dumbfounded. I gave Charlie a confused look, but he just shrugged his shoulders.

How was Terry not there?

"Don't make me start counting down," said the spokesman for the group out front.

"Hang on a second," I yelled out, trying to give myself a bit of time to come up with the best play at the moment. Not that there seemed to be one. "He's not here."

"That's not what we've been told," said the man. The tone was that of someone losing their patience. It wasn't a surprise when his next word was "Five."

"Can you just give us a minute? Please?" I yelled.

"Four."

I looked around at everyone in the downstairs area then shrugged my shoulders, hoping someone would have an idea ready to roll. It didn't happen. I raised my weapon and my eyebrow. Claire and Asim nodded. Liv swore then her and BIlly got their weapons ready.

Mine was shaking in my hand.

"Three."

I figured I'd fire a few warning shots past the first person through the door to keep them at bay. We really had all the advantages. We could see their silhouettes gathered outside, while they could see nothing. Plus they'd have to come through the narrow entryway, not knowing where we were on the other side. Of course, they were under the false assumption they had the advantage of weapons. I signalled Charlie and Em to position themselves at the back window to protect the rear of the property.

"Two."

My gun was shaking in my hand and my heart was beating so hard I thought my ribs would break. "Just warning shots," I whispered.

Everyone was waiting for the count to hit one when a hail of nearby gunfire cut its way through the atmosphere. Lots of bullets. Very close.

"The fuck was that?" said the guy in charge.

Screams could be heard down the street. The sounds of shots lasted for several more seconds before it thinned out. A double shot ended the barrage no more than 15 seconds after it began.

"Shots fired. Man down," came a call over the man's two-way. "Get here now!"

"Go, go, go!" the guy screamed before the intruders sprinted back up the Parade.

"Everyone downstairs!" I yelled.

Within seconds the group was together, minus Terry.

Another round of gunfire opened up.

"Where's that coming from?" said Asim. "It's got to be on the Parade."

"What do we do?" said Liv.

"Wait, that weapon sound, that ain't pistols," said Claire.

No one spoke. We all knew she was right. Whatever was happening up the street was happening with the weapons we had swiped from the gun store.

"Fuck!" I said, eventually. "What's he done?"

###

###

CHAPTER 32:
GEORGE HOUSE

"They're heading out," said the man with the binoculars.

Terry moved in next to him, reached out his hand and gestured for him to pass the binoculars over. He looked through and saw the two soldiers headed east up the Parade on their mission to update the other hubs about the change in circumstance of the city.

He tracked his view back to where Patrick and the other leaders were seeing them off. They stood around watching the departure before Patrick signalled them all to follow him to George House.

"Should we get ready to roll?" said the man.

"Not yet," said Terry. "They'll be there for a while. Let's give it a few minutes to make sure the soldiers will be too far away when shit goes down."

He looked around at the others, a group of eight, all armed to the teeth with high-powered weapons and sidearms. A firepower far in advance of those in charge. They were bunkered down on a second-storey office space that had been converted into a bedroom for one of them. A prime spot to monitor the goings on at George House. The occupant, one of the team, had been assigned the room by Terry. "Get yourselves mentally prepared. Let's make this as quick and clean as possible. Remember the plan. No dumb mistakes."

*

Soon they were on foot. A pair headed down the Parade towards George House, where a guard was positioned out the front. The rest of the group circled around the side streets to be positioned at the ready from the other direction.

The pair – a man and a woman – waited for the signal, then advanced. With their heavy weapons carried by the others, they were exchanging small talk about the ash conditions as they approached the guard.

The guard moved his hand down near his weapon.

"Excuse me. Do you know which one is Queen St?" said the woman.

"You're close, next one in the way you're headed."

"Thanks." She smiled at him. "Not too cold I hope."

The guard shook his head and returned the smile.

The man nodded as the pair passed by. Then, just as the guard relaxed his stance, the man pulled his hands from his pockets to reveal a blade. It was in the guard's ribs before he realised the situation had changed.

As he fell the blade stuck him again in the chest, then again.

With the guard downed, the man frisked the body, coming up with a pistol. Across the street Terry looked at the others. "Move!"

He moved forward, four of the group in tow, the others now circling around an Indian restaurant to a laneway that led to the back of George House.

Terry and the main group had reached the pair waiting out front of George House. They turned to the gates and walked in.

George House was one of the few properties along the main strip of the Parade that wasn't built butting up against the footpath. Instead it stood approximately ten metres back from the street. Not that it made a difference for visibility of the attackers in the moment. The shrubbery, now caked with ash, blocked out any clear view of what was happening on the street.

The group shuffled silently down the walkway and were at the door in seconds. Terry signalled the man on point to try the door. Meanwhile he positioned himself behind a bush, aiming a weapon through the window where he knew Olivia spent most of her time.

The door clicked open and one of the team behind the door positioned himself in a crouch then leaned inside.

The stillness of the dawn air was broken by a series of shots. The crouching invader dropped to a prone position then unleashed a rapid fire volley of shots. Bullets hit the door frame in return fire, then Terry unleashed a burst of fire from behind the bush.

The sounds of a woman screaming in pain could be heard inside. Then yelling and instructions being called out.

Then the attacker who opened the door started yelling and Terry looked down to see the prone soldier lying still in a pool of blood.

Terry processed the scene. The enemy had been prepared. They had been waiting for an attack. They had stayed off their two-ways or given false information. Now he didn't know how many were inside. What he did know was that it was more than Patrick and the board members. He swore, then signalled one of the others to stand back at street level to keep an eye out for approaching back-up.

Despite the advance in firepower they had, they found themselves in a horrible no man's land. Without even taking the entrance area, they had no idea of enemy numbers, no position to lead an attack from and a very exposed position to fight from if it became anything other than a quick mission.

If they didn't break through the front of the building they would have to run or die where they stood.

"Fuck," he said again as pockets of gunfire rang out around him.

Then he charged at the window he'd presumably shot Olivia through.

*

"Fuck, fuck, fuck," said Alex. "This is beyond horrific."

She was pacing back and forward with Jacob crying in her arms. "Let's just stash our weapons and pretend we had nothing to do with this."

Jacob's crying wasn't the only noise in the room, Sara was struggling to breathe and Yamato was offering her words of reassurance.

In the distance, we could hear the fighting picking up again.

"We need to find out what's going on before we do anything," said Asim.

"He's going to get himself killed. He's going to get us all killed," said Alex. "What's he doing?"

"Best guess is hitting Patrick at George House," I said.

"What kind of asshole marches himself into enemy HQ and starts firing? What a waste."

"I don't think it was just him."

There was a pause as everyone digested the implications of my comment.

"Wanker!" said Alex. "Couldn't get us to fight for him so he found others."

"Where does that leave us?" said Yamato.

"Depends on what happens," I said.

"Well, if Patrick wins, we're fucked," said Keira. "If Terry wins we might still be fucked."

"Awesome," said Claire.

"Can we leave?" said Liv. "I just want to get as far away from all this as possible."

"Where would we even go?" said Billy. "You heard that soldier last night – Norwood is the best setup to survive this thing."

"Dude, we're not even going to survive today," Liv returned.

The conversation petered out again as everyone searched for a non-existent simple answer to the situation.

"Asim's right," I said eventually. "We can't leave without understanding what's going on. What about this? I'll head up the Parade to try to find out what's going on. Some company would be great. Meanwhile, let's get another team to head out to the gun stashes and load up whatever they can carry. Maybe stash a few somewhere else, just in case. The rest of you can pack everyone's stuff up so we're ready to go at a moment's notice."

"I'll come with you," said Asim.

"In," said Claire.

I nodded my appreciation. "Anyone else?"

There were no takers.

"Three's enough," I said. "Alex, you stay here with Jacob and pack. Yamato and Sara, you too. The rest of you, go and sort the gun situation. Plan?"

"Plan," said a number of people.

"What about the lookouts on Osmond?" said Billy.

"With everything going down right now I doubt anyone is there. Maybe just in case head south of the Parade and loop back around the way we came in last time."

He nodded.

"If shit gets too heavy here, we'll follow straight after you. We'll move in your tracks. If you're heading back here, take the same path. Understand?"

Keira and the teens nodded.

I checked my weapon and holstered it in anticipation of whatever lay ahead for me, Claire and Asim. "Alright then, let's do this."

###

###

CHAPTER 33:
CIVIL WAR

Just as Terry made his run for the window, the sound of glass smashing came from above. Then shots rang out and down from the balcony of the upper deck. Terry made cover by the side of the building just in time.

The same could not be said for the intruder on watch out on the street. A bullet passed through his calf as he stood at the top of the walkway gates, eyes focused on potential threats up the street. He screamed as he sought cover behind the large cement upright post. He reloaded and returned fire at the balcony defender.

Terry moved his head up to the side of the window and glanced inside. He could see the body of Olivia slumped against the back wall. He retracted his head then bobbed it back in further to get a wider view of the scene. No targets and nothing fired on him. He checked to make sure he wasn't casting a shadow on the glass before he leaned in to where the edge of the glass bordered his protection. He took a deep breath, moved into a more exposed spot, saw movement in the space beyond and fired until it was clear. Then he ducked back to safety and reloaded.

He'd seen four people inside and was pretty convinced he'd hit two of them. The screams of pain seconded his beliefs. He held up hand signals to the others to indicate what he'd seen.

With his new clip in place he held his gun at an angle, passed it through the broken glass, guessed the direction of fire and pulled the trigger on a short burst of blind spray.

The aim was successful enough to put an end to the screaming from those injured. As the echoes of the shots dissipated, he could hear whispered instructions being passed around on the other side, before footsteps signalled the enemy had fallen back.

He ducked under the bottom of the window and moved to the other side, before leaning back into exposed space again. This time he had a far better few of the main footprint of the room. Three additional bodies lay in blood and there were no signs of life. He called up one of his men to climb through the window while he held his covering position.

Soon Terry's raider was inside. Seconds later he was at the front door, ushering the others through.

They were all inside seconds later. Terry frisked the bodies and swiped a couple of pistols as he went. He made a gesture for the two closest fighters to follow him through to the back of the building and hand signalled the other three to go up the stairs.

Terry led the way down a passage leading to the back carpark. He tried to land each step as delicately as he could on the floorboards, but knew he wasn't as light on his feet as he might have been years ago. The first creak moaned out shortly before they came to the first door. It was open.

He sidled up to the frame and gestured for the others to join him. They hashed out a strategy to approach the door breach then stepped into the open space, looking down their barrels. It was clear. They swept the space to make certain before Terry turned his attention to the paperwork on the table. A quick rifle through confirmed this wasn't Patrick's space. Just as Terry signalled the others to focus on the next door down the corridor, they heard a creak of floorboards. It was in the direction they were headed. And close.

*

The other three raiders neared the top of the stairs, inching forward in small circumspect steps. The stairs made the ground level floorboards seem silent. If there was someone up there, they would know company was coming.

They ascended as far up as they could without exposing themselves to whoever might be waiting for them on the first floor. They looked at each other to offer the next move into the danger zone. Eventually, the woman fished a zippo lighter from her pocket and signalled the others to get ready.

Then she yelled "Grenade!" and lobbed it up onto the first floor. It made a satisfying metallic sound as it clunked into the floorboards. At the same, she and the others rose to get a view of the landscape above, guns raised.

They saw two men scurrying from cover positions into an office space that led to the back of the building. The woman fired a shot in hope at Patrick's retreating men – it struck the last to scurry through the door. He made a guttural sound of pain as he disappeared from sight.

"Tagged him," said the woman. "Snicked him maybe."

The three were soon up the stairs and on the first floor.

"The other one was the cop," she said.

The two men nodded and focused their attention on the door the enemy had fled through. With the cop in play, they knew they were getting close to Patrick.

*

Terry's injured man on lookout turned his attention back to the street after the upstairs gunfire dissipated, only to see the group of Patrick's people who had been at our place running towards him.

With the visibility as it was, by the time he saw the threat they were already in shooting range. There was a brief period where the incoming enemy was working out who the slumped human was, but as soon as the guy lifted his rifle in defence, they knew he wasn't one of theirs. Pistols were raised at the injured rifleman, which triggered a shooting standoff.

Then the lone raider fizzed a bullet into the advancing group, sending them scattering. He took his moment and hobbled through the gate and out of immediate line-of-sight danger.

*

By the time Patrick's men who'd been shot at on the Parade had managed to seek cover and regroup, we had managed to traverse the side streets so we popped out past them and George House on the other side of the street.

We could see Terry's wounded gunman backed up against the gate upright making hand signals to someone inside the house. Blood soaked his lower leg plus his sleeves and his hands where he'd tried to wipe it away. Some of it was caked in ash, some of it still freshly flowing.

"That's not great," I whispered.

"That's one of Terry's other crew," said Asim.

"Yep," I said.

We paused on the moment as the extent to which Terry had been working with the other group hit home.

"This is fucked," I said, eventually.

"Pretty much," said Asim. "The question is, what can we do about it?"

"Stay alive," said Claire.

He nodded. "So, the shooting's coming from George House. Terry's work. How many do you think he has with him?"

"Who knows," I said. That main group of his was less than ten though. And if he wanted to surprise Patrick, he would've wanted to limit the group to those he could trust."

Asim nodded in agreement with his eyes fixed on the front of George House. "Weird how no one's come out yet."

"Mmmm," I said. I looked down the street to see Patrick's other group heading in. "This is not going to end well."

Most of Patrick's second group advanced in unison down the Parade, while two smaller groups headed down the side streets north and south – no doubt flanking as we had. I started updating Claire and Asim on what I'd seen. As I did, the sounds of gunfire from George House filled the air once again.

*

Terry and the pair he was with had finished their sweep of the ground floor, finding no signs of Patrick or his men. They ascended the stairs and met up with the squad on the first floor. A few hand signals were exchanged. Terry followed the signals and the blood trail to the door Patrick and his men must've gone through.

"No sounds of movement on the other side," reported one. "We think they're holed up in there waiting for us."

It was the boardroom. Terry nodded, then picked up his rifle. He aimed at the door and fired. He kept pulsing the trigger until he had unloaded the clip. A pained scream could be heard on the other side. Then the shuffling of movement and whispers as Patrick and his men attended to the injured.

The door itself was weakened around the handle, where Terry had focused his early shots. There was also a crisscross pattern of bullet holes across the rest.

Terry's troop looked at him for instructions. Instead of offering any, he casually replaced the gun's magazine, aimed it back at the door and drained all of its contents.

More screams sounded out. Perhaps three people.

The door now had gaping holes in it. Enough to make out small sections of what lay on the other side.

"I give up," came a voice. "I have no weapon and I want to come out. Please."

"Pass your group's weapons through the door and you will be allowed to exit," said Terry.

Whispered conversation came from the other side of the door.

"Erm. I don't think the others are coming with me," said the voice.

Terry pondered on the statement for a moment, aware all ears on both sides were waiting for his words. "Their loss," he said. "What are you holding?"

"H-holding?"

"Yeah. What sort of pistol do you have?"

"I… I don't have a pistol."

"Hmm. So, what's your weapon?"

"I, um, don't really have one."

Terry sighed. "Alright then. Approach the door. Hands up and behind your head."

There was some inaudible mumbling from the other side of the door before the sound of furniture scraping on floorboards preceded footsteps. Soon, they could see someone standing on the other side of the door through the holes.

"OK… what's your name?"

"Andrew," said the man, fear in his tone.

"OK, Andrew, you know the deal, just like the movies except, if you screw up, you die."

Terry paused long enough to hear the sounds of fear float past the door.

"But I have the highest confidence you'll be able to follow simple instructions without panicking as you know your life is on the line."

A whimper replaced words.

Terry sighed again. "I'm assuming you're still listening, Andrew. When I give the signal, I want you to slowly – and I can't emphasise the word slowly enough – move your right hand onto the door handle and await further instruction.

"And go."

Terry and his crew watched what little they could see through the holes in the door.

"Done," came the wavering voice of Andrew.

"Very good Andrew. Almost there now. Now I want you to turn the handle and pull the door open. Again, slowly is the theme. Do you know what? Let's just make slowly the theme with everything. I don't want to keep repeating myself. Everything slowly. Starting with this. And go."

They watched the handle start to turn, then falter.

"It's stuck," said Andrew.

"It's quite messy, maybe just give it a little jiggle," said Terry.

"Got it!" said Andrew.

"Well done," said Terry. "Now gently ease it open. Don't move, just ease it open."

After a few jarring movements, Andrew managed to release the mangled door from the frame and open it. He stood where the door once obscured him, now completely exposed to Terry and his crew. Blood covered his shoulder and seeped down his sleeve but he looked oblivious to any pain it might have caused. When he looked at Terry, he gulped hard. Terry still wore the bruises he'd helped inflict on his face. He was hoping in the moment Terry wouldn't recognise hi—"

"Well, well, well," said Terry. "Look at who we have here."

"I am so sorry. Truly," said Andrew, his words falling apart as he became acutely aware of how recognised he was and, now, how exposed.

"Now I realise why you didn't need a weapon. Your fists are pretty good," said Terry as he brushed his hand over his jawline. "When you've got two other people holding the person down, of course."

Andrew made eye contact with Terry, then sized up all the guns pointed at him. He stood in silence watching his feet.

"So," started Terry. He let the word linger in the air until it drew Andrew into looking again. "What do we do with you now then?"

The tone made it seem like Terry already had the answer. It also compelled Andrew to lift his game, clearly now fearing for his life.

"I was just following orders," he defended. "It wasn't my fault."

Terry laughed as he looked at the weapon in his hand and the change in power it had caused. "It's a good little system, that. You've got a leader claiming he's making his shitty decisions for the people. And then you've got the people who follow the orders they don't believe in because they have no choice. So, apparently nobody wants to do it, but everybody does."

Terry stepped forward, weapon trained on Andrew and perhaps any threats behind him. Andrew went to respond but no words were summoned into his vocal chords. He flinched and turned his head away from the long and threatening barrel bobbling not too many metres from his face.

Terry turned to his crew and gave a brief smile.

"My hands were tied," he said, as if mocking Andrew's tone. "Just doing my job."

Then Terry pulsed a few rounds from his weapon.

Andrew screamed.

But the bullets weren't meant for him.

In the next room they could hear the cries of pain from another of Patrick's people.

The echoes of gunfire simmered down and the room fell briefly silent.

"It's just a circle jerk of bullshit," said Terry. "Just a self-saucing pudding of shit you serve each other to make yourselves feel better about being absolute scum."

He looked up to see Andrew's cargo pants wet and stained at the front. In his humiliation at pissing himself he lowered his hands to cover his crotch.

"Keep those arms up over your head where I can see 'em, soldier," said Terry.

"For fuck's sake, Terry, leave him alone!" said Patrick from the other room.

"If it isn't our glorious leader," said Terry. "What should I do, oh wise one?"

"Lay down your weapons and negotiate a truce," said Patrick.

Terry laughed. "I don't think you fully appreciate the concept of bargaining power."

He fired a single shot into the roof to accentuate his point.

"Terry, this is Senior Constable Kyle Jenkins. There's still a way back from this. We can get through this without any more bloodshed."

Terry laughed again. "You still don't get it, do you? Back! There is no way back. We left *back* in a different world and just in case you haven't worked it out yet, we're never getting that again." He turned to his team. "New world – new rules. Adapt or die."

"I hear what you're saying, but shouldn't we be building a world we want to live in? Doesn't matter what the world throws at us, it's what we do with it. That's what's going to make this thing worth surviving."

"Says the guy who decided he's in charge, next to the other guys in charge. Of course that's the world you want to live in. Just like before everything went south. Doesn't matter how fucked it is out there, as long as we follow, like we always have, things will work out. Same shit, different day."

Things fell silent for a few seconds. Perhaps the truth of how unfixable this situation was was hitting home. Then Terry added. "Today is going to be a different kind of different day."

"Let's not get too hasty," said Kyle. "This doesn't have to be a class warfare situation or whatever you're trying to turn this into. Or an us versus them situation. It's just a survival situation."

"Spot on," said Terry.

"I think what Kyle is saying, Terry, is that you don't have to take away everything it means to be civil while you're trying to survive," said Patrick. "This is still Adelaide. There are still laws. There is still a—"

"Laws?" said Terry. "What laws? Upheld by who? Protected by who? Defended by who?"

"Well, I am a senior cons—"

"Oh fuck off," said Terry. "Backed-up by a real estate agent, a doctor and a council member. That's all you are."

"Actually, you killed the lawyer."

Terry shrugged. "Meh. What I'm really hearing over there is our gang had the best guns so we took charge. We didn't massively give a fuck about you guys while we were setting ourselves up as best we could. I'm not sure if you know much about history, but things don't work out too well when the people with all the power have no checks and balances or accountability.

"But look at us come along and fuck your shit right up. And what are you thinking now? What would be great for us if is they could give them to us so we can continue to do what we were doing."

There was a very long pause in the conversation.

"I get it. And I didn't think you're here to play besties anyway. For the record, I'm not sure history tells maybe better stories about revolutions," said Patrick.

"I beg to differ," said Terry.

"Look, we all know you're loaded. How about we start talking about what it's going to take to get everyone here to walk away from this?" said Patrick.

"You've really opened yourself up to compromise over the last… well, 23 seconds."

As Terry spoke, he removed a sidearm from inside his coat, checked it was loaded, then slid it across the floorboards to where Andrew was standing. The pistol bumped his shoes as it came to a stop, then Terry gestured Andrew to pick it up while looking down the barrel of his rifle.

"We are going to be stronger if we're all alive and working as one," said Patrick.

"Less mouths to feed will make the food last longer," said Terry. "Although it's touching to know working together is suddenly now important for you."

"Cut the shit Terry. Let's end this."

Terry had found a notepad laying nearby. He picked it up, pulled a pen from his pocket and wrote in it.

"I am ending this," he said, before sliding it to Andrew.

Andrew inhaled deeply before opening the notepad to read the words. Every sense told him to brace for the words and their implications.

Kill them if you want to live.

###

###

CHAPTER 34:
MAYHEM

Asim and I had climbed to the roof as Patrick's men neared where Terry's injured soldier lay in wait out by the front gate of George House. We had skirted along the backside of a theatre until it met a low ledge. From our perch we climbed to a platform, which led us to another short climb to a building roof at the back. We rounded the back of the theatre and headed via the rooftop to a view over the Parade, almost directly opposite George House. Not only did we now have the best view of what was about to unfold, we were away from the side street where a smaller group of Patrick's men would soon be doubling back.

The injured man must've sensed the enemy getting close. Whether he heard them I'm not sure, but he had the presence of mind to remove his sunglasses and sink them in the ash in such a way he was using the lens reflection to monitor the advancing enemy.

I don't think Patrick's men were aware of his presence, judging by the way they were advancing. In all the ways the injured guy was outnumbered, he did have that advantage.

You could see his hands on the rifle, the weapon angled in readiness for attack. He sat as still as he could, focused on his breathing and with his eyes on the reflection.

While the set-up to the moment seemed to take forever to transpire, when things escalated again, it all seemed to play out so fucking fast.

It was all triggered by a number of shots fired in quick succession, none of which came from anything playing out in front of Claire, Asim and I on the Parade.

"George House?" Claire whispered.

"Not sure," said Asim. "Those shots sounded different, echoed differently. Outside maybe?"

"Out the back perhaps," I said. "I saw a few of Patrick's men headed that way."

Back on street level on the Parade, the sound of firing halted the advance of Patrick's back-up. The one who was the leader held up his two-way with one hand and gave the others a stop signal with the other.

He stood like that for several seconds before putting the two-way to his mouth. "Lucas, was that you?"

He never got to hear the response. Terry's injured raider took the moment of hesitation and confusion to launch his own attack. Leaning around the corner, he sprayed round after round into Patrick's men. The men scattered or fell. Screams rang out.

After those who could run for more cover did so, four bodies remained in the middle of the Parade. Two were not moving. Blood-covered ash was everywhere.

Terry's man attacked again, this time with a little more confidence. He leaned out further from his cover and searched out fleeing targets.

That's when I saw three of Patrick's crew coming up the street from the other direction. They were obviously the ones who had circled through the side streets to come out where we had been positioned a few minutes earlier. They had since crossed the Parade to the George House side and were nearing the ground to the gate and the injured man.

He was completely ignorant to the new threat closing in on him. The man in front had a pistol, the other two cricket bats.

"What do we do?" I whispered.

"Jesus, is that Craig?" said Claire.

Sure, his head was covered in a beanie, he was wearing a camo colour palette I'd never seen before and my eyes were too busy absorbing a thousand other things but, once I was tuned in, I recognised his gait in a second.

*

The sound of gunshots flowed through the second storey of George House. Terry maintained his gun's aim at Andrew, signalling to his team that he thought the shots came from the rear of the building. He received a round of nods, then refocused.

Andrew's face twisted, tears welled in his eyes and he slowly shook his head. "Please don't make me do this," he mouthed.

"Here's what's going to happen," said Terry to Patrick and his men. "I'm going to send your old mate…"

He looked at Andrew. "What's your fucking name again?"

"Andrew."

"I'm going to send your good old buddy Andrew back in there. You're going to give him your weapons and he's going to bring them to me. Once we've done that, perhaps we can have a bit of a chat about how we all get through this in one piece."

He smiled before turning his focus back to Andrew. "Kill them," he mouthed.

"Lucas, was that you?"

The call across the two-way could be heard from devices on both sides of the door.

The silence that followed was an eerie one. People were preparing their last stands with silent gestures.

Seconds later, gunfire sounded out from the back of the building before more rounds sounded out from the Parade as Terry's injured follower unloaded on Patrick's approaching crew. Inside, Terry took a deep breath while he focused his thoughts. Then he looked at the woman in his team and gestured with hand signals to go and see what was happening on the street.

"Roger that, Lucas here," came the response over the two-way. "Took out the guy at the back door – the coast is clear. Repeat: the coast is clear. Hope everyone is OK."

It was Patrick's team that had flanked from the north.

Everyone on both sides heard the statement. And while there may have been varieties of interpretation depending on certain understandings, it didn't matter from an action in the moment perspective.

Within a handful of seconds there was the sound of a door creak from Patrick's side of the door, then a whispered swear word, then the sounds of the survivors fleeing for their lives.

"Fuck!" said Terry. "After them!"

Then eyes fell on the problem between the damaged door and the escaping enemy – an armed and confused Andrew. He was stuck in no-man's land – angry and panicked.

"Drop the gun then drop to the floor, or help us chase them," said Terry.

There was a look in his eyes that had Terry and the others on high alert with weapons raised.

"We really need to go," said Terry. "I'm going to give you one more chance to—"

Andrew fell to the floor, the impact on his head forcing his body to land on his back. Blood flowed from a hole near the side of his nose, just under his eye.

"Changed my mind mid sentence," said Terry. "Let's go!"

*

"Get ready out back, we're coming," said Patrick through the two-way.

A group of three of Patrick's men received the call metres from the rear entry of George House that connected to the laneway carpark. The body of one of Terry's fighters lay metres from them. Dead before he had heard the group sneak up from the back fence.

Lucas held the two-way in his hand. It was still shaking from all he'd seen and all he'd heard transpire while nearby but out of sight. He surveyed the area. "I don't trust the laneway, I think we're best climbing back over the fence."

He didn't get any opposing views from the other two men in his team – as good as wax sealed approval at the moment.

"Right, you head up the alleyway. Just to where it turns. Stay in the shadows," he said before turning to the other. "Open the door and wait for bossman."

Both nodded.

Lucas turned to the one he'd directed to the door and handed over his pistol. "Take this. Don't leave until Patrick and the others are out. If you cop any heat, use it."

Once again they nodded that they were on the same page.

"I'll be waiting by the fence. Send them to me. We need to be over and out of here in less than a minute."

*

Inside the door, another of Terry's men lay on the ground. This one was alive. Unharmed. In fact, Patrick's men were completely unaware of his presence. He was huddled over in a small storage area at the bottom of the stair bay, barely obscured by some gated maintenance equipment. He trembled as he heard the three men outside make plans that would in all likelihood expose him. He tucked his rifle under his arm and used his opposite hand to aim it at the door. His shaking finger toyed lightly with the trigger and he tried to control his breathing.

*

On the Parade side of the building, Asim, Claire and I watched three of Patrick's men continue to sneak up on the injured man from his blind side.

"Wait, whose side are we on here?" said Claire.

"Neither," I said. "The winners… maybe."

"Look at where we are, look at our weapons," Claire said. "We can have a say in who that is."

"Craig is out there," I said.

"I'm not saying shoot Craig, but if his side wins we're fucked."

"Fuck," I said.

I just remember hoping and praying the universe would give me an answer before I had to make a decision, because the only decision I could make after getting involved was who to aim at and when to pull the trigger. That trigger was not a position my finger felt at ease with.

"What if we put a warning shot in front of the—"

Claire's words were stopped in their tracks by a crack of gunfire echoing its way from the street to our ears. By the time it hit us, we already knew the source, Terry's injured soldier felled by a shot to the back of his neck. He fell forward, no part of his body resisting the face-first impact with the ash-covered ground.

Seconds later another series of bullets impacted the fallen and bloodied body.

"Boom!" cried the man at the front, before fist pumping his success, then turning to Craig and the others in his group.

I don't know what hit me in the moment most. The shot in the back of an unaware man, the cheap celebration or Craig being involved. Perhaps it was watching on as our world turned to shit in real time around us. But none of that mattered, what happened next did. I fired my rifle. I fired it at the fist-pump man. And I hit him.

Did I add to the layers of fucked-up shit already exploding around us? Yep. Am I proud? No. Would I take it back? Every. Single. Time.

But that's not how the end of the world works, it seems. It's supposed to be navigated without the usual psychological processes – no emotion, no self-reflection, no guilt. Just do things. If you survive, work out a way to cope until you're faced with the next thing. Step and repeat down the vortex spiral of your humanity.

The impact dropped his legs from underneath him and he screamed in pain.

It didn't take long for scanning eyes to work out the rough direction of the shot and find us on the rooftop across the road.

They all looked up, all of them. I locked eyes with Craig for what seemed like an eternity. At least it felt like we locked eyes. Either way, I couldn't deal with the consequences of being recognised and I dropped behind the rooftop cover.

Then a few shots headed our way. Claire and Asim returned fire. With our longer-range weapons and the completely dominant location advantage, the now official enemy were soon scurrying for safety.

That's when another shot fizzed its way through the airspace above the Parade and a sickening gushing impact sounded out in my ear.

I knew one of the other two had been hit. My stomach knotted as a spray of blood landed on my arm and torso.

I screamed.

I saw Asim hit the galvanised iron roofing, seeking cover, as Claire's body slow motioned backwards. Her head had been struck.

Claire! Fucking, fucking, fuck! Claire!

The sound. I'll never forget the sound. It's one of the things people never tell you to expect when in close proximity to death, especially that kind of death. The sound of the impact – there will never be a time that won't haunt me. The sickening deep penetration of a foreign object, flesh being ripped apart, bullet hitting bone, fluid jettisoning from entry and exit points – all of it warped together into one gush of noise that comes from nowhere and leaves you in shock at its power. Then another more gut-wrenching shock as you realise why those noises combined and try to deal with the reality of who they happened to.

You just don't really process any of it. But, that fucking noise, you never unhear it. Ever.

I was over by her side in a second, trying to find hope, a reason or any angle that would lead me to believe she would be OK. There were none.

She didn't die straight away. Although I truly believe her last moment of awareness happened a nanosecond before being struck. Whatever was left of her fought against the fatal blow. The side of her face was, well, not her any more. Her mouth opened at a strange angle as she fought to take quick shallow breaths.

That, too, will stay with me.

I just stroked her hair and said "It's OK," over and over.

Maybe she heard some of my words there somewhere.

But it wasn't OK. Not for Asim, not for me and definitely not for Claire.

Already the ramifications were hitting home. What if I hadn't taken a shot? Maybe Terry's lookout across the road would never have seen us? Maybe Claire would still be here.

It took perhaps three minutes for Claire to pass. I held her tight as her breathing became more infrequent and shallower, and I held tighter when it didn't come any more.

Then I cried.

Asim held onto me. He didn't say anything, just let me go through whatever I needed to go through. We weren't in a battlezone for those lost minutes. I'm not even sure we were existing at all. Just teleported to some other time and universe where there was just corrugated roofing and overwhelming pain. Whatever or wherever it was, we weren't in our reality.

###

###

CHAPTER 35:
ONLY ROOM FOR ONE

"Hurry up," screamed Terry as he and his crew chased their way to the back of the building, dodging filing cabinets and whatever else Patrick and his fellow runaways had tipped over in their wake.

"Through here!" said one of his chargers, opening a door into a side corridor.

The others were through in seconds, the stairwell door greeting them only metres ahead.

Terry gave the shush gesture as he toed his way toward the door, ears on high alert. He paused at the door, listening out for any clues as to what might lie on the other side.

One of the others made a walking down stairs gesture with his pointer and index fingers. Terry nodded back before readying his weapon and putting his hand on the door handle.

As he did, a burst of shots echoed up the stairwell. Then another and another. Then panicked screams, pained screams and returning fire met the noise. Terry's trapped fighter at the bottom of the stairwell had opened fire on Patrick and his men from close range. The attack lasted until the end of his life a few seconds later.

The sounds of skirmish echoed into nothingness.

"Is that Patrick?" said Terry.

"I think so," said one of his underlings. "Sounds hurt. I think they're trying to get him out of there."

"Agreed," said Terry as he clicked the handle and eased through the door as quietly as possible.

Not quietly enough, as it turned out.

"Hurry up!" said someone. "They're coming."

Terry led the way, hitting the stairs by feel and looking for targets through his rifle's sight as he went.

"Hurry!" yelled Patrick.

The comment was followed by a couple of rounds from his pistol.

One of the rounds clipped the metal stair railing near Terry. The tinking noise echoed up and down the concrete stairwell chamber. Terry didn't miss a step as he continued his descent.

"Pull!" came one of the voices from downstairs. It was Kyle, the cop.

This almost gave away how dire the situation was for Patrick and his team at the base of the stairwell. The door down there was still open and streaming in light from the outside. Not only that, if they were able to leave they would've already.

"One more," said Kyle. It was followed by a few grunts and a thud. "Go, go, go!" he added before another series of shots were fired up the stairwell.

Then things darkened as the door at ground level closed just as Terry rounded the landing on level one, four of his team close behind. "Hurry!" he said, despite his hobbling older body slowing the pace for those behind him.

Shortly after he rounded the landing he had to step over a body, his foot nearly slipping in the blood. There was another body slumped up against the bottom of the staircase and another laying just short of the exit door. None of them were Patrick. He did recognise one as a member of his crew.

Terry swore, then readied his rifle and his fortitude as he prepared to head outside into whatever awaited. He paused for a moment before the distant sounds of struggle prompted him to push the door open with a flurry. At least, that was the plan. A weight was pressed up against the other side. He called the others over to help him push. It took several seconds to get the door open enough to pass through.

Terry was the first to pass through, another body greeted him on the other side.

Before he could get a visual on the entire battle space, bullets pounded into the wall behind him. He didn't flinch, scanning the environment until he saw the threat. At the back of the car park, a man huddled by the trunk of a tree, firing on him. Nearby, three others tried to lift a fourth man over the fence. The man was injured.

It was Patrick.

A voice sounded out on the two-way radio network everyone was connected to. "Attack!"

*

On the Parade side of the building things were eerily quiet. I was still lost in a moment in time with Claire's body in my arms. Asim soothed my shaking body as best he could but the enormity of it all was too much for me or us to take.

Claire – she had survived the end of the world – we had survived together. And we had a lot of surviving ahead still to do. That was the assumption, but I guess that was based on pre-12/4 conditions. If I needed any more evidence of how much the world had changed, I had it. I definitely didn't need it, but I had it.

That was just one of the thoughts going through my head at that moment. Grief for losing one of the few people that made this whole fucked-up thing tolerable. Grief for the loss of someone who connected me back to before the world changed. Guilt at the guns – just everything and anything to do with the guns. Guilt at letting her come. Guilt at firing into the battle space and exposing our location. Dread at wondering how in the fuck I would tell the others about this – tell Alex.

Above it all one thought was stuck in my mind and I couldn't let it go. From the moment the world had turned to shit until… this, I hadn't asked her once about how she felt about what had happened to her parents. Not once! I felt so guilty about it, I felt nauseous.

"I'm sorry," I said over and over again.

I held on tight to her body, knowing that while I did so I didn't have to deal with all the other shit that would overwhelm me the second I let go.

I just let the tears flow.

Somewhere on the other side of George House the gunfire continued in sporadic bursts. Then it hit all at once. Rounds sounding out near and far in all the tones and tempo of gunfire – a symphony of horrors playing out on the Parade.

For my part, at that moment, I shut down. I stayed in my embrace with Claire's body, now even more scared of the world I would face when I let go than seconds earlier.

Asim kissed me on the head before getting up to take a look over the edge. "The group the dead guy scattered is advancing again. They're firing on the chick who… the one on lookout at George House. Fuck, this is going to be carnage."

*

Terry released an empty clip and replaced it with another – his last. While he did, the others in his posse stepped from the door and continued to unload bullets on Patrick and the others near the fence.

Terry raised his arm to cease fire and the rain of bullets stopped. As their echoes faded to reveal more gunfire further away, four bodies lay slumped at the end of the car park.

"Boom!" said one of Terry's crew. "We did it!"

"Fuck, I think you're right," said Terry. "Was it ever in doub—"

Terry screamed in pain as a bullet hit him in the leg. As he did, one of his crew fell to the ground, blood spraying from a neck impact. The remainder of the team dropped to the floor as their attention switched to the small group of Patrick's men firing from the top of the alleyway.

The firing started up again, Terry's team countering this time with their heavier weapons.

One of Patrick's men was downed in the initial foray. His screams replaced Terry's in the air, behind the noise the sound of the others arguing about their next move could be heard. Did they stay or retreat?

Terry had one hand pressed against the wound in his leg to limit the bleeding. With the other hand he signalled his crew to advance.

They exchanged hand signals about how to approach the corner, then crouch moved forward.

Seconds later one of Patrick's men moved his head out of cover to get an updated assessment on the threat – it was Craig. He was fired on and pulled back to safety, heart racing at the near miss. "They're coming! Fall back!"

Seconds later he sprinted across the alleyway to the Parade side of the street, a trail of bullets failing to catch him on the way through. As the sounds of gunfire dulled down, Terry's crew could hear the sounds of retreating footsteps and the call came to advance.

The first was at the corner recently held by Patrick's team in seconds. He readied his gun and courage before exposing his head and weapon to the unknown. He saw the last of them scurry around the corner back on to the Parade and fired a few unsuccessful rounds into their direction. Then he turned back to the two others who had followed him and called them to advance.

*

That skirmish spilled back out onto the Parade seconds later. Craig and Patrick's other guy came sprinting around the corner, headed west towards George House once more. They stuck to the footpath where the ash was lowest and there was sporadic shopfront and verandah protection, but the goal seemed to be to make it back to George House where the garden space out front offered a place with enough cover to mount a defence.

Unfortunately, the woman from Terry's crew with the rifle still held the territory. She had Patrick's attackers coming from the west pinned down by the wall at the corner of the front garden.

It was at that point Terry's men rounded the corner in pursuit, bullets soon ringing out once more on the Parade.

With the help of the pinned-down crew, Craig and the other guy figured out they were headed into trouble before they ran completely exposed into the riflewoman's firing range. Instead, they skidded to the ground to make a smaller target for the attackers from beyond, then fired back from their prone positions.

This stopped Terry's group in their tracks, also dropping to prone. It was the same for Patrick's pinned-down group – everyone on the Parade was now scrounging around for whatever they could use for cover. That included bodies of the fallen.

*

"Breathe," said Yamato. "Nice and easy, in and out."

His hand was on Sara's back, hoping his soothing strokes of reassurance would match the tone of his words. "You know, I think the fighting might've stopped. I haven't heard anything for a few minutes."

"That's the third time you've said that!" said Sara through laboured breaths. "Don't jinx it again."

He nodded his agreement and his eyes fell on the line-up of everyone's belongings. A mishmash of bags ready to be hauled in whichever direction life would take them if they had to bug out. That was the term for it, he was told.

He studied his daughter, more than a little concerned with how her body would cope with everything involved in finding a new home right now.

"I'll be OK, you know," she said, seeing right through his attempted poker face concern. Despite the words, there was a doubt in her tone of voice, struggle in her eyes.

"I know," he said. "Let's just hope it doesn't come to that. Any minute, Zoe is going to come through the door and tell us Terry has won and everything is fine."

At that moment the front door opened. Yamato shared a smile of anticipation with his daughter. There was a minor disappointment when Billy revealed himself, but that was quickly replaced by a deeper concern when they saw the look on his face.

Billy just stared at them for a minute before the words fell out. "He's completely fucked us!"

Yamato and Sara exchanged a confused look. "Who?" said Yamato.

"Terry! Fucker took the weapons."

Yamato and Sara weren't catching up quick enough to the gravity of the situation for Billy's liking. "He swiped the weapons from where we stashed them. Moved them somewhere else. With his other crew no doubt."

"That fucker," said Alex.

She was holding Jacob in one arm, a rifle slung over her shoulder in the other. "So, what? He's completely betrayed us. Restashed the cache, armed his other group and has now just done what he'd been talking about all along."

"Pretty much," said Keira as she came through the door, leading Charlie, Liv and Em. "Feel used yet?"

"Dirty," said Alex. "So, are we going to walk-of-shame our way out of this place or what?"

"Not until we hear from Zoe's group," said Yamato.

*

"Not sure what's gone on out the back, but it looks like a nil-all draw out here," said Asim.

I heard the words and the change in firing pattern that had led up to them, but I couldn't find my own words to respond.

"Must be running low on ammo out there," said Asim a short while later.

"I reckon we'd be the only group with just about all our ammo left," he said, by now surely aware he was having a one-way conversation.

"You know, it would only take a word for me to change this thing altogether," he said. "A word from you to me like, say, Terry… or Patrick."

It was all too much for me. I already felt sick about why I was doing what I was doing at that moment, I was in no position to double down. But I was also hiding and I knew it.

"I know you're dealing with some serious shit back there," said Asim. "I'm not here to say I understand or I can make it better or anything. But right now – like, right this fucking moment – the history of the Parade is being written in front of us.

"We're already into this thing up to our eyeballs, Zoe. Don't give away our voice in this history now. Not after all we've been through."

"What are you saying?" I said.

"I'm talking about writing history instead of letting it just happen to us again. History tells me if we don't seize this moment to be a player in it, we'll just be well, cast in the same shit roles people like you and me are always cast in."

I looked at him, studied him. At that moment we were operating at a level where you needed a whole lot of knowledge of a person to be able to trust them – their truth, their words, the intent of their plans, their desire to execute and a million other things you couldn't gain from knowing someone long enough to run on hunches.

My intuition trusted the expression he gave me back, but that was a long way back from the data I would've preferred to act on.

He gave me a nod. "Let's write ourselves into this future," he said.

"I have my pen at the ready," he said as he held up his gun. "Team Terry? Team Patrick?"

###

###

CHAPTER 36:
TERRY OR PATRICK

In some fucked-up way I knew what Asim was saying was right. Like, on more levels that I was prepared to admit on what people are like and capable of and what it takes to truly survive that as a decision-maker, not a pawn. That's just our shitty world, scaled up many fold on this shitty situation. And I was so overleveraged on decisions that will haunt me until they day I die, I had no fucking fear of adding another one to the list.

My decision was an easy one to make in the end.

But just as the words reached my lips there was more commotion across the street.

A burst of rifle fire was followed by someone yelling out for all to hear.

"Alrighty fuckers, put your fucking guns down, right fucking now."

There was no mistaking Terry's voice. I exchanged a confused look with Asim, left Claire's safe embrace and headed to the edge of the building to see what was happening.

He was hard to miss. He was standing on top of the three-story tower at the front of George House. The parapets adding to the medieval vibes of a landscape that had been taken back several hundred years in technology in a few days already.

The guns were the exception to the rule. One – Terry's pistol – was pressed against Patrick's head.

"Guns down now, or fatty gets it."

You could see Terry favouring one side as he winced through his words. You could also see Patrick was in a far worse state. The sight of the pair of them up on the building's pinnacle was just something to behold. Two huge men. One seemingly impossible vantage point. It was just such a shocking entrance to the Parade side of the skirmish that you could do nothing other than watch on.

"How the fuck did they get up there?" whispered Asim.

"Not sure," I whispered. "But I have the feeling one of them is not coming down in one piece."

Asim nodded.

What we hadn't seen while everyone's attention was focused on staying alive at street level, was Terry's two helpers aiding the injured men from the back carpark, up three flights of stairs to the prominent vantage point in the building.

The effort was herculean in itself, let alone what they had endured to get to that point. While Terry's two helpers headed back downstairs to flank Patrick's men positioned to the west of the building, Terry began his rant.

Whatever my thoughts on what transpired that day, both before and after, I will never forget that moment. Terry was shot. He also probably had a dozen ways he could've finished the battle which would have made it easier for him.

But this wasn't about just winning a battle, as I realise now. This was about so much more. And his presence, in complete control of Patrick and the situation in such an eye-popping location was just... I'm not fully sure how to say it – part leadership – real leadership, part show, part stunt, part statement. Even those words fall short. He transformed a pivotal moment in our history to a fuck-off statement piece and he had the attention of everyone along the strip.

Soon his flanking crew had made their presence known to Patrick's fighters on the west side. It was at that moment everyone knew the game was up.

"Now fuckers!" said Terry.

The weapons dropped in quick succession.

The Parade had been conquered from within.

"Good decision," said Terry.

All eyes were fixed on the tower expectantly.

There was some sort of crazy in Terry at that moment. Perhaps it was the exhilaration of victory or the endorphins of battle. Maybe it was just a power trip. Whatever the case, the guy who made the effort to make a big location statement was clearly expected to make more.

Everyone knew it.

And Terry knew they knew.

"I just want to make this change of management official."

As soon as he said that, he pressed Patrick's head over the edge of the parapets. He didn't receive much resistance, with Patrick seemingly struggling to cling on to consciousness as it was. Then he fired the pistol.

The action produced a modest noise, in comparison to some of the weapons, and a modest visual jolt of Patrick's head. But the result was all the same. After a few grunts of exertion, Terry had leveraged the rest of Patrick's body far enough that gravity had more of a hold on him than the parapet of George House and his body went on a short flight to the ground.

The thud of impact was as gut churning as the silence that followed.

Everyone waited for the next move. No one was as fully invested in that as Patrick's crew, who now surely realised their demises were, in all likelihood, imminent.

"Line the rest of 'em up," said Terry. "I'll be down in a minute."

###

###

CHAPTER 37:
IN DECISION

It was a weird moment. It was an end but it wasn't. The fighting had stopped for now, but what did that even mean? And what was going to happen to Patrick's crew. Or us? And Claire. Fuck.

I took in my lofted view of the Parade for another minute as I let it all wash over me. The strip of street out front of George House looked a mess. Bodies lay everywhere. Windows were blown out and shop fronts and verandahs had been destroyed. It looked like what it had been – a warzone.

I had no thoughts around what all that meant at that point in time, only that me playing a part in it would be something that would stay with me for a long, long time. While there would be plenty of time to start that process soon enough, this was still a time for making battle decisions.

The fighting may have been over, but Norwood had just been reborn – again – and that change would need me to make the sort of battle decisions that would protect and keep my people alive.

That meant dealing with Terry.

And none of any of the above mattered to me as I turned, shared a silent hug with Asim, then went about the task of getting Claire's body off the roof.

###

###

CHAPTER 38:
DEAL

Asim and I had found a piece of corrugated iron in the rubble that fit the bill as a makeshift gurney to transport Claire's body to – well, we hadn't worked that bit out yet. We were headed in the general direction of our new accommodation – a place she spent one night.

We removed her jacket and used it to cover her face.

As we neared George House, the people of the Parade were now moving forward to help the injured and deal with the deceased. It was all done under the direction of Terry's surviving fighters, now unequivocally in charge.

That in itself was a shift in everything. It was a complete change of the social order of, well, all things. None of which my mind was capable of thinking about at that moment, but I could embrace the unmistakable scent of more change in the air.

I saw Craig as he was getting his hands tied behind his back by someone I didn't recognise. He saw me as we passed. Judging by the look on his face he recognised the body as Claire's. At the very least he recognised the look on my face as one of defeat, even in what could be considered a victory.

He mouthed an apology to me. I looked past him without reacting then he lowered his vision to the ground. I had even less time to dedicate to Anita as she came running up the street screaming after him. When she looked at me I just stared through her.

We were soon passing by George House, where most of the carnage had taken place. Clusters of people surrounded the injured and dead. Some began the migration west – in the direction of the medical centre, the centre of the Parade and the rest of the population. Other groups soon borrowed our gurney idea, using parts of destroyed shop fronts and verandahs to carry the fallen west.

There was a commotion at the main doors to George House as we passed. Terry made his way out of the building, assisted by two of his people. He took in the scene that confronted him, but it didn't take long for him to lock eyes on me.

"Zoe!"

He held his hand up for me to stop while he caught up.

I felt my stomach churn and that was before I noticed that one of the people carrying him was the woman who had killed Claire. By that point my stomach was trying to escape my body via my throat.

I exchanged a glance with Asim and knew he recognised her as well. We silently agreed to obey Terry's request.

All the options of what could transpire hit me as we waited for Terry to hobble the ten or so metres to us. At that point in time, if he'd cast us as the enemy and decided we were going to go the same way as Patrick and his people, well, I would not have cared. Not one single bit.

I was every bit as culpable as everyone else who had battled in and around George House that day. The guns! Fuck! Being involved in adding an arsenal of weapons to this world – that was on me. Firing into the battle – me. Hell, I was walking back to my people on the Parade with so much new baggage I would need an entirely new compartment in my brain to deal with what had happened since 12/4!

A quick end from Terry or the woman who killed Claire didn't seem so bad in the circumstances.

Terry soon reached us. We stood there for a while, looking at each other through a new lens.

I shared a look with the woman as well. It was enough to let me know she knew who was on the gurney and under the jacket and how they got there. No sign of remorse was shown. No sign of anything aside from a glare of determination in the moment. Deal with it was the vibe I got.

I turned my attention back to Terry.

"We did it," he said, eventually.

No emotion, no celebration, just three words.

"We did," I said.

Then he nodded to those supporting his body weight and he hobbled west with their support. We sat in the wake of the moment for a few moments, then followed.

*

If the activity on the battle space was overwhelming, it was dwarfed by the comings and goings at the nearby medical centre. We watched Terry enter as we continued down the Parade. It was frantic inside with people rushing about, the yelling of instructions and screams of pain. The place looked like its own separate war zone.

Asim and I pulled Claire's body further down the street. We were soon near the intersection where the town hall stood. The crowd was thick with onlookers watching goings on up the street. They formed a wall at the intersection as if there were some hidden police barrier to hold them back – but there was no barrier, there wasn't even a policeman any more. News was also being ferried back to them. The realisation had hit that Patrick was dead. It spread like a shockwave. The ramifications were different for each person. So, there they stood on the border of the action. It was like they felt that if they took one more step forward they would be too involved and if they took a step back they wouldn't have any idea what was going on.

It left a distaste in my mouth watching them. The court of the king. They didn't even truly care about who was the king. As long as they were in the court. Close enough to be dragged through all the end of world survival stuff, far enough away not to own any new scars from what it took to get there.

We just walked right at the middle of the wall of people, right along the heart of the Parade. It must've been ten deep. They stared at Asim and I. We just stared back. They stared at the body of Claire.

We were almost on top of them when they pushed out a little corridor that would allow us to pass.

We had just pressed through to the other side when I saw the rest of my crew. Leading the change was Yamato, holding Sara, who was gasping for breath. It was bad.

We looked at them. They looked at us.

There were no words to say.

I turned back to the people in the crowd. "Keep that corridor open!" I screamed. "Emergency."

Yamato and Sara reached us and we processed each other's truths with a nod of respect before he ushered his daughter through the small gap in the wall of people.

The next face I saw was Alex's.

She looked at me with an expression I'll never forget. It was then that I lost it. Every strength I needed to get through to that moment broke down. I squeezed her in an embrace and wailed.

###

225

###

CHAPTER 39:
AFTERMATH

Yamato patted the thin film of sweat off his daughter's forehead. They sat in the middle of the mayhem that was the waiting room at the medical centre. Blood covered the chairs and floor. The injured lined the corridors, people barked out instructions, others called for help and others ferried equipment. It was chaos.

Sara's eyes spoke of someone losing awareness of the here and now.

"Everything's going to be alright," said Yamato as he gently stroked her head.

He could see the panic in her eyes as her lungs screamed at her to breathe fully and completely – the one thing they were incapable of doing.

He saw someone scurry past in blue scrubs.

"Excuse me…"

It was too late. The woman ignored him as she carried out whatever mission she was on.

"Someone will be with us shortly," he said.

He saw another person in scrubs on the move past his chair. This time he grabbed the man's arm. "Excuse me, my daughter needs your help. It's an emergency."

"I… I… I'm an accountant," said the man.

"Why are you wearing scrubs?"

"I'm trying to help."

Yamato stared at him, horrified.

"There's only two doctors," the man said. "Neither of them are surgeons. A handful of nurses, a vet… and yeah, that's why I'm helping."

Yamato squeezed the man's arm harder. "I need oxygen. It's an emergency."

The man looked in the direction he was headed. Then sighed heavily.

Yamato pulled the man into him and whispered into his ear. "She is going to die if you don't help us."

The man pulled himself away. "OK, OK!" He brushed himself off. "I'll see what I can do."

He then rushed off to carry out whatever task he was already on.

Yamato turned to Sara again.

She looked up at him, showing more awareness than she had since their arrived at the medical centre. "I'm scared," she said.

"Me too," said Yamato. "But everything's going to be alright."

At that moment Asim arrived at their side. He nodded to Yamato as he took in the chaos of the waiting rooms.

"What are you doing here?" said Yamato.

"Helping my family," said Asim. "What's going on? What can I do to help?"

"We nee—"

A gunshot ripped through the space. Everyone turned to see a woman pointing a pistol at the ceiling. Asim recognised her immediately as the one with Terry. "Can I get some fucking help right now?"

The room fell quiet.

"For fuck's sake, Terry is hurt!"

After another bout of silence she stormed out of the space, heading into the medical rooms.

"This is insane," said Asim.

"We aren't getting anywhere, if we could just get—"

The man in the scrubs was back by their side. "I got these."

Yamato looked at the medication.

"Doc said it was the strong stuff."

"Thank you. She's already taken that, but I'll try more," said Yamato. "I think we need oxygen."

The man nodded. "If you give me a few minutes I can see wher—"

"You!"

They all looked up to see the woman with the gun standing over them, eyes on the man with the scrubs.

"I need you to help me right now."

"But... I'm just—"

"I don't give a fuck, follow me."

She accentuated her point with the aim of her weapon.

The man put his arms up and head down then stood up. Soon the two were on their way to Terry.

Yamato sat speechless in their wake.

"Oxygen you say?" said Asim.

Yamato nodded his head.

"Leave it with me," said Asim, before he disappeared into the chaos that had already replaced the silence of seconds earlier.

Yamato turned to his daughter. "I love you."

"I love you," came Sara's weak response.

"Your mum would've been very proud of the woman you are turning into."
*

Alex had taken over from Asim in helping me pull the gurney. In our wake, Keira held Jacob and those not at the medical centre followed us back to our new home.

No one said a word.

We were soon inside and sitting in a circle around Claire's body.

No one had asked me questions, just given me support and something to drink until I was ready to talk.

"He won," I said eventually. "This place is now Terry's. Everything is Terry's."

I looked at each of my new friends in turn. It was a look that shared how deep we were now connected in everything. A look that said here's where my trust lies in this world.

"He's cool with us, by the way. So, we don't have to flee or anything."

"So, what are we going to do?" said Keira.

"We wait for the others, then we bury Claire," I said.
*

"...you see the colours on your swimmers there. Now look at your mum's bikini. Same palette. Always the same," said Yamato.

He was looking at the photo salvaged from their house in the aftermath of the tsunami. The only physical reminder of a life no more. "I remember this trip because it was the first time she started to feel sick.

"So this photo always reminded me of our transition. It had happened, we just didn't realise it yet. We went from the family in this image to a family that cared for Akemi.

"Her smile always came with her, but things were never the same.

"In one way you could say the moment in this photo was as far down the line as we came to living the dream."

He wiped a tear from his eyes, then studied Sara. Her eyes were barely in the moment, her breathing shallow. He sniffed in more tears and returned his focus to the photo.

"At least that is the version of the dream you're raised to think is how it's all going to work out.

"Sometimes that doesn't happen. And it's then you realise the dream isn't what you thought it was going to be. The dream is what happened. Even when it delivered hurt. Even when you lose forever things, forever people, forever love. All of it was the dream. It was the dream when it happened and it was the dream when you could think back and relive it.

"The fact that it happened at all. That was the dream."

He looked back at Sara through wet eyes and saw a truth he already felt. Her breathing had stopped, her lips blue. Tears consumed him as he wrapped her up in his arms and held her close.

There they stayed, an oasis of peace in the mayhem of the waiting room. Somewhere lost in the dream.

After a couple of minutes Asim skidded to a halt by their side. "Got some, it's connected to this mask so we—"

He stood with an oxygen cylinder in hand looking at Yamato. Asim knew before Yamato shook his head.

###

###

CHAPTER 40:
DREAMS

It wasn't long before Asim was opening the door back at our place. Behind him, Yamato cradled the body of his daughter.

As with me, no words were exchanged as he entered the house, just gestures and body language of care and support.

Within the hour we had decided how we would honour our kind.

We headed out to the Parade as a group of twelve, in body, for the last time. We headed west, passed under the tsunami line until we reached the oval. It didn't take long to find the equipment in the groundsperson's shed we needed to bury our loved ones. Then we dug. After removing enough ash to reach the pavers beneath we discovered a plaque on the ground – a monument to local war hero Captain Lionel Matthews.

We repositioned our dig a respectful distance away and started over.

Soon, the bodies of Claire Byrne and Sara Mochizuki were returned to the ground. Asim had carved wooden markers with their name, age and birth and death dates. Underneath each was a single word – dreams.

After hearing Yamato tell the story of his daughter's passing and remembering Claire's connection to The Forest of Dreams sign in the city, it seemed the only thing to do.

They were laid to rest near another sign – the words Mateship & Memory out front of the Parade oval providing a fitting backdrop to those we would love forevermore.

###

###

CHAPTER 41:
DISTORT

Life is beautiful. Life is brutal.

If I keep distilling back that period of time, those are the words I come up with. Life and death, the extremes of humanity, the cosmos itself, how few fucks the universe spares those navigating a life in it, blind fate or destiny or whatever other bullshit interpretation we put on top of it all to make sense of it. All of these things are both beautiful and brutal.

Looking back, it's hard to fully believe that so much transpired in such a short period of time, but it did. I was there and I still find it hard to accept the rapidfire nature of those last few days before 12/4 and the first few days after.

I'd love to say these hard moments were the foundations of happier times ahead, but this was only the beginning of everything that would tell the story of the Parade in the shadows of the end of the world. Such a significant chapter, but just a chapter. Just a series of beautiful and brutal events coming at us in quick time. What happened in those days and moments, what happened between Patrick and Terry, what happened in the things me and my people had their fingerprints all over, would change the fate of almost everyone who survived 12/4 on the Adelaide plains.

It would also shape the future city.

It would also shape us.

Or is that distort us?

###

###
POSTSCRIPT

It was a quiet and soul-searching couple of days that followed the battle for George House. For our part, we kept to our own. The entire group never went east of our home.

Each of us faced the days in their own way. Some sought company, some solitude but, whatever the case, we were doing it away from the rest of the Parade.

It was the second night of solitude when we received our first visitor. The teens were out doing something and the rest of us were dotted throughout the house passing the time and contemplating.

The knock belonged to one of Terry's men. "A town hall has been called for tomorrow morning," he said after I answered the door.

He left as soon as I acknowledged the message.

Alex went to the window to watch his image fade into the ash up the Parade, now falling harder than ever. "A fucking town hall? Are you fucking kidding me?"

"Is our new leader too good to come down and tell us personally?" said Keira.

Alex clicked her fingers and pointed at her. "That! Right there, that. This fucking guy."

Asim and Yamato were heading downstairs after hearing the commotion.

"Did you catch all that?" I asked.

Yamato nodded.

"I think we got the headline," said Asim. "What do you think that's all about?"

"I'll tell you what that's all about," said Alex. "This fucker – who we supported every step of the way – has got his fancy fucking position and is now flipping us the bird from up on high."

"He's no better than Patrick,' said Keira.

"Exactly!" added Alex. "He's exactly the same. Fucking entitled, old, white… cockwomble. Just another fucking fat man. Get rid of one, get another!"

"It's like whack a mole," said Keira.

"Yes!" said Alex. "Whack a man, maybe."

Keira shrugged. "Maybe it works."

"Either way, you can guarantee we're about 24 hours away from having the next step in this apocalypse mansplained to us."

"That I'll pay," said Keira.

Alex nodded her appreciation. "So, what are we going to do about it?"

"Are you kidding?" I said. "We're not getting involved."

Alex stared at me. "What, so just let him do whatever the fuck he wants?"

"Do you not remember what just happened?"

Alex went to speak but no words came out.

"Not only are people we love dead, the new cockwomble ripped us off for an arsenal of weapons! He owns everything. He owns the Parade and he probably owns us," I said.

"Well, that's just fucking great," said Alex. "So, basically you're saying even at the end of the world the same shit people doing the same shit things still own the world?"

"We could do worse than accept it as a truth right now, let's just lay low and—"

That's when the teens came bursting through the front door.

"We found the guns!" said Liv.

"What? What guns?" said Alex.

"The guns. Our guns. The ones Terry took," said Billy.

"Well, not all of them," said Charlie.

"Wait, wait, wait," I said. "Can we slow down and take this from the top?"

Billy cleared his throat. "We've had this little hangout spot at the storage space on Sydenham Rd–"

"What?" said Keira. "What's that all about?"

"Nothing," said Charlie. "We've just hung out there a couple of times. There's room to kick the footy."

"Yeah, yeah, yeah," said Alex. "Get to the guns bit."

Liv looked at the others before talking. "We were just hanging out and we heard some voices headed our way. Anyway, we laid low. And four of Terry's crew came—"

"How could you tell they were Terry's?" I said.

"They were definitely his, I'd recognise them anywhere,' said Billy. "Plus that woman was there."

"Anyway," Liv continued. "They unlocked one of the storage rooms not far from us and took out four of the bags."

"We recognised the bags straight away," said Em. "We knew it was the guns."

"Then what?" asked Alex.

"Well," said Charlie. "They loaded up and left and when the coast was clear we went to check out the locker."

"There's a masterkey in the office," added Liv.

Charlie nodded. "Yeah. Anyway, we checked out the room and, sure enough, the rest of the stash is there."

Keira nodded. "Then you came straight to us, right?"

Charlie opened his mouth to speak, then paused briefly. "Yeah! Eventually."

"What do you mean eventually?" said Keira.

"We may have repositioned them," said Billy.

"Repositioned them?" said Keira. "The weapons? You repositioned the fucking weapons?"

"It was my idea," said Liv. "We didn't have much time to think and we definitely didn't have time to come back here and tell you. So we just took them and put them somewhere else."

"Oh fuck," said Asim.

"Where?" I said. "Is it safe? Did you cover your tracks?"

"We moved them back to the oval," said Em.

"No way they're finding them now," said Charlie.

"And we definitely covered our tracks," said Billy.

"Sorry!" said Liv. "We thought we were doing what you'd want us to do."

"It's not your fault," I said. "And you did the right thing."

Then I exhaled deeply. "Fuck!"

"So, now we have guns," said Alex.

"So now we still have guns," I said.

"Whack a mole?" said Keira.

The End

###

WAR PARADE

APOCALYPSE SURVIVORS

Coming late 2023

Or go back to where it all began...

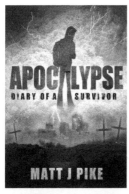

****

Alms for an author

Your reviews matter big-time to this indie author. If you can
post your thoughts on Amazon.com or Goodreads.com
it would be greatly appreciated.

Review on
Amazon

Review on
Goodreads

****

AUTHOR Q&A

#spoiler alert!

Seriously. #spoiler alert!

First of all, welcome back. We thought we'd seen the last of post-apocalyptic Adelaide with the book Apocalypse Diary of a Survivor 4. What made you decide there was more to write about with this world?
Quite honestly, this book was always part of my plans for the series. I just had other stories I wanted and needed to write first (I cowrote a very inappropriate sci-fi comedy adventure – Hart & Sol – with my good friend, the late, great Russell Emmerson and my Zombie RiZing series got a fourth instalment – Dragon's Wrath. If you have kids in the 8-12 range I'd highly recommend). Hopefully readers think the wait was worth it and I promise it won't be so long between drinks next time around. I'm already writing the next instalment!

Does that mean you had plans to write villain origin stories before Hollywood made them so popular?
It's funny you should say that. Because when we were writing the description of the book for sites such as Amazon, my editor and I had some spirited debate about the use of the word 'villains'. She won (she always wins!) but I do think that such a black-and-white description almost always comes down to who the narrator is. After all, no one is ever a villain in their own story! So while the Norwood hubbers were definitely the bad guys in the original ADOAS books, the background of who they were and what they did was never, ever going to be a straight-up case of bad people doing bad things.
But, yes, as readers who have met me at events around Australia and New Zealand pre-Covid will know, the concept for this 'villains' story has been coming together since 2018. It was readers who gave it the green light.

Does that mean we can expect origin stories from the other settlements in the ADOAS series, like TTP, Burnside or Goodwood?
Possibly ;) I also have a couple of killer ideas for standalone stories in the Apocaylpse Survivors universe. Like, seriously killer cool. What I can say is that as long as there's love for this series, I'll keep writing them.

Was it deliberate to choose a woman as the lead character after having a man in the thick of the action for the first four books?
I know there are some people who assumed any Norwood hubbers story would have Terry (AKA the Fat Man in Jack's world) as the central figure. But the idea of Zoe as the lead was part of my thinking while writing the end of the ADOAS books.
I loved the idea of exploring a different perspective on the apocalypse – from a woman, someone who was a little bit older, and who also didn't have the same sense of family as my original hero Jack did.
And, while we see her as a leader of powerful change in that world and a likeable person, we also know she was part of a machine that did some abhorrent things. That journey had the makings of a good series of stories in my eyes.

Speaking of which. We notice you snuck a Jack cameo into this book with your description of comet night. Does that mean we'll be seeing more of him?
I want to say keep reading, but honestly, if you've read the previous ADOAS books (and you have, right? :)) it's pretty obvious he'll have to feature more as the story unfolds, given how significant a role he plays in the creation, development and fight for New Adelaide.

Ohhhh - can't wait to see the final showdown from the other side. But for now, one last question. Why do you have so many books set in Adelaide?
That one's an easy answer. It's because I live here. And when you need to do some research, say like exploring any and all tunnels that might give access from the burbs to the CBD for the purposes of sneaking up on an enemy force (whoops, I've said too much already), it's much easier to do it when you can hit the actual streets yourself to map them out. I actually live among the very streets I write about in the Apocalypse Survivor series, so when I take a break and go for a walk, I'm right where the action is/was. Plus, I like the idea that Adelaide would survive the impact of a comet. If only so that FruChocs could live on (I even made sure the Menz factory was above the tsunami line, because I would not let the world's finest confectionary be destroyed)!

About the author:

Like the legendary R M Williams, Matt was born in Jamestown in rural South Australia. But that's where the remarkable similarities between these two end. While Reginald went from bushman to world renowned millionaire outback clothing designer, Matt is a complete dag who was lured by the city lights of Adelaide. Kindergarten in the big smoke was a culture shock, but it is here he first discovered his love of storytelling.

In high school that love found an outlet in a series of completely unflattering cartoons about fellow students and teachers alike. He survived long enough to further his art into a successful career in multimedia design but, like a zombified leech, the lure of the written word gnawed at him, forcing him to pen his first novel, the award-winning sci-fi comedy epic, Kings of the World. It was followed the next year by Amazon Australia dystopian sci-fi best-seller Apocalypse: Diary of a Survivor. He has now published eleven books and won several international awards for his works.

Matt donates part-proceeds of each book sold to find a cure for Rett Syndrome, a neurological condition the youngest of his three children, Abby, has. As a gorgeous Rett angel, Abby cannot walk, talk or use her hands in a meaningful way. So, not only is each of your book purchases a ticket to fantastically rounded, character driven, hilarious and poignant sci-fi awesomeness, it wraps you in a warm feeling that you've made a difference to people who deserve your help the most. Like the zombified leech it's a no-brainer.

****

More ways to connect:

Facebook.com/
MattJPikeAuthor

Instagram.com/
matt_j_pike/

Subscribe to Matt's
mailing list

####

Ingram Content Group UK Ltd.
Milton Keynes UK
UKHW042331230623
423807UK00020B/189

9 798890 744647